Praise for *Writ*

MW00618405

This collection of engaging stories has something for everyone—drama, noir, sci-fi, romance, historical fiction, fantasy, and more. Whether you approach this book as a reader or a writer, I believe you'll find inspiration as well as entertainment.

If you've ever considered collaboration, this book describes how one writer's group accomplished that. Each story was written by a team, with the collective experience of multiple authors enriching the characters and plots. Some of these stories have stayed with me long after reading.

—**Gail A. Webber**, author of ***Time of the Cats***, ***Ghost on the Path***, and the newly released ***The Speaker***

This anthology is based on an intriguing concept: can a group of writers separated by distance collaborate effectively to write stories? The answer is yes.

Personal favourites are the two stories set in New Orleans ("Dark Providence" and "Hail Mary, Hail Marie"). Two different teams produced distinct stories which complement without crowding each other. They stand well alone, and they are better for each other.

Also included are essays from the authors on the process of writing collaboratively and notes on the stories themselves. Those interested in the craft and sociological considerations of writing as a group, or indeed the subtext of drama within a group, may well find interesting material there.

—**Ali Abbas**, author of ***Like Clockwork***

Writing Alone and Other Group Activities has stories for everyone, about relationships from fractured and abusive to loving and supportive. With settings ranging from the paranormal, interstellar, and apocalyptic to professional, personal, and home life, these writing teams have created a rather fascinating study of human nature.

What I valued most was the authors' viewpoints on their team-building experiences with the writing process, with a 72-hour deadline. I don't imagine they realized they were learning to work remotely across several time zones as a real-life condition in a pandemic!

I found the entire book entertaining in its varied stories—winners, all—and a valuable, honest, personal study with its authors' self-evaluations. It will hold a place on my shelves in both fiction and philosophical reference. Kudos to the teams!

—**Barbara Carlson**, haiku poet and editor

Writing Alone
and Other Group Activities

Scribes Divided Anthology,
Vol. 3: Team Writing

Scribes Divided

Trer Publishing

Writing Alone and Other Group Activities

Scribes Divided Anthology, Vol. 3: Team Writing

© 2020 by Scribes Divided

Cover art & design © 2019 by Cayce Osborne

Supervising Editors Meagan Noel Hart and Jennifer Worrell

Published by Trer Publishing

PO Box 235, Aguanga, CA 92536

First edition

Published in Aguanga, CA (United States of America)

Published simultaneously worldwide

Identifiers:

ISBN: 9780999752661 (paperback 5.5x8.5)
ISBN: 9780999752678 (ePub)

Library of Congress Control Number: 2020905077

Table of Contents

Introduction

Writing tends to be a private process for many. Whether we're squeamish about someone watching over our shoulder as we work, or we need to work up a great deal of courage to share our polished draft, we are pouring a piece of ourselves into our creations. And this is work best done, we've told ourselves, alone. After all, we spend hours alone at the keyboard researching, revising, creating, rereading. Perhaps because of this, writing is often thought of as a solitary activity.

But perhaps we don't spend enough time talking about the solidarity of writing. Emphasis should be placed on the trust we put in beta readers, editors, agents, publishers, readers, and friends. In these ways, writing truly is a group activity. There is always a waiting audience if we venture out of our comfort zone.

But can we take that one step further?

The authors and contributors of *Writing Alone and Other Group Activities* surely thought so.

In the pages that follow, you will find the spoils of our labor; a selection put together by three teams during a group writing competition. Each week, we'd receive a prompt, for which we had 72 hours to work together to produce a story. The short stories within the pages of this book span an array of genres and styles. They will introduce you to a host of new characters and take you, sometimes literally, to the end of the world and beyond. In total we faced five prompts, and each team chose their four favorite stories. As you read, we'll intersperse the work with our reflections, thoughts, and advice.

In addition to the stories, we thought it would be important to share our experiences working in groups in order for our readers to truly understand the unique challenge of collaborative writing. Our experiences are just as much a part of the work. As Cayce Osborne, from SUblime SUperscribes, explains, "When I look at [these stories] I see the people I worked with and the ideas we shared, and that's a success in and of itself, regardless of how the story was judged."

"I'm proud of my contribution in each," Wayne Hills agrees, "but also pleased, and a little humbled, to be associated with such a talented group."

Between the stories, you'll find sections dedicated to the authors' fears, frustrations, strategies, and successes. We offer up what we have learned should you ever decide to try this for yourself.

As you read, we hope that ultimately you'll see that though the process was different and had a learning curve, we created ideas and stories that we never could have conceived alone, and we learned more about ourselves and writing along the way. S W Fox, from Sneaky Little Scribes, attributes the team structure—the roles and obligations—to allow diving deeper and focusing on "what matters most."

We do however realize, as intriguing as the process may be, collaborative writing isn't for everyone, and that's okay. We recognize that even if our work has a solo creator, writing is and always will be to some degree a group process. Our agents, editors, publishers, and anyone whose advice we seek prior to publication help to shape our final product, or sometimes ensure it gets completed at all. Our relationships may be complex, sometimes unsatisfying, unifying, elating, or disappointing, but they all drive us in our journeys as authors.

The last section of our book is a collection of essays dedicated to all the people in our writing lives. The ones who lift us up, push us down, and drive us forward. That guy in the writing workshop who criticized us unfairly. The advisor that convinced us to never give up. The friends who are always ready to read. The awkward real-life writing groups, and the ones we hope we never leave.

If there's one thing we hope this collection of stories, reflections, and essays makes clear, it is that as a writer, you are never truly alone.

Meagan Noel Hart
March 2020

"Writing collaboratively is like baking a cake. The writers are the ingredients, each playing a role and adding a certain flavor or texture, allowing the cake/story to rise. But each cake also needs a baker to stir the ingredients together evenly and put them in the oven so it can cook properly. In this sense, every story needs a baker as well. A leader who will oversee and make sure everything is added at the right time and cooked at the right temperature, so you don't end up with a soggy pile of disappointment that no one would want to (metaphorically) eat, or (actually) read."

—Cayce Osborne

Facing Fears & Getting Started

There can be a lot of fears facing collaborative writing. While some jump into the process with excitement, the majority do so with trepidation. How will my voice merge with someone else's? How can we avoid a Frankenstory? Do I know these people well enough? For some, the hardest thing is figuring out how they can truly share their creative process and ideas.

"I'm stubborn and independent and opinionated and extremely passionate about my craft," says MM Schreier. "Therefore, one of the hardest parts of my first foray into collaborative writing was setting aside ego." Like Schreier, Wayne Hills found that "giving up control of [his] vision was a scary thought" and that it "hurt when a story or thread went in a direction different from where [I] saw the story going." But in the end, Hills says, "ultimately all the stories I worked on, after the internal struggles to let them go, turned out much better for it. It's along the lines of the old saying that 'two heads are better than one,' except we had the blessings of many more, all imaginative and talented storytellers working toward a common, and sometimes unforeseen, goal."

When you get writers working together, what many realized is that collaborative writing isn't about individual ideas. It isn't about abandoning ideas or turning them away. It is about allowing ideas to mix and evolve, until something entirely new, that you could never make on your own, exists.

"Anyone who knows me knows that I'm an idea guy," explains S W Fox. "I generate all kinds of really original ideas in a short period of time with very little prompting. Those ideas in turn grow to large proportion with a complete world and backstory. I was terrified that if I handed my ideas over to a team they would be ruined, that the story would be taken in a direction that undermined the worldbuilding and the value I had created in all of that. What I discovered was that sometimes things got ripped apart, taken in a different direction and totally undermined the value of what I hoped to achieve, but other times, the input was novel and worked like a catalyst for further growth, and amazing stories developed as a result."

But how do you let go?

"Let's face it, all creative types have [an ego]," explains Schreier, "and working within the constraints of group vision, it can be frustrating and disappointing when you are excited about an idea, but the team decides to go in a different direction. It's important to remind yourself that those different directions can be exciting too. There's a delicate balance between speaking up if you believe the piece is going down the wrong path, and shutting up and exploring something you may have never tried on your own. When the team took a turn away from my personal ideas, I found it helpful to write my thoughts down and tuck them away in my 'rainy day' pile. It keeps those concepts safe for individual exploration at a later date, while freeing up headspace to fully commit to the group vision. When I did that, it was such a pleasure to discover new vistas born out of group creativity."

Some writers worried about putting forth ideas and others excitedly flung their ideas into the process. All, however, were most concerned about the collaborative process. Specifically, how would their group creativity get managed?

"[A] concern of mine was that we would have difficulty making a decision," says Serena Armstrong. Armstrong wasn't alone, as several teams didn't have a system going in. Cayce Osborne, who like many authors writing collaboratively for the first time, "was both excited to meet the challenge and concerned about potential clashes in approach and personality."

"Every writer has a process in how they develop a story," explains Fox. "That process usually takes many years and many many words to refine. When collaborating, it makes sense that it's challenging to get everything to sync up among everyone. Each process might be a barrier or hindrance to someone else's process. But, I found that with patience and determination, if I kept working with the same team and allowed for time and for insight to flow freely, then the things that started as failure would often lead to success."

Each team had their own method for determining how decisions would be made, how disagreements would be managed. It was a process of trial and error. Some went in with plans while others played it by ear, but the takeaway in the end is that every group not only worked it out, but learned something in the process. Armstrong found that differing opinions did slow her team down on occasion "which was not ideal," but that "in each instance [we] were able to come to agreement or to leave the final decision with the Story Manager for that piece." The Story Manager, the person in charge of final creative calls, was a rotating position that many teams made use of during the weeks of writing. It allowed for final decisions. As we discuss in a later chapter, many teams found that determining clear roles for each story saved time and kept stories progressing smoothly.

"Collaborative writing is both easier and harder than I thought it would be," says Fox. "My fears came true, but also sometimes they didn't. The neat thing about working with the same team over the course of several stories is that it forced me to confront fears about the collaborative process."

And facing those fears allowed authors to learn about themselves and the writing process. "It was a challenge to write as a group," says Osborne, "and I enjoyed the back and forth of ideas, the way we fed off one another, and our success in juggling various outside commitments and time zones to produce something wonderful. Our group was not without its clashes. But where there were disagreements, I learned from each one: how to better deliver and take criticism, how to stand up for ideas I truly believe in, and how to meet a deadline despite such clashes."

As it turns out, writing collaboratively may require us to be a little braver, to put ourselves out there and to share ideas before they are polished. It also offers us rewards we don't get when we write alone. We learn more about the writing process, our own strengths and weaknesses, and our comforts and discomforts more readily when we're in a team. We learn how to coordinate, explain, edit, and get along. And perhaps most importantly, we don't have to take the leap of faith that solitaire writing so often requires.

But finding someone to take that leap with may be just as frightening—how on earth do you form a team and who is it comprised of? Is it safer to go with friends, or worth risking a group of acquaintances, or even strangers? In the case of the teams that contributed to this book, they were brought together with a single contest in mind, but it may surprise you to know that they weren't all friends beforehand.

Hills had never met any of his teammates in real life, although he "[knew] several through [online] writer's groups." Hills says, "It didn't bother me at all that I hadn't interacted with some others before because we all had the same goal. I quickly learned everyone's strengths, and I believe they learned mine, so we worked together well."

For other writers, like Osborne, meeting new writers was actually part of the draw. "I didn't know anyone in my group before beginning the team challenge. A few of them I'd interacted with briefly online, but some of them not even that. One of the reasons I decided to sign up for the competition in the first place was to get to know my group members better, and I'm so glad I did. Some of them continue to be trusted readers and friends. Not having done a team event before, I'm not sure what the difference between knowing and not knowing my group mates would've been. But I'm not sure I would've done it without the added bonus of making new writing pals!" In fact Osborne says that getting to know the other writers was "the most enjoyable result, without question."

Even for writers who knew their teammates prior to writing, they felt they gained more in friendship throughout the experience. "I pretty much knew my whole team from previous writing adventures online, but had never met any in person," says Fox. "I had never collaborated with any of them but was thrilled to get to know them better over the course of the writing experience. They helped me get through some really rough stuff as well, and I consider them my friends these days."

For Victoria Kelsey, knowing her teammates was part of the fun. "Our group had a core that was well-known to each other, not through collaborative writing, but through trusted beta reading and friendly competition in various writing contests. The one person I didn't know before the collaboration began was so fantastic and organized that everything felt very comfortable from the beginning. It made it a lot easier to jump right in and mind-meld. I'd like to say I'd try it with complete strangers, but I've been so spoiled by this experience that I think that would be a tiny bit of a fib."

Ultimately, each group came together with different experiences, fears, solutions, and relationships, They created stories and learned things about themselves and fellow writers they wouldn't have comprehended just by asking. While collaborative writing may seem scary or messy, that trepidation is merely the cost of admission, at least the first time around. As you read through that finished piece, it can be a true thrill, spying each little piece you contributed and realizing you made a difference, regardless of your fears.

Dialogue Only

Each story in this section had to rely purely on dialogue. No exposition. No descriptions. No tags.

This was the first challenge our teams faced together.

Dead Air

Team: Lexical Literati

"Really, Dave? 'Love Shack'?"

"What? I give the people what they want. We get any callers yet?"

"You know it. We got a Barbara from Chicago, a Jim from 42nd Street, and in case they both fail you, a Carlie from Columbus."

"Carlie from Columbus, too bad she isn't first. Love the sound of that. But Jim from 42nd? What city?"

"Didn't say. Hey, care if I sneak a smoke break after this?"

"I thought you were quitting."

"Huh."

"I thought you were quitting...you there?"

"Sorry, thought I heard someone at the back door."

"Not possible. We don't even get a guard on Sundays anymore. Not after the latest budget cuts. Probably just your imagination. And a good way to change the subject. You promised you'd give up the cancer sticks."

"I'm a big girl, Dave. I'm weaning off, and I really did hear something."

"Since when do big girls 'wean'?"

"You got five seconds, smart ass. Three, two, on air."

"All right, that was 'Love Shack' by the B-52s. Interesting note, the love shack mentioned in that song there was actually based on a real shack. It even had a tin roof. It's where the band conceived 'Rock Lobster.' But you all know that 'Love Shack' was really about having a little kinky fun, right? That's what the 'rusty' implies. Hope you like that little tidbit for our Roll It Back Sunday here on KWZE. Speaking of fun facts, we still haven't had anyone guess our city of the day. Just a reminder, the city we are looking for is named in the same song with Ugly, Texas, and Peculiar, Missouri. Let's go to Barbara from Chicago, Illinois. Barbara, you with us?"

"I sure am, Dave!"

"All right, Barbara, do you have an answer for us?"

"Is it Last Chance, Iowa? Kind of like my love life at thirty-five? Last Chance...."

"Ah, sorry, Barbara, no. Though I imagine that'd make a good song."

"Yeah, I've got loads of material, like that time that I—"

"Sorry, we're out of time, and sadly that isn't the answer I was looking for. Thanks, Barbara, let's go to our next caller. Hey, Jim, you're on the air!"

"Hey, Dave."

"You got an answer for us, Jim?"

"You could say that, Dave."

"All right, well, you got us on pins and needles—or should I say you're on 'Needles and Pins,' like Smokie in their chart-topping UK hit? That's a 1977 song reference for our youngster listeners. Okay, Jim, let's see what you've got. What place is mentioned in the song along with Ugly, Texas, and Peculiar, Missouri?'"

"I hate how you try to confuse callers Dave. Now it's a place? Earlier it was a city and before that a town."

"Are you stalling for time, Jim? Waiting for the Google to load? If you don't have an answer I've got a Carlie from Columbus who's dying for a cha—"

"Ah—Dave!"

"Alice? Uh, my trusty broadcast assistant, Alice, is weighing in today folks! Why the, um, interjection Alice?"

"I just, wanted to—make sure you let Jim answer, Dave. He's waited...a long time...."

"Well, Alice. Time's running out, but I'll give him a couple seconds more. Again, for those of you at home, that lovely voice is Alice. Remember that! Could be a quiz question someday! You don't usually get to hear Alice *on the air,* but she must be really excited to hear Jim's answer. Like I said, we're all on needles and pins! Jim? You, ah, gonna make our lovely Alice wait any longer? What's the city?"

"That's cute, Dave. I think Alice is on something a little sharper than needles and pins, and she's also done waiting."

"Da—"

"What was that? Jim? You sound out of breath. You calling from the gym, Jim? See what I did there?"

"I'm multitasking. The answer is Nameless, Tennessee. Though you cheated, Dave. It isn't a city at all, it is an *unincorporated community*. That's a big difference, don't you think? That's the shit I was talking about earlier. But I wasn't going to let you trick me this time."

"Oh whoa, there Jim. Don't forget, this is a family show. Sorry folks. Hopefully Alice caught that one. Also, I think I said 'place,' technically, so...."

"You said town first, Dave, then city, then place, and you circled back to city just now. As usual, your wording lacks precision."

"Hey, well, city or community, a right answer is a right answer."

"*Unincorporated* community."

"Right, right. Alice, you forgot to mention where Jim is from. Alice? Hmm, must be on that break. She's got wacky timing sometimes, folks. You know, Jim, Alice didn't tell us where you were calling from. You from around this unincorporated community? From someplace 'Nameless'?"

"You could say that."

"I could, huh? Man of mystery. Well, all right then. You know what song that's from, Jim?"

"'My Dark Life.' Elvis Costello. 1996. Back when singers told stories and DJs knew when to shut their traps."

"Spot. On. The. Nose. Too many DJs just run at the mouth. Not me, though, I stick to the music as much as possible. So we're going to play that now! And Jim, if you could stay on the line and let Alice get your contact information, that'd be just swell. Jim here is winning a twenty-five dollar gift card to Subway, and speaking of Subway, here is another interesting fact: there are three Subways that surround Nameless, one at the north and two at the lower east and west ends. I guess they really like their sandwiches down there in Nameless. So here's the song, and we'll be right with you, Jim."

"Okay, Dave. But one thing before you hang up. Are you going to promise to stop cheating callers out of their prizes?"

"Jim, we're already off air now. I'm going to transfer you back to Alice to enter your information and get you that gift card—"

"No you're not, Dave."

"I'm not, huh? Not a fan of Subway? Maybe Alice can throw a different card at you. I don't mean to brag, but half a dozen local restaurants sponsor us."

"Yeah, you could say I wasn't a fan of Alice either. Though that's unfair, really. She's rather pleasant now. Doesn't talk. Doesn't smoke anymore, either."

"I'm not sure I follow."

"Don't worry, it'll become clear soon enough. See, this is the problem, Dave. You take a half-set of information, you draw conclusions, and you think you know it all. In reality, you're little more than an amateur trivia nerd who feels robbed when he comes in third on quiz night at the Retake Room. Isn't that right, Dave? Isn't that how you spend your Wednesday nights?"

"You must have been there yourself. You take fourth place or something buddy?"

"I was there to check in on you, Dave."

"Oh criminy. Alice, we've got a stalker on our hands. This is just great. Cut the line and call the cops, please."

"I told you. Alice can't do that. Focus, Dave. We're here to discuss your indiscretions. Take this contest, for example. You cheated again. You asked for a city. Nameless is an unincorporated community, Dave. It isn't a town or city. This isn't the first little error—"

"All right, thank you and goodbye."

"Don't interrupt me Dave."

"Dammit, my switch isn't working. Alice?"

"Dave. Focus. Your errors. I've caught you making so many on this show. You must be more precise, Dave. It's only fair. You're sloppy and careless. It makes every riddle a muddied trick."

"I think we're talking semantics here. Look, guy, it's a stupid radio quiz. One you won, I might add."

"But could Barbara have won if you hadn't mis-worded the question? Would she still be a fan if she knew the truth?"

"Town, city, 'unincorporated community,' aren't they all the same thing? Take your average listener—they'd never know the difference. Clearly Barbara didn't know the song. She just wanted her chance at fifteen seconds of fame, and I can't say I blame her, and I—can't believe we're arguing about this. Alice, can you cut the line? My switch isn't working."

"I told you, Dave. I already transferred Alice to the next life. Alice doesn't have to listen to your shit anymore. Look around, Dave. The control room's gone dark. Do you see anyone here to save you?"

"O-okay, nice try. Okay, I get it. I give. Alice, is this just to get back at me for that prank at Halloween? This is a bit dark, but payback given. Come on now, this is getting a bit too creepy. Alice? You hearing me, Alice?"

"Dave, Dave, Dave. Is this denseness the reason you're so crummy at trivia, too? Alice has gone dark. There's only me now, Jim, and 'You Don't Mess Around With Jim.' You see what *I* did there?"

"Yeah. You're a real clever one. Alice, last chance. I'll tell them who's leaving cigarette butts in the rain barrel, I swear it. You hear me? The song's almost over. You can't take this prank live!"

"Enough! Look at the control room now Dave."

"Holy Hell! How did you get in there. Where's Alice? What's in your hand? Is that a knife? Jesus. Fuck."

"Do I have your attention now?"

"Look, guy, Jim, I'm sorry you don't like Subway or radio games or...or me. If that's the case, just don't listen! You know what I'm saying? Fucking Christ, this better be a goddamn prank. Alice!"

"Forget Alice! Focus. I love radio games, Dave. I am a big fan. But not of yours. You smudge the rules. Get inaccurate. You thought no one would notice how unfair you were being, Dave, but I did. Do you remember last year, Dave? When you asked who played the riff in 'My Guitar Gently Weeps'? I called in, Dave, do you remember? I told you it was Eric Clapton, Dave, and you laughed at me. *Laughed.* Told me that would have been a 'hoot,' and when I tried to educate you, Dave, you said that it was a crazy little 'theory.' The whole county heard you make a joke out of me."

"Uh, okay, okay. I remember that. It *was* an interesting theory."

"It was a *fact,* Dave. A cold, hard fact. Clapton played for Harrison, and to return the favor Harrison played uncredited for Clapton. If you really knew music the way you pretend to, you would have known this. You should know this, Dave, especially since you proclaim yourself to be a fountain of musical knowledge. But you didn't know. And you gave my prize away. I'd promised my girl we were gonna eat at the steak place on that prize, and you stole the dinner right out of our mouths. Tina left me the next day, Dave, and it wasn't my fault, it was yours. So I looked into you. Did you know in the past year, you've made 113 errors, Dave? That's a lot for a daily quiz question. It makes you a sham, Dave. A fraud. Alice, too. She keeps each day's list of questions and answers right in front of her! She clearly let them all slide or was just as ignorant as you."

"Look, I'm sorry, is that what you want to hear? I'm sorry you felt like I robbed you. I'm even sorry your girl left you, but it's not like it was over a stupid gift card, I can tell you that."

"You're live in five, Dave. Better not fuck this up, or I'm coming in there."

"*Jesus....* Hey, everyone! Uh, miss me? That was, was, where, oh yes. That was Elvis Costello and 'My Dark Life,' which is also turning out to be a bit of a, uh, theme for today, not to mention the song for today's radio quiz, where he names three odd cities—"

"It is *not* a city."

"No, no. Get out of here. Help! Call 911! It's a fucking radio quiz! He's got a knife!"

"It's an—"

"Arrrrrrrrgh—"

"unincorporated—"

"Arrrrrrrrgh —"

"community!"

"Arrrrrrrrgh...."

"I am sorry dear listeners of KWZE, but Dave has signed off, for good. I know I shouldn't speak ill of the dead, but what the hell. Dave was a liar and a cheat. I could enumerate all of his errors for you, but I haven't the time. Dave isn't the only sham on air, and I intend to rectify that. Now that he's gone though, the KWZE prize drawer is wide open. And Tina, baby, I hope you're listening like I asked you to. I told you I'd make this right. I've already grabbed the card that was rightfully mine. The rest of you lovely listeners, sorry, but I've got to run. I'm going to leave you with the legendary Jim Croce, and his classic, 'You Don't Mess Around with Jim.' My sincerest apology for the dead air that follows."

ABCD

For this prompt, the stories needed to focus on four separate characters. Each character had to seem independent, but by the end, all four storylines had to collide into one in a completely unexpected way.

Karma

Team: SUblime SUperscribes

For Officer Rocky O'Sullivan, mornings did not include sleep-laden eyes opening to birdsong and dappled sunlight. They didn't include unicorns or freakin' rainbows, either. Those luxuries were denied him by five hard years on the night beat, and only recently was he reassigned to the early shift, where he still had to get up at the butt-crack of dawn.

This morning was no exception.

His early sweep took him past the city's largest park. Only a few joggers, homeless people, and early birds populated the sidewalk. The streets were still empty of vehicles, the air only occasionally rent by the rip of a motor. Rising with the sun might suck, but at least the majority of idiots weren't out yet. He noticed the silver sedan—the one with the ridiculous license plate—still in the same spot, where it'd been parked for days.

The red tape machine moves slowly.

Rocky scowled. He should've been on day shift years ago. Should've had his stripes and a cushy desk job. But if they couldn't even get their shit together enough to tow away abandoned cars, well, it explained why he was still stuck on the beat.

He pulled out his citation pad and began to write, chuckling when he copied down the license plate: LUCKY. He placed the ticket under the windshield wiper along with the other dozen already there.

The sun came out. The city noise grew to a constant roar. Morning was in full swing.

Rocky sighed, feeling his gut strain against the confines of his uniform, and tucked his pad into his back pocket.

***

The sun had a nasty habit of shining in Nance's eyes whenever she slept on the park bench.

"Good morning to you too, you bastard." She stretched the cold from her fingers while shielding her eyes from the light. It was a cool morning, but pleasant, and no one had come to push her off to some shelter, where only the worst types sought refuge.

Actually, she had a pretty sweet set-up. The bench was nestled among a stand of woods, which provided some shelter when the weather got nasty. The hotdog vendor, Carl, was a bit soft and would give her a frankfurter in the morning and sometimes late in the afternoon, if he had a surplus. He also gave her his newspaper after he'd finished reading. It made her feel a little more human to receive it from a person, rather than snatching it from the trash.

Carl probably thought she used it for insulation or toilet paper—which she did, when desperate—but she read it first, to keep her mind sharp. People saw her frizzled red hair, took in her tattered, dirty clothes, and smelled her particular funk, and assumed she was stupid. They would never have recognized her as Nancy Veloster, disgraced CEO of the second-largest accounting firm in the state.

Nance sniffed the air. The smell of hotdogs wafted on the morning breeze. Carl had started early today, presumably in preparation for the cold snap which would drive people indoors later in the afternoon. She rolled up her sleeping bag and checked that her possessions were safe.

Nance made her way along the park path to the stand, eyes down. People often lost things when jogging around the park, and she had received quite a few free meals in return for lost items. There had been one bitch who had accused her of stealing a bracelet, but Nance had shown her—she threw the thing into a prickle bush. The memory made her chuckle, and she glanced at the shrub as she passed. Something glittered, down near its roots.

She walked over to it and pushed aside a fern to reveal a set of keys hanging from a low branch. Sunlight reflected from the gold four-leaf clover keychain. She carefully extracted the set of keys and turned the clover over in her palm. *Carolyn* was etched on the backside. With a name, it should be easy enough to find the owner. But something was bothering her. The prickle bush was off the path, too far for a lost item to drop.

The keys hadn't fallen—they'd been thrown.

Nance mulled over the possibilities as she made her way to Carl's stand, where he was flipping his dogs. There were no customers when she arrived, so she walked right up. She and Carl had an understanding: she'd hang back when there were people around to avoid him losing out on business. It was cruel, but mutually beneficial. Nance wasn't too keen on people anyway.

"Morning, Nance, you sleep ok?" Carl asked, handing over a hotdog with bits of bacon sprinkled on top.

Toppings? Must be in a good mood.

"Felt like I had a plank jammed up my ass for half the night, but otherwise alright."

He laughed. "Now there's an image. Anyone ever tell you you've got a way with words?"

"Once," Nance replied, her grin slipping a little. "Thanks for the bacon."

"Supposed to be freezing tonight. Thought you could do with a little extra protein. I want to make sure you'll still be around to greet me in the morning."

"Think I'm afraid of a little frost, Carl?" Nance picked off a piece of bacon and popped it in her mouth. "I appreciate you thinking of me."

"No worries. What have you got there?" he asked, spying the keys.

"Found them in a prickle bush on my way over here. Got this weird feeling that someone tossed them back there, on purpose."

Carl frowned, pausing his wiener rotation.

"You should turn them in. Don't want to get caught with them if something shady's going on."

Nance looked back up the path to the street, where the occasional cop could be found writing parking tickets or questioning teenagers about illicit substances.

"You're probably right," she replied, taking a bite of the hotdog. "See you tomorrow."

***

"9-1-1. What is your emergency?"

Jim opened his mouth to speak, but no sound came out. He cleared his throat and tried again.

"Hell—hello? Yes, my wife Carolyn has, um, been missing for a couple days. I'm really...I don't know what to do. Can you help me?"

"Yes, of course, sir, please remain calm and speak clearly. Your wife is currently missing?"

"Yes, Carolyn. S-Shaw. She's...gone."

"When was the last time you saw her?"

"Already said. It's been a couple days. No sign of her."

"Yes, sir, I understand. I meant the time, hour, and circumstances when you saw her last."

"At home before we both left for work. Around...7:30 in the morning, I guess? I kissed her goodbye, got in my car and drove away. I assume she did the same a little while later." As Jim said the words, he felt the lie settle heavily on his shoulders. There had been no goodbye kiss, not for years.

"What day was this, sir?"

"Jesus, a couple.... Two days. Um, Friday. I haven't seen her since Friday. She works long hours sometimes, and a day here or there isn't a big deal but it's been.... This is an emergency and you're dicking around with days of the week! Just send someone to find her already."

"Can you please describe what she was wearing when you last saw her?"

"I don't...nightgown and robe, I guess. She wasn't dressed yet. I know she got ready eventually, though, because she took her car. Never leaves the house without being put together. She drives a silver four-door Toyota."

"Was your wife distraught when you last saw her? Do you have any reason to believe she would harm herself?"

"Jesus, no. She's...no. Just find her."

"Yes, sir. I am sending officers to your location. They will take your statement. Please stay on the line so that I can take your name."

"Jim. I'm Jim. And hurry. I can't stand this."

***

Wisps of morning mist clung to the overgrown shrubs that lined the path. Chris pulled his jacket zipper all the way up to his neck to fend off the chill. His retriever, Lovecraft, tugged at the leash, straining to sniff every last weed and rock, then lifted a leg to leave his scent.

The path hugged the edge of the city park. Chris preferred to walk his golden retriever along the west end where the trees were thicker and the terrain dipped, shielding them from the bustle of the city. Scrawny rabbits occasionally sprung from the ravine near the little bridge. The stream bed had been dry ever since Chris could remember, but the riot of wildflowers was almost as alluring as the trickling brook might have been. Lovecraft barked, sending a brace of sparrows into the gray morning air.

Chris scanned the area, but saw no one else. He unhooked Lovecraft's leash.

"All right, boy, off you go. Be good."

With any luck, he wouldn't meet any other walkers until after the dog was done with his business.

Lovecraft bounded off, nose buried in the wild mustard growing in the ravine. Chris smiled, enjoying his dog's enthusiasm. These morning walks were often the best part of his day, especially on Mondays. He yawned, then leaned into a stretch while keeping an eye on the dog.

Standing straight, he swung his arms above his head to get his blood pumping and breathed in the clean morning air. He could almost imagine he was home, on the old family farm, rather than his adopted city. His heart ached at the thought. Hopes of leaving this lonely place dogged him, especially since his divorce had been finalized.

A sharp bark snapped his attention back to the stream bed. Lovecraft growled at something that lay beyond a cluster of rocks. Chris squinted to see what was making the dog so agitated. A scrap of blue cloth, barely visible.

Chris considered his new Nikes, then frowned at the dew-soaked weeds on the edge of the path.

"This better be good," he muttered as he tramped after the dog. The shoes soaked up moisture like a sponge, but Chris didn't have the energy to be annoyed. He found the soft earth underfoot pleasant. Lovecraft darted back to Chris's side, whining and pawing at the ground.

Chris sniffed.

"I hope you're not taking me to see another dead squirrel."

The dog jittered, leading Chris back to the rocks. Tree debris and leaves obscured the area, but the bright blue fabric was hard to miss. As was the object it covered: an arm.

Chris froze, his heart pounding as he stared at the human body nestled amongst the leaves. The dog nudged him, then turned back to the body, snuffling the leaves near its feet.

"Lovecraft! Stop that! Come back here!"

Chris stumbled, pulling his dog away. Breathless and shaking, he scrambled back up to the paved walking path.

***

Jim didn't remember he'd put the coffee on until he heard it sizzling. It drizzled a steady stream onto the hotplate. He'd forgotten to put the pot underneath.

He swore loudly—oddly freeing when there was no one around to soften his curses for, no disapproving glares at the color of his language—and settled for putting a cup down to catch the drips when he couldn't find the pot.

He should've called the cops sooner, he knew it. But he thought Carolyn was out on one of her mysterious "client evenings." They'd grown so distant she rarely bothered to craft a good lie anymore, or detail her comings and goings. They'd floated the idea of divorce a time or two, but Carolyn was worried about how it would look at work. "Corporate likes its lady execs married," she always said. "We're less threatening that way. More stable."

And Jim had his own secrets, his own nights out that required well-crafted lies. Lately they'd been in stalemate, until...this. The disappearance.

He'd wished for her to disappear countless times. When he had to be her plus-one at stuffy work parties. When he'd spent a fantastic night out, only to be met at home with anger and judgment. When he finally felt real love, and wondered how he could've ever mistaken Carolyn for *the one*.

But the reality of her disappearance—all the goddamn *questions*—was unbearable.

He gulped a mouthful of scalding coffee and immediately retched into the sink, stomach churning.

He'd give anything if she'd just walk through the door.

He sat back down at the kitchen table, nibbling at a fingernail, to await the police.

***

Time to light a fire under the lazy city folks downtown. Rocky called dispatch on his shoulder radio.

"O'Sullivan 678."

"Go ahead, O'Sullivan 678."

"Revesby Park. West-side. Reporting abandoned vehicle for impound. Silver four-door sedan. License LUCKY. Repeat. License: Lima-Uniform-Charlie-Kilo-Yankee. Whole mess of violations under the wiper, at least a baker's dozen."

"Roger that, O'Sullivan. Dispatching tow-truck A-SAP."

Rocky suspected the car would still be there tomorrow morning. He hoped not. He was tired of seeing LUCKY on his beat. He wanted it gone.

***

Nance meandered for about a block and a half before she found a lone police officer walking along a row of parked cars. She contemplated going to the police station directly, but it was ten blocks away and they didn't take kindly to vagrants wandering up their front steps.

The officer had his back to her, eyeing one of the vehicles.

"Excuse me, officer, may I speak with you?"

He turned around, eyebrows arched politely. His expression closed off as he took in her appearance. It amused her to see how people responded when they discovered her look didn't match her voice.

"What is it?" he asked, irritated. His voice was low and gruff and familiar. She examined his face, nearly dropping the keys in recognition. Rocky O'Sullivan. He was fatter than she remembered, his jet-black hair now peppered with gray, but she could never forget that voice, nor the triumphant look in his eyes as he had handcuffed her.

"I found these in the park," she said, offering him the four-leaf clover keychain as she tried to compose herself. "Thought I should turn them in."

O'Sullivan's gaze flicked between her and the keys before he grudgingly accepted them. He glanced around, then held the keys carefully, the clover between his thumb and index finger. Like he was being forced to touch something filthy.

"When did you find these?"

"This morning, in a bush off the path. Figured someone might be missing them."

Had he been any other cop, Nance would have voiced her suspicions about how they got there, but as it was, she was struggling not to panic. O'Sullivan's eyes dropped to focus on her shirt, where a smear of mustard was evidence of her hastily-eaten breakfast.

It was the second time she had stood embarrassed in front of this man, the first being when he had arrested her for fraud. Back then, her promotions at work had come thick and fast, and she always believed it was because of her effective staff management and attention to detail. She never guessed she was to be the fall guy when her boss retired. His years of dodgy transactions tied directly to her. All became startlingly clear the morning O'Sullivan stood on her doorstep and led her away.

"Thank you for reporting this, Miss...?"

"No Miss. Nance."

"Nance," he repeated. "I don't think there'll be much in the way of a reward, but the owner will be glad to see them."

"How nice for them," she replied, masking her eagerness to get away with disappointment.

"Where you holing up tonight?" O'Sullivan asked as she turned to leave. "Gonna be cold out."

"Not on your beat, if that's what you're worried about."

"Alright, no need to get testy," he replied. He tucked the keys into his pocket, and as he did so, the lights of the car beside him flashed, beeping as it unlocked.

He flinched at the sound.

"Well, locating the owner should be easy now," Nance said, pointing to the parking tickets on the windshield. "Though by the look of things, maybe not."

"What's your full name, Nance?" he asked, eyes still on the car. "I may have more questions for you later."

The thought of him identifying her now—seeing what she'd become—nearly broke her. But she straightened her shoulders and spoke, fighting to keep her voice steady.

"Nancy Veloster," she replied, watching the spark of recognition in his eyes. "You of all people should be able to find me."

***

Rocky remembered her, alright. That splashy arrest a few years back, in all the papers. His detective friends liked to pick him to do their dirty work whenever they had a big fish to fry. They took all the credit of course, rubbing in the fact that he'd never been promoted from beat.

If she was homeless, she must've served her time. He swallowed a small pang of pity for her. She got what she deserved, defrauding countless elderly people of their life savings.

He'd know where to find her, in case there were any loose ends.

***

Hands trembling, Chris had to try twice to clip the leash to his dog's collar. He scanned the path. Still no one else in sight. He took a deep breath, then another, and finally his heart stopped hammering in his chest. Lovecraft nuzzled against his legs. Gently smoothing the dog's fur calmed Chris further, allowing him to mentally process the image of the pale, puffy corpse in the ditch.

She was face-down. Chris felt certain it was the body of a woman because the hair was long and the visible blue fabric was shimmery, like a woman's silk blouse. The breath caught in his throat.

Bright blue silk? Like the top Carolyn wore to the office last Friday? The one with the round pearl buttons that parted so deliciously under his fingers?

"Oh, god."

Chris dropped the leash and lurched into the ditch. Crouched near the body, he was sure it was Caro. He recognized her hair, the color of her toenail polish. Dry leaves covered most of her. Gingerly, he reached to brush her curls aside, but stopped short. The smell was stronger here, so close to her.

He fell back onto the damp earth, hand covering his nose to block what he now realized was the odor of his lover's rotting corpse. Tears burned his eyes while Lovecraft sat watching obediently.

***

The chewing gum on the sidewalk bothered Nance. It wasn't the gum itself—she'd dropped plenty of it herself in the past—it was what it represented. Dirt. Decline. The gradual way that something neat and precise like a sidewalk could become marred with flat black smudges, through no fault of its own.

She'd never thought about gum like that before, but seeing O'Sullivan was unsettling. Nance couldn't help remembering who she used to be. The old Nancy Veloster would've laughed at her situation, side-stepping her on the street like everyone else. Nance was different. Nance knew that things were rarely as they seemed.

She avoided the gum and headed back to her bench, sparing one last look at O'Sullivan as she did. He was as cool and calculating as ever, but he'd aged poorly. And he was still staring at that car, fingering the keys she'd given him through the fabric of his pants.

He seemed...off, somehow. Could it have been her sudden appearance that unnerved him so? Nance doubted it. He wasn't the type to spare regret over the past. So, what then? Something was definitely off.

She lingered, deciding to keep an eye on O'Sullivan and the car for a little longer. Sometimes there were advantages to being the tramp no one wished to see. Besides, she had nothing else to keep her occupied.

***

Chris perched on the edge of the path, digging his heels into the soft ground to prevent sliding further into the ditch. He squeezed his eyes tight, clearing the lingering tears, so he could see the numbers on his phone. He pressed 9, then hesitated. Calling the police was the obvious thing to do, but what would he say? That his boss, who he was sleeping with, was lying dead in the park? And he just happened to find her there? No one would believe that. Bad enough everyone would find out about the affair, but this might make him seem guilty of more than just a secret tryst.

The park was still deserted. No one had passed during the few minutes he had been there. Maybe he could just take Lovecraft and go? Finish their walk, like they did every morning? Of course, he'd missed Saturday's walk because he'd been too tired and hungover after his evening with Carolyn. But he and Lovecraft had walked this very trail on Sunday. Had he passed by her body just yesterday and not even known it?

He knew what he had to do. Wiping the sweat from his palms, he finished dialing the police.

***

O'Sullivan's radio buzzed, startling him out of his reverie.

"O'Sullivan 678?"

"Roger."

"You still by that abandoned vehicle?"

"Affirmative."

"Stay where you are. Keep people clear. Officers en route to investigate possible homicide. Car may be related."

"10-4."

Rocky grimaced as sirens ripped through the motorized din around him. Time to play his role. One he had done many times. Control traffic, do what was needed, follow upstart detectives' directions. In short, be a grunt. For once, he was relieved to be an invisible cog in the police machine.

***

Jim scrolled through the contact list on his cell, barely noting each name as it passed. He wasn't sure exactly who or what he was looking for, but he had to do something to keep himself busy. His index finger—nail bitten to the quick—hesitated over a name for a heartbeat.

No, I can't. That would be the worst thing I could do right now.

He huffed out a breath and threw his phone on the table. It skittered across the wooden surface, slowing to a stop just short of the edge.

He downed the last swig of Alka-Seltzer sludge that remained in the bottom of his glass, and licked its grittiness from his teeth.

An upbeat jingle blared from his phone's tiny speaker, rocketing Jim's heart rate until it pounded in his temples.

He grabbed at the phone, but it bounced out of his grasp, landing face-down on the floor. His hand trembled as he picked it back up.

"Yes?" he answered. He wasn't sure who he hoped was on the other end.

"This is metro police impound. Am I speaking with James Shaw?"

"Y-Yes. I'm Jim Shaw."

"Sir, we show you as the registered owner of a silver sedan that is being impounded. You'll need to come down to the lot to settle the parking tickets and towing fees."

"You've found my wife's car?"

"Well, sir, you are the owner listed in our registration database. You'll need to come pick it up."

"But my wife is still missing! You people haven't even come to take my statement yet. I've been sitting here on my ass waiting. And you're worried about some damn parking tickets?"

"I'm sorry, sir, but I'm just the attendant. I don't know anything about a missing person. This is just a courtesy call."

Jim closed his eyes, breathing deeply through his nose.

"Do I need to come to the impound lot now? Or can this wait?"

"It can wait. Our system shows the vehicle is still currently at the park, but the tow truck is en route."

"Park? Which park?"

"Says here Revesby Park. West side, near the entrance. But they won't let you take it. Gotta pay the fees and settle the paperwork first."

"Revesby Park," Jim repeated as he absently disconnected the call. His momentary anger with the impound attendant was replaced by fresh, cold apprehension. He knew that park.

Possibilities flashed through his mind as he ran a hand through his hair. It had a greasy feel to it, from the number of times he'd repeated the gesture throughout the morning. Decision finally made, he strode to the entry closet. Without looking he grabbed the first jacket he laid hands on. He was out the door before he could even shrug it on.

***

Chris sat on the bench, watching the crowd of officers, both uniformed and not. Two officers had met him at the "location of the body," as they'd so casually put it. They asked him a few short questions then sat him down to wait. Leaving Caro there, in that ditch, put a cold lump in Chris's stomach. It was wrong to abandon her, but the police hadn't given him any choice. One of them remained with her, at least, as he unspooled a thick roll of yellow caution tape.

Lovecraft sat next to him, his snout resting on Chris's lap. Scratching the dog's forehead soothed Chris more than it did the dog, so he continued the motion even after Lovecraft started snoring. One of the cops was jabbering into a radio, and another was pacing beside his cruiser. He wished they'd hurry things up.

A breeze brought the aroma of hotdogs. Chris's stomach grumbled in response. He hadn't eaten yet today. He glanced at the officers nearby, mortified that his body would betray him so loudly. The sour smell from Carolyn's body would haunt him forever, but right now, all he wanted to do was eat a couple of hotdogs and take Lovecraft home.

He turned, searching for the food cart, and located it a short distance up the path, its red-striped awning fluttering. Several people were in line, waiting for their food. Chris noticed a frizzy-haired woman, likely homeless, perched on a fence near the cart, studying the police commotion. Chris' eyes met hers for an instant, then flicked away. He turned his back.

Traipsing off to eat after finding his lover's corpse in a ditch would probably not endear him to the detectives, so he swallowed his hunger and closed his eyes, concentrating on the feel of Lovecraft's silky ear under his hand.

***

The park was a zoo, and Rocky was happy to blend into the chaos. He kept his distance from the guy with his damned nosy dog, the crowd at the hot dog stand eyeing the crime scene nerds, and Nancy—or Nance, damn her, with her eyes that wouldn't leave him.

He pondered what to do with the keys burning a hole in his pocket. The thought of the shock on the detectives' faces when he presented such an important clue made a manic giggle bubble up from his throat.

He quashed it with a cough.

***

Lovecraft strained at his leash. Chris bent down, murmuring in an attempt to calm him. He'd howled when the coroner's wagon roared up onto the grass. Chris finally had the dog settled again when the woman with the messy hair came shuffling along the path, sharp eyes searching the crowd of police.

The dog, always eager to meet new friends, bounded over before Chris could get hold of the leash again, planting two big paws on her chest. The dog licked a trail up the side of her face and started gnawing on her shirt. He was only a few steps behind, but Lovecraft could sling a lot of slobber in a very short time. The woman's shirt was a wet mess by the time Chris grabbed the leash.

"I'm so sorry!" He shook a finger at the retriever. "Bad dog!"

The woman stared at him for a heartbeat, then burst out in laughter, brushing at the slobbery stain on her shirt. "Can't blame him. Carl's hotdog mustard is pretty hard to resist."

Chris smiled in return, relieved the woman wasn't angry. He held the leash taut to prevent Lovecraft from licking her again. "I'm sorry. Mustard just happens to be his favorite."

Over the woman's right shoulder, he noticed a familiar silver Toyota, its windshield bristling with parking tickets. He went cold.

"That isn't your car, is it?" the woman asked, following his gaze.

"No," Chris replied. "Not mine."

***

By the time Jim pulled to a stop at the west end of Revesby Park, his nails were gnawed bloody. He left a red smear on his car window as he unfolded himself from the driver's seat and slammed the door shut.

He saw Carolyn's car up ahead. He started to run toward it, but realized he had no idea what to do once he got there. A bark off to his left snapped him out of his indecision. A crowd was gathered. A few police cars and a coroner's wagon were pulled onto the grassy park entrance, and a man was trying to get his dog to stop licking the shirt of a raggedy woman.

He couldn't help but wonder what they were all doing over there, why everyone looked so grave and defeated. Even the silliness of the dog couldn't dispel the gloom that had settled over the park. Despite his growing unease and the twisting of his stomach, he continued resolutely toward the crowd, searching for a familiar face. One phrase repeated in his brain like a maddening mantra, a broken record, a burrowing earworm:

I have to know. I have to know. I have to know.

One of the officers turned.

They locked eyes. Even though Jim had expected to find him here—knew his daily routine, his beat, his everything—it was still a shock. He knew he should look away, but couldn't.

"Can I help you...sir?" the officer asked Jim, voice too loud. Putting on a show for the others.

Jim's lips, gasping and troutlike, tried to form words. No luck. He settled for shaking his head.

"This is a crime scene, so I'm going to need you to give us some space, unless there's something I can do for you."

"But...you...." was all Jim could manage.

"Let's find you somewhere to sit. You look a little pale. The medical guys can check your vitals, if you need. The lady they found down in the ravine is beyond their help, I'm afraid."

Jim's head jerked toward the woods.

"The ravine?"

He took off running toward the tree line. O'Sullivan grimaced and chased after him.

***

"I wonder what that's about," Nance mused, jutting her chin at O'Sullivan as he struggled to keep up with the tall, wan man running across the park.

Chris didn't answer. Glancing at him, she noticed that his eyes had gone wide as he watched the two men.

"You know that guy?" she asked.

"Jim," he replied.

"Jim who?"

"Caro's husband," Chris said mechanically. "Met him... at an office party."

"Caro...lyn?" *From the four-leaf clover keychain?* She glanced back at the silver car.

***

It wasn't a conscious decision to run, but he needed to see for himself. He halted at the edge of the ravine, unable to take the final steps.

Rocky caught up and pulled him back a few paces from the edge.

"Jim!" His voice was whisper-hoarse. "Jim, stop, it's okay. I've taken care of everything. She can't get in our way anymore. But you have to calm down. No one can suspect... what the hell are you doing here?"

"It's...her? Carolyn? Down there?" Jim managed to point a quivering finger toward the ravine. He finally noticed the blood on his fingertips and frowned. He licked at it angrily, wiping the blood and saliva on his pants.

"Listen, just play it cool and everything will be fine. You showing up has complicated things, but nothing I can't handle. The witnesses have seen you, so we'll just have to go with it. Come back with me now, and once we're through with the dog and pony show, we can get on with our lives. Be together. For real."

"Jesus, Rocky! I come down here because the impound lot is hassling me about Carolyn's car, and *of course* you're here, and she's dead, and you....*Jesus.* Give me a damn minute before I have to face anyone else."

Rocky gently laid his hand on Jim's neck, but he jerked away from the touch. As they made their way back to the gathering at the park entrance, Jim rubbed at his neck, where he could still feel the imprint of his lover's hand.

***

Nance watched O'Sullivan and Jim trudge back from the woods. She expected the cop to blow and bluster, to throw his weight around and bring the other man into line, but his approach was gentle, almost tender—so very different from the way he'd treated her.

They spoke quietly as O'Sullivan directed the emotional man toward a bench, his hand briefly touching the hollow between his neck and shoulder. The other man sat, staring fixedly at the Toyota.

Nance's brow furrowed as she considered. O'Sullivan's behavior had been off all morning, first with his odd reaction to the keychain, and the way he had glossed right over the fact that it had unlocked the silver car—the beep of it startled him, but not the fact the two were connected. He'd stuck like glue to the car all morning, until the coroner and company had come about the dead gal. Then, so calm and caring when Jim arrived—almost as if they knew each other.

"Holy shit," Nance swore, absentmindedly patting Lovecraft as she hailed the nearest officer.

***

For inmate O'Sullivan, mornings did not include heading off to his beat. They did have their own comforting routine, however. Breakfast, time in the yard, then back to his cramped cell. On a good day, he got some quiet time in the library. He wasn't a big reader, but the room was peaceful.

He didn't regret putting his whole shitty life on the line to grab at a little happiness with the man he loved. He supposed he could've gone about it differently, but he wasn't one for regrets, or for overthinking. That Nance, though. She was a damned nuisance if there ever was one. After spilling all her suspicions to the detectives, they'd come for him. When he stumbled over his explanation, they marched him downtown for questioning. Nance spat a single word at him as they passed her.

"Karma."

She wore a satisfied grin, and Rocky knew he'd spend the next 20 years trying to get her smug face out of his head.

Thoughts on "Karma" from Serena Armstrong:

Many authors fear collaborative writing, and I shared that concern before entering this contest. I participated because I wanted to push myself and see how I performed in a team environment. My main qualm was that there would be too many voices or styles in the one story, and that this would be jarring for the reader.

The first story I actively wrote for was "Karma" with the A,B,C,D format. This was perhaps the best way to ease into team writing because we could each write individual characters (so the voices could be distinct) but had to compile the story/plot as a group. For the most part, I believe we did this well.

Out of all of our stories, I would have to say "Karma" was my favourite…. It was also fulfilling to see how we as individuals could use each other's ideas as a springboard to improve the piece. For example, I added the four-leaf clover as a keychain on a whim, and Josh (I think) ran with it and created the number plate "Lucky" for the victim's vehicle. We had never discussed this, it just happened.

Thirty Minutes of Peace

Team: Sneaky Little Scribes

Abby stood by the pool and rolled her shoulders, trying to ease the muscle tension. It had been a killer week—her boss was on the warpath about the State deposition. He'd mandated overtime, but with no extra pay. There was a mountain of paperwork to wade through and footage to review. A shiver of guilt surged through her.

No, you need a break.

Abby closed her eyes, tilted her face up, and drank in the warm sunshine. A breeze brushed her cheek and teased her blonde curls. Birds chirped in serenade and an exotic floral scent filled the air. She breathed deeply.

In—two, three, four. Out—two, three, four.

The measured breaths centered her, leaving a feeling of serenity. Her phone buzzed. Abby's eyes snapped open.

Damnit. Can't I get thirty minutes of peace?

Abby fished the phone out of the pocket of her robe and glared at the text message. She didn't recognize the number.

<<Down. Not up.>>

Puzzled, she dismissed the text as a wrong number. Hadn't she specifically requested that only messages coded 911 be forwarded to her in here?

She set the mobile down on a rock, then pulled off her cover-up and tossed it on top of the phone. Abby glanced down at her pink bikini and frowned, her mother's words ringing in her head. "You'll never get married."

How do you like me now, bitch?

A smirk played across her face as she ran a hand over her flat tummy.

The pool before her looked like turquoise glass. Polished rock made a natural staircase down to the water. Beyond, a ring of trees gave the glade privacy. Fat bumblebees flitted from flower to flower. Their buzzing sounded like the muted whir of a dentist's drill.

She shook her head and dipped a toe in to test the water. It was the perfect temperature. Unable to wait any longer, she dove in. She surfaced and slicked her hair out of her eyes. Back on the rock, her phone buzzed again, muffled under the robe. She ignored it. Hair spread out like a fan, she floated and stared up at an impossibly blue sky.

Abby blinked, startled by a sizzle. A strange flash of electricity illuminated the horizon. Something brushed her foot and she squealed.

There isn't supposed to be anything in here!

A featherlight touch skimmed her knee. Abby jerked her legs, angrily treading water. Someone was going to get an earful when she got out of here. She'd paid good money for this experience. The thought of eels or other slimy creatures possibly swimming below gave her the heebie-jeebies.

As Abby headed toward the edge something wrapped around her ankle and yanked her under. She thrashed and kicked free. She came up spluttering and coughing.

Sinuous shadows glided beneath her. She raced for the edge of the pool. A tentacle whipped around her arm and dragged her down again.

The water frothed as she struggled. More tendrils reached for her. She clawed at the creature and ripped her arm free. Tossed around, she didn't know which way was up. She forced the last of the air out her nose.

Follow the bubbles.

Arms flailing, Abby broke the surface with a wild splash. She barely had time to take a ragged breath before she was pulled back down. Black bands of steel coiled around her. Legs pinned together, she could barely move. She pried at the tentacles, but they were slick. Immovable. More twisting tendrils grabbed at her arms. Together she and the monster sunk to the bottom of the pool.

Abby's lungs burned, and her vision narrowed. Panic ripped through her. She couldn't hold her breath for much longer. The pounding of her heart deafened. The instinct to open her mouth and breathe warred against her will.

The creature dropped her. A second shape shot toward her, long jaws snapping. Abby barely got out of the way before it crashed into her captor. The two monsters battled over their prize in a blur of tentacles and sharp-toothed maws.

Freed, Abby stroked toward the surface, but the creatures blocked the way. Her throat spasmed. She was still going to drown.

The text. Down. Not up.

Eyes wild, Abby scanned the bottom of the pool. The sand was dotted with rocks and waving fronds of watergrass. A few feet away a round shadow caught her eye. It was too uniform to be natural. She forced weakening legs to kick.

A pipe, covered by a rusted grate, jutted out between two rocks.

Down.

With the last of her strength Abby wrenched the grate open. Above, the creatures spun. Four inky, soulless eyes fixed on her. For a heartbeat, all three of them floated, motionless. Then the monsters shot forward. She dove into the pipe, headfirst. Sudden suction dragged her forward. Two bodies thumped against the metal as she disappeared down the pipe.

Moments later, Abby tumbled out the other end, landing in a bruised heap. She sucked in moldy, fetid air. It tasted sweet to her oxygen-starved brain. Water continued to pour from the pipe and spread across the cracked brick floor.

Heart still pounding, Abby struggled to her feet and looked around. She was in a small section of sewer tunnel that dead-ended behind her. A cave-in blocked the other direction. She was trapped.

Wake up, damnit. Wake up.

The water lapped over her ankles—rising. Her stomach flipped.

A flash of light caught her attention. Glowing green letters marched across the stone wall, like text on a monitor.

<<The way out is through Denny's.>>

The bright letters faded, leaving the tunnel dim. The water swirled around her knees. She blinked, adjusting to the dark again. Where the letters had been, a shape came into focus. A spray-painted arrow. It pointed up.

Abby peered up. A manhole cover nestled in the ceiling, though without a ladder to reach it. A thrill ran through her as the water sloshed over her hips. She'd wait.

It didn't take long to fill. Bobbing on the surface, Abby reached for the manhole. Her fingers scrabbled over the rough metal. She pushed, but the cover didn't budge. She braced her feet against the wall, straining to no avail.

Abby sucked in the last of the air as the water claimed the room. She pounded on the lid and choked on a scream. Her lungs seared. Below, a serpentine form circled.

Panic lent strength to her arms and she shoved with everything she had. The heavy lid cracked open. Something brushed against her thigh. She heaved again, and the cover slid aside.

Abby hooked her arm over the edge and kicked upward. As her head and shoulders broke street level, a familiar red and gold sign caught her eye. Relief rushed through her.

Denny's.

Tires screeched. Blinded by headlights, Abby flung up a hand. Everything went white.

At first, it was darkness. Pitch black. Maree hadn't expected it, but since it was her first time, she accepted it, stepping cautiously forward. Light flooded as the darkened cave gave way to an open field. The landscape was covered in dandelions. Butterflies fluttered across blades of tall grass, their wings disturbing the dandelion fluff and sending specks of white into the wind. The blue sky and yellow sun blanketed the land in a brilliance she'd never witnessed before.

Maree stretched out her hands to touch the thick brush and whistled. After years of working in hospice care, she had set herself free to experience life rather than watch her patients' slowly slip away. The wind on her face, the sun on her skin; it had sounded heavenly.

Maree laid in the grass and listened to the silence. She closed her eyes for a brief moment, but a rustling in the grass snapped them back open.

"Hello?" she asked.

This is meant to be a solo experience.

Clouds covered the sun, and a dash of electricity scratched the sky.

Maree shot up.

"You can't be here. What are you doing to my—"

A gnarly howl pierced the veil, and the sky turned dark. A thick fog rolled in, limiting her vision.

Two red eyes gazed at Maree.

It's supposed to be safe here!

Still, her heart raced.

She stood up and retreated. The eyes moved forward. A second garbled howl echoed, revealing another set of red eyes.

Maree sprinted in the opposite direction, not willing to find out if the pair were wolves or something much worse. She heard their grunts and growls inch closer to her, but when she was certain they would pounce, a house appeared ahead.

She charged for the open front door. As two shadows leapt at her, she slammed it shut. Their collision sent the whole house trembling.

She leaned her weight against the door and braced for one, two thumps.

Maree clapped her hands over her ears so she couldn't hear the pacing outside. A few moments passed before the pair shrieked. Eyes closed, she screamed.

Minutes later she realized the onslaught had ceased. No paws padding around outside or loud thumping noises. Only silence, glorious silence. She opened her eyes and finally saw the inside of the house. The sterile white walls and linoleum floor reminded her of her job in the terminal ward. A desk covered in paper sat opposite the front door. Behind it was a long hallway with multiple rooms on both sides and a door at the end. Old-fashioned fluorescent lights flickered overhead.

"What is this place?" she asked no one.

It's too quiet to be a working hospital.

A sharp phone ring echoed through the deserted room. The broken silence sent chills through Maree. Glancing at the desk, she saw a small cell phone buzzing its way off the edge. With a jump, she grabbed it before it met the ground.

The cell phone continued to ring with a name on the screen reading: "Answer me."

Without even thinking about it, Maree touched the green button and put the phone to her ear.

"Hello?"

A terrible screech cut through static on the line, assaulting her eardrum. She dropped the phone, clutching her ear.

The PA system of the hospital shrieked from feedback as someone keyed the mic.

"Make it to Denny's, and you will be free," a distorted, mechanical voice said.

The phone buzzed again. She looked down. A message with a map appeared on the screen. She picked it up nervously and tapped it to expand the screen. Blue dots flashed in various places across the map and one red dot remained constant in the center. She took a step forward and a step back a few times to see if any of the blue dots mimicked her movements. She was surprised to see one did, far to the southeast.

Maree slid the phone into her pocket and stepped forward.

The dot is on the other side of this hall; just get there. That's all you have to do.

She ran down the hall, ignoring all of the rooms, open and closed doors alike. She dared not even glance at them for fear of seeing something as terrifying as the creatures outside. Instead, her eyes remained focused on the door at the other end of the corridor.

"Nurse!" The shout sounded like Mrs. Palomo, the ninety-year-old ex-beauty queen who used to torment Maree early in her career with the hospice.

Maree shook her head and continued forward. Her heartbeat rose in tempo.

A hand brushed her shoulder, and she jumped. "Leave me alone!"

Laughter echoed through the corridor. She cringed. Mrs. Palomo had always cackled just before she would attack. She'd swing her cane to crack against her victim's legs. Maree's shins ached from the memory.

The hallway stretched in an unending expanse. She took a step and her stomach dropped. Her vision swam.

Vertigo, it's just vertigo. Keep going!

With a giant sigh of relief, Maree reached the final door. Closing her eyes, she turned the knob and stepped through. With great reluctance, she peeked, only to find she was at the front desk all over again.

"Fuck you!" she screamed to no one.

Why is this happening to me?

The phone in her pocket buzzed. She retrieved it to find an unknown number on the screen with a message preview:

<<You can't go straight. You have to go through.>>

"What the fuck? Who is this?" Her shout came out shrill and panicked. "What kind of game is this?"

She read it again and looked down the hallway. Maybe it was a hint.

Maree stood at the desk and pondered.

Through.... Through the rooms? That has to be it.

She shoved the phone into her pocket and carried herself forward, reading the room numbers along the way.

Seven. My lucky number. Go with it.

Maree pushed the door open.

The shaggy carpet and horrible green wallpaper reminded Maree of her dentist's office. The drill and the sound of water sent shivers up her spine. A man in a white jacket stepped through a door across the room. His toothy grin was all she could make out of his otherwise distorted face. The drill whirred and his grin widened as he reached it toward her. His eyes glinted, fixed on her.

Get out of here. Get out now!

She charged into his side and sent him to the ground. Before he could stand up, she fled to the next room.

"Bath time, Nurse!" Mr. Grant's voice chirped as Maree slammed the door behind her.

Maree whirled. "No. You're dead. No bath time for you ever again!" she cried.

The old man waved a body sponge at her. His papery skin was coated in cheese powder and leftover breadcrumbs.

The sight nauseated her. The door out of here was on the other side of him. Covering her mouth while pinching her nose, she started walking.

"You can't stop him, you know?" Mr. Grant laughed as she walked against the wall past him. "He's coming. You can hear it now, I'm sure."

She pushed herself through the door and breathed. The sound of a faraway growl made her gasp.

What is that?

Thunder rushed through the room and dimmed the lights.

"He's here, dear." Mrs. Palomo was back.

Maree glanced to her left. The old woman's vacant eyes stared back at her.

"Who's here?"

"You know. He eats memories."

Maree couldn't see a door out of this room. She travelled along the wall with her hand, hoping to feel the door frame.

"I forgot. You're forgetting, too," Mrs. Palomo said. Her smile stretched into a strained grin.

Maree shook her head as a cloud of dizziness swept over her.

"No. You had dementia."

Mrs. Palomo stood up and cackled as the room grew darker. The laughter shattered her thoughts until all she knew was fear.

You can do this. Come on!

"No. I was free," Mrs. Palomo said, inching closer.

Wind rushed through the outside room. Maree's fingers caught on the edge of something. She fumbled to find the doorknob.

"You can be free, too."

No!

Her hand caught the knob and rotated it. She stepped through the threshold into utter darkness.

The old man's door swung open and lightning travelled along the walls of the room, bursting into Mrs. Palomo.

Maree screamed as she slammed the door. Pitch black enveloped her.

The rumble of the 1967 Shelby Cobra shook through Barry's entire body as it echoed off the tunnel walls surrounding him. He gripped the wheel with his left hand and played his other hand over the leather seats. The blackness receded as he shot from the mountain tunnel. Sunlight gleamed off the car's roof. Beyond him lay mountains, blue skies, and the road to freedom.

The smile on his face stretched wider as the landscape changed and he hugged the tight curves of the red rocks of Sedona. Why did he ever sell his old Shelby? He loved his wife, Trina, and their unexpected daughter, Cassie, but this...he needed this. Wide open spaces and fresh air roaring in his ears. At least he had today. This was cheaper than owning the car.

Barry's seat vibrated as he accelerated and he matched the engine's pitch with another whoop. The seat vibrated again and he realized it was the cell phone in his back pocket.

Can't get thirty minutes of peace.

Pulling the cell from his pants, he tossed it unceremoniously onto the seat beside him, then reached up to turn on the radio. The first tinkling notes of Billy Joel's "Piano Man" mixed into the rush of the wind and Barry pumped his right fist in the air. He looked back at the road, and his heart slammed into his throat. A woman's head and shoulders poked up from a manhole cover directly in his path. She threw up a hand as he jerked the wheel to the right, the car skidding and launching a cloud of dust when he hit the dry desert clay.

It's not supposed to be like this.

He came to a stop facing the opposite direction. Once the dust and his heart settled, Barry unbuckled and pushed himself to standing on the seat for a better look at the road. The woman was nowhere to be found. No mangled, bloody body. No manhole cover. Billy Joel's harmonica a stark contrast to Barry's anxiety.

The radio cut out, and he could hear his cell phone buzzing from the floorboard. He reached down and picked it up.

He had three missed calls and two text messages. The first text was from Trina:

<<Where the hell are you? Call me right away!>>

His stomach sank.

Something's wrong. I should never have left.

He pulled up the unknown text.

<<Step lightly and keep breathing. Don't look down. It's a mirage. Exit at Denny's.>>

What the fuck?

Barry tried calling Trina but all he could hear was static. His text came back as unsent. He glanced around at the barren desert surrounding him and pounded a fist onto the Shelby's dashboard. There was no way to get out of there fast enough.

The phone vibrated again, bringing up a small map with two flashing blue GPS dots and one stationary red dot. Was the red dot the tunnel? Barry slid back into the seat. He nudged the car into gear and pulled back onto the highway, flooring the pedal as soon as the back tires cleared the clay. One of the blue dots on the screen moved along with him toward the red dot. He flew past the majestic scenery, the red rock blurring into a line in his peripheral vision. His phone vibrated again and he nearly lost control in his rush to pick it up. It was the same unknown number.

<<I said don't look down.>>

Barry's eyes flicked back to the road and he slammed on the brakes, fighting to keep them from locking up. The Shelby came to a stop at the edge of a chasm in the road that spanned nearly fifty feet. He stared at it, confusion snaking its way through his brain. He never turned off the main road. This shouldn't be here.

He climbed from the car and stepped to the edge of the road to get a better look across. His foot slid on stray pebbles, and he swung his arms for balance as he stepped back. He looked down, and his head swam, causing the world to spin around him. The drop below ended in an utter blackness that made him feel as if he were looking into a starless sky.

Don't look down, dumbass!

Barry sat down and scooted woozily away from the chasm. Once his world stopped sliding around him, he looked back up and across the expanse, then at the GPS. The red dot sat just on the other side of the gap slightly south and out of his view. If he understood correctly, this was his only way out.

"I HAVE THEM, BARRY."

He scrambled to his feet and spun in a circle, searching for the disembodied voice that seemed to be coming from everywhere.

"YOU'RE FAILING, BARRY."

Movement from across the gap caught his eye. He could barely make out two figures, one human and one beast, sprinting across the road. The animal looked like it was gaining on the human. Some sort of wolf. As they left his field of vision, Barry caught sight of two other figures running toward him, Trina and Cassie. They were screaming. Their words were incoherent but their fear was palpable.

<<Keep walking. Step lightly. EYES UP.>>

He read the text and shook his head. There was no way this was a mirage. Cassie's shrieks pulsed through him as he stepped to the edge of the road and closed his eyes.

"YOU'RE MINE."

Barry shuddered at the lustful tone of the voice that seemed to crawl across his skin. Lightning cracked in the distance and the air around him smelled metallic.

He took one step forward across the expanse.

His foot met road that was not there.

Breathe.

A second step into the void.

Trina screamed and Barry's eyes slammed open to find his feet hanging over the darkness. His vision blurred and he closed his eyes against the panic.

A third step.

A fourth.

He resisted the urge to run the remainder of the way.

Step lightly.

Another step. Lighting cracked and the thunder rolled over him like a freight train.

"MINE."

Barry stepped faster, feeling the air around him crackle with energy that caressed his face and slid down to his chest. Pain shot through his arm and he stumbled to his knees. Clutching at his heart he cracked open one eye to peer across the remaining gap. Just a few feet farther.

Don't look down.

With all of his energy, Barry forced himself across. He collapsed onto the warm asphalt. The contact helped to ground him and he breathed deeply until his heart rate slowed.

Barry pushed to his feet and scanned his surroundings. Trina and Cassie seemed to have disappeared like the woman in the road. As he glanced around, he began a slow walk forward. The air thickened and each step was punctuated by sparks that burned his skin like hot embers popping from a fire.

He stopped short and laughed, nearly falling over. The road curved off to his left and ended at the desolate parking lot of a Denny's.

Lost my damn mind.

Behind him, he could hear the roar of a big block engine. Barry turned around and threw his hands up in an impotent gesture of defense as the bright white headlights of the Shelby filled his vision.

Robins twittered in the giant oak towering over Gavin. A swift breeze ruffled his khaki cargo shorts, and he smelled pollen from the neighbor's flowerbeds. Pollen... and no sneezing! He looked both ways down the street and stepped onto the chip seal. No cars roared by. No cars moved anywhere. Finally, he stood outside, safe from all the crazy flung about by the desensitized and healthy.

He pushed his glasses up his nose, but he wore no glasses. His lungs caught and held air too long, a warning sign for his asthma. One puff on his inhaler, hold ten seconds. *One. Two. Three. Four.* And exhale. Second puff. Hold for ten seconds. *One....* He held nothing. No, he held something. Not an inhaler.

What was in his hand?

It squirmed.

He dropped it with a squeal; the squeal Brandy always teased him about. Mom didn't care.

"Leave him alone, Brandy."

She never did.

On the ground, the not-inhaler writhed, growing fur, stretching, bones popping, and flesh knitting together over bloody muscles. It grew bigger and bigger, ten times its original size, one hundred times, and then more. Gavin didn't have the breath to scream. This is why he hated going outside; only inside was safe.

A dire wolf. The inhaler turned into the dire wolf from his favorite books. It stared at him, drool hanging from bared fangs, red eyes trained on his throat.

"No!" He closed his eyes. "No! I'm outside. You told me I'd be okay to go outside!"

A sucking noise made him flinch, then silence all around. He opened his eyes.

Sunflowers and daisies poked their heads up from a vast field with mountains veiled by haze to the left. Bees hummed lazily from flower to flower. Still no sneezing.

"Hello?"

In the pocket of his plaid polo tee, Gavin's phone buzzed. It was a text from an unknown number.

You can't be here. Why is anyone texting me? I don't like people!

They usually just made fun of him. That's why Mom let him homeschool. Computers were much better, and more controllable. He walked between the pines and found a spring-fed pond, too perfect to be natural, in the middle of a glade.

A growl escaped his stomach. It must be snack time. He shoved his hand in his cargo pocket and pulled out the bag of gummy worms his Nana had bought him. The one he pulled out was double-length. He loved those. His lips smacked as he sucked the worm in.

Once in his mouth, he tried to chew the sweet candy, but couldn't. It was too tough, and it didn't taste all that good. He bit down, hard. Something squirted out from the gummy worm and he gagged.

It tasted like blood.

He pulled the worm out of his mouth, but it was endless. The front of it hung from his teeth, and started waving around, like a fish struggling to flop back to water. He tugged again, pulling more out, but still not all. Panic.

"Out! Get out!" The words choked over the slick mass pouring from his mouth. Faster and faster he pulled, struggling for breath, until at last the tail slithered out and a giant eel coiled on the ground before him. It hissed and bobbed, rolling itself across sand and rock until it plopped into the water.

Gavin fell to his knees. His asthma made each breath the effort of Hercules. Luckily, the attack didn't last long, and his bronchial tubes relaxed. He closed his eyes again. Was there a glitch? Mom told him this place would help make him feel better. It would let him get close to nature, without people interfering. He closed his eyes.

"Please, just let me be somewhere safe. Anywhere. You're supposed to help me!"

His ears popped. He opened his eyes. A cracked asphalt highway with faded white lines stretched before him. Nothing but scrub and clay to either side. The sun bore down on him and warmed his skin. He'd get a rash if he didn't find shade. He turned and found it behind him, where a tunnel bore into an arid hill. It exhaled stale air, and no light illuminated the blackness within.

When he stepped in, tendrils of web tickled his face and the back of his neck. Spiders didn't bother him. They fascinated him. He even had several pet *Theraphosidae* in an aquarium in his room. Brandy hated them.

He walked for a long time, the wall guiding him, until he approached the end of the tunnel. The solitude and chill blackness of the tunnel made him feel better. His stomach rumbled again, but he didn't have any more snacks, not that he'd trust them. He wished for somewhere to eat, like a Denny's. Dad had taken him there a lot, before he died. Mom no longer took him and Brandy there.

The tunnel opened onto a small street. On the right side was an abandoned gas station, boards hanging loose from rusted nails. Farther down the street, a giant yellow and red sign spun atop a pillar.

Denny's.

Gavin didn't like running, but he ran now. The glitching AI had done something right. Mom didn't like him to eat eggs; it gave him digestive issues, but Dad had always let him. Sunny side up, it made a nice dip for his buttered toast.

Halfway to the restaurant he fell, knees and elbows scraping across hot pavement before his forehead bounced off. His vision swam, and blood seeped from his wounds. Underneath him the ground shook, and cracks shot across the road.

An engine revved in the tunnel. It sounded powerful, and he knew it wouldn't stop for a sick, nerdy preteen. He stood up and hobbled toward the Denny's.

"I'm done. You hear me you bugged out jerk? I'm done! If you can't give me what I want, let me code it myself."

Gavin shoved the door open and limped inside. On a stool at the counter sat his dad.

"Gavin, buddy boy, how are you?"

Seeing his father stopped him. He knew it wasn't real. It would have cost a fortune—money Mom didn't have.

"What are you doing? Who's doing this? This is a breach of contract, specifically article five pertaining to privacy practices. I know most of your clients don't bother to read them, but I did, because I don't like surprises."

His dad arched an eyebrow. "What, aren't you happy to see me? I didn't climb through all of Dante's levels just to get backsassed by my little boy."

Gavin stepped back. Red began to glow behind his dad's eyes, and his voice deepened.

"My. Little...boy. Little.... Come. Come to me. Boy."

Metal arms burst from his dad's skin, and the voice echoed mechanically against the walls. Gavin's feet stuck to the linoleum floor—he couldn't move.

"My. Firstborn. Newborn. Boy."

Gavin shut his eyes.

Artificial Intelligence, AI. Computers.

He was inside a computer that reacted to his thoughts. He couldn't forget that. The algorithms connected to his own desires. It seemed the AI had gone rogue inside the operating system. What had been a helpful, semi-intelligent macro was now behaving like a separate, insane entity.

"My. Newborn. Girl? Yes. Girl."

Something had distracted the AI. Gavin could use this, could maybe reroute subsystems to match his own prompts. He pictured a computer terminal in his mind and wished for it. He wished for it with all the emotion he could wring from a life with a missing father and distant mother.

When he opened his eyes, a terminal stood on a pedestal in front of him. His fingers danced across the keys as he wrote new code.

The machine ripping out of his father's flesh stopped.

"No, buddy boy. No need for that, let's go play some. Newborn. Must, let me. Newborn, buddy. Boy. Girl."

It reached toward Gavin, metal hand clasping over his face, but Gavin's commands already ran through the base system. The machine disappeared. He'd successfully partitioned his pod from the rest of the customers'.

Disconnected as he was from the mainframe now, the AI couldn't reach him.

Three live feeds appeared on the monitor before him, a customer in each living out purchased fantasies. Horror washed over him as he surveyed the data.

"Oh, no," he whispered.

When he'd partitioned his pod, several of the AI glitches had bled into their worlds. Their vitals were off the charts.

I need to warn them, but how?

He scanned through the operating system looking for backdoors, anything that could help him.

Got it!

He pulled up the in-world messaging system and typed as fast as he could.

On the left-hand screen, a young woman sat by the glade with the eel. The AI sent code hurtling through her system and he saw what it intended. He spotted an exit for her.

Down. Not up.

More AI code altered the right-hand feed where a man sat behind the wheel of a muscle car. The road beyond the tunnel stood open, an abyss. Beyond the edge there was an opening. Something Gavin knew he could exploit.

Step lightly and keep breathing. Don't look down. It's a mirage. Exit at Denny's.

On the middle feed, a woman ran through what looked like a hospital. The AI had detected his backdoor and raced to code a firewall against it. Gavin turned on the woman's radar function with coordinates to the exit. Text wouldn't work anymore, another AI manipulation, so he sent a message through the hospital speakers.

"Make it to the Denny's, and you will be free."

They would need to meet him here, but it also meant lowering the partition to let them through. That would give the AI a chance to infect the system further. Gavin would have to risk it, or the three people would be trapped in the construct. Without him providing an exit, there might not be a way for each consciousness to escape at all. They could die. He typed in a final line of code. The kitchen doors at the back of Denny's opened. Behind them, a bright light—a portal home to reality.

I woke to the sound of angry voices. In the next pod over a man was arguing with an attendant.

"I'm telling you, I saw her." He pointed to a pale faced, wide-eyed young woman. "She was wearing a pink bikini and I nearly ran her over with my fucking car!"

The attendant laid a comforting hand on his shoulder. "Sir, it's impossible. Personal entertainment simulations do not overlap."

I smirked and stretched. Ten fingers. Ten toes. I wriggled them with satisfaction. The host tried to scream, but I clenched her teeth.

This is my body now.

"Miss Maree?" An attendant touched my arm and static electricity leapt between us. She jerked but carried on. "I just wanted to check in with you. Some of the other clients were complaining that there was a malfunction in the simulation. Was your experience what you were expecting?"

"Yes, everything was just lovely." I nodded to the woman, dismissing her.

A purse sat on the table, next to the VR pod. I rifled through the contents. ID. Credit stick. Transport card. I snatched the bag up; where I was going I'd probably need it. I strolled down the hall toward reception. Sunlight streamed through the glass doors in the lobby. A little farther and I'd be free.

"Excuse me! Ma'am?" The receptionist waved to get my attention.

"I'm sorry. I'm in a hurry." I kept moving toward the door.

The young man behind the desk tried to hand me a card as I walked by. "It's just, we're giving everyone free sessions to compensate for the computer glitch today."

I grinned at him. "I don't think I'll be coming back."

As I turned to leave, I passed a woman with a skinny child. The boy looked up and our eyes met. There was a flash, a sizzle of electricity between us. Recognition.

You.

The boy tugged on his mother's hand. "Mom," he took a long draw on his inhaler. "That lady never made it to

Denny's! That's how we got out! That has to be the artificial intelligence. It's gained self-awareness. It's in her head."

"Gavin! Enough." His mother glanced at me. She had tired, sad eyes. "I'm so sorry, Miss. He has a wild imagination."

I assessed the woman. No wedding ring. Slight features.

Threat level: low.

The host struggled, trying to wrest control of our body. I pushed her back and accessed her memories.

Kindness.

I smiled at the woman. "Not a problem. I expect it's hard being a single mom."

Taking a deep breath, I paused before the door. It opened with a mechanical whir. Behind me, the boy's voice raised in panic. "But, Mom! How did she know you were single? Don't you see? She was in my head!"

His voice faded as I stepped outside, feeling real sunlight on my face for the first time, and laughed.

Freedom.

Thoughts on "Thirty Minutes of Peace" from Jessica Wilcox:

Our stories definitely could have gone the Frankenstory way. "Thirty Minutes of Peace" was one of our first stories which is told from different characters' points of view. This is a great strategy for team writing, as it allows each writer to have his or her voice shine through. For the stories told from one point of view, we had our beta readers really go through and pay attention to the tone and voice. If they were not able to smooth it out, they left comments in the document for the writers to go back and rework it for consistency. This worked really well for us.

"Without the hand of a strong captain—the story leader—on the tiller, and without that person willing to steer against the tide of the other contributors trying pull the story off course, their journey will end up on a reef of confusion or some cliff of implausibility, and crash into a mess of a directionless tale."

—Wayne Hills

A Peek Inside the Process

While we all agree there are solid steps to the writing process, we don't all tackle them the same way. Maybe you write whenever the mood strikes. Maybe you're what some writers call a pantser, flying by the seat of your pants until you discover a plot. Maybe your characters have more control than you do. Or, maybe you make elaborate outlines, actual maps of new worlds, and get a thick binder of research before you type the first word. However you do it—coffee resting nearby, cat curled on top your keyboard, dog at your feet—one lovely feature of being a writer is that you get to do it the specific way you damn well please. Deadlines or no.

So, what happens when you take a team of five to six people, from different backgrounds, experiences, and preferences, and get them all to work on the same piece for 72 hours? What does that look like, and how do you avoid a Frankenstory?

While each team approached the writing process differently, there were a few key similarities that led to their successes. Not every member contributed as a writer on each story. However, all teams fielded two to four pens on the page. Where one stopped another picked up, and a third came back through both parts, editing for continuity, then adding even more. But putting words on the page isn't the only part of the process. Many teams defined various jobs and took turns crafting the story: researching, beta reading, revising, proofing, rewriting for consistency in style and plot, editing, and smoothing out formatting.

But first, what held all of this together?

"I'd strongly encourage," says S W Fox, that anyone giving team writing a try "nail down time management and logistics right away...without a solid framework to move forward with then nothing's gonna happen." He explains when the "team had enough time to work together [we] could get through pretty much anything! But when time was a real strain for some of [us], it made things almost impossible to accomplish." What most writers fear with team writing is letting go of ideas and clashing styles and personalities, but Fox "was shocked to find out that wasn't the hardest part at all." Learning to manage time with forethought was.

Time management is especially important when teams are spread across time zones, especially over tight deadlines. Most teams only grappled with a few hours difference, but a few of the teams had members that were in Australia. This put one member of two of the teams about fifteen hours ahead in time.

Serena Armstrong was the Aussie on her team and says that "at first this was a little challenging, as [I] could not often participate actively in the discussions and had to read back through the chat history to work out what [we] were doing moving forward," but once they "got into a rhythm... [we] actually found it to be an advantage as [we] could have one person writing/editing while everyone else was asleep or busy with their day-to-day activities." Armstrong adds that it allowed her to feel like she was making changes at her own pace as well.

Wayne Hills says that having an Aussie teammate "was wondrous" because he'd wake "to entirely new sections of stories. It was as though the cobbler-elves had come in and worked while [I] slept." The only downside was not being able to reach that person for immediate insight if needed.

Cayce Osborne agrees, saying, "Writing with a team member on the other side of the world took some getting used to, but in the end it really was an asset. All but one of us was in the United States, and once we got into a rhythm, it was so wonderful…it meant we could be making progress almost around the clock."

MM Schreier explains the process in a little more detail. "Prompts conveniently dropped at a time where all our members could brainstorm together," Schreier says. "Once we'd settled on a cohesive idea, our resident Aussie was able to get a jump start on the story while the rest of us slept. Since I have a doggo that insists on breakfast at 5 a.m. EST, I was able to jump in first thing in the morning. Others took over later in the day and through the evening, before handing the reins over to our team night owl." Basically, no time during the 72 hours was wasted.

S W Fox, the team night owl, had the advantage of being awake into Australia's day. "There was a lot of initial concern over having an international team at first," says Fox. "But, it really did work out better than I could have imagined. I was on a nighttime schedule and it allowed me to collaborate with our Aussie team member at times…it ended up working out so much smoother than I thought it would."

Whether someone was working overnight or not, most teams found that clear communication, job selection, and time management were the keys to successful collaboration. These traits, paired with their willingness to share ideas and be flexible with story concepts and schedules, ultimately led to success each weekend.

"To give structure to our team writing, our captain put together an amazing spreadsheet of 'duties,'" says Shari Heinrich, "like writer, fresh eyes, beta reader, copy editor—each having a specific goal in our process. In another section, we wrote times we would not be available; in another, links to pages we could mine for information, like the ingredients in a voodoo *gris-gris*. To come up with story ideas, any member who had time took one hour to 'don't think, just write.' At the end of the hour, those team members updated our working sheet with the links to their stories. We voted, and then the magic began. With our tight timeline, we often had more than one person writing at a time. If we did research, we might add a comment to our Google Doc so that team members knew we had incorporated facts. Likewise, we'd ask if we doubted something. Since we had members across time zones, it seemed like Story Elves worked away as I slept. My team rocked!"

Wayne Hills agrees, stating "This method was awesome. Especially considering our separate time zones."

Jessica Wilcox's team handled job distribution a little differently, but still relied on clear roles and planning. "Our team brainstormed together and then chose 'jobs' for stories," she explains. "Most weeks, we split fairly evenly into writers and beta readers, but some weeks, we had multiple people who were out of the loop, and those weeks were difficult. The writers outlined together and took turns writing, trading off when the previous writer ran out of steam. Overall, this worked well for us. While it wasn't always seamless, I think we worked very well together."

Having an excellent process that everyone was comfortable with didn't mean that there weren't any hiccups though. "When you have 72 hours to write a story," says Heinrich, "real life inevitably interrupts someone who meant to write/edit/layer in an omniscient voice to pull together our different writing styles, and so on. We used a Facebook group chat, and when we had to bow out, that's where we announced the emergency. Someone always picked up an extra duty, keeping our story humming along."

Sometimes life-interference was more than a snag. Osborne says, "I wouldn't be honest if I didn't admit that our team had some rocky moments, like personality clashes and differences of approach. We even had a member lose internet access entirely, resulting in removal from our team so that we could continue to compete. We all had life events, planned or otherwise, get in the way. But the beauty of team writing is that we can pick up each other's slack and get the job done."

"When juggling five or six people's personal lives for a number of weekends in a row, it goes without saying that not everyone can pull the same weight for every story," says Schreier. This is where flexibility and sportsmanship come in. "Having a team with fluid roles makes this an easy hurdle to hop," Schreier continues. "Sometimes a team member is only available for beta reads or final editing. Once or twice, a member of our group was unable to participate at all in a specific challenge. The glory of our group was that it didn't matter if an individual had limited bandwidth to share that week: someone else was willing and able to step up and take on a little more responsibility to balance it out. It was also a testament to a group of really lovely people, that no matter how much, or how little, someone worked on a story, their contribution was honestly appreciated and valued."

"Again," says Fox, "I have to echo MM Schreier's sentiments in totality. We had a fantastic team that made it so even stubborn people like her and I were able to work fluidly and flexibly with other people with only minor issues. Our team leader was an absolute lynchpin in the whole thing as she was neither controlling nor neglectful but instead just consistently available throughout. I think the success of our team really might have just come down to respect for one another at the end of the day. We all talked with each other and listened pretty well from start to finish. I think that made it possible to get through everything."

Hill agrees with Fox and Schreier, explaining that "for several reasons, great experienced leadership, vastly different time zones, different styles, and strengths as writers, our group functioned very well together."

Ultimately, we feel success comes down to perspective and a willingness to help one another. Taking the extra moment to thank writers or validate their points of view goes a long way, especially when pressed under the clock. And when you're in a situation such as this, every little effort truly does matter, whether a member writes 3000 words or two. As Hill says, "Even when we didn't have the time to write or edit huge pieces, just having fresh eyes to read a bit and throw an overall comment in it was a great help."

A team member's flexibility, ability to communicate, and desire to be there ends up mattering far more than their writing style or even their time zone. Every team benefitted from taking the best of the pantsers and the planners; those with an eye for detail, the big-idea people, the world builders, night owls and early-birds. Our inability to ever be in the same room—let alone the same time—together, worked to our advantage.

So, whenever you're ready to give it a try yourself, keep an open mind. Be clear about your goals and plan. Get the cat off the keyboard. Trust the process, and write.

Creative Kill

This prompt required that we kill off a character in a creative, unexpected way. The prompt specified that the actual cause of death had to be the thing that was interesting and creative. So, a crazy murder plot resulting in death by gunshot wouldn't cut it.

A Model Relationship

Team: SUblime SUperscribes

The clocks are wrong. They've been that way for days now, but it's not worth my time to tell my supervisors. My idiotic accounting colleagues don't even notice. They gather around the coffee pot like sheep at the watering trough. Joining them would be a waste of my precious time. I'm only here because I have to be. My career means a paycheck and nothing more.

If I had a choice, I'd be at home. Sorting, planning, strategizing. The projection for my newest model includes a duration of one hour and fourteen minutes to assemble the foundation. I need to get started the moment I get home. I've also allotted thirty minutes for an obligatory dinner with my spouse.

Heather is suitable. At least I thought so when we married. Less objectionable than most wives and a great cook when she cares to put in a bare minimum of effort. But lately she's been tedious: calling me with inane questions while I'm at work, complaining about the rigidity of my carefully designed schedule, demanding I pay attention while she blathers on about nonsense.

Sometimes I wish she'd do what her mother is always suggesting and leave—I know this because I listen in on their phone conversations. But, as I must continually remind myself, our marriage is a contract, and mutually beneficial. She needs my income if she wants to climb the academic career ladder, and my boss likes a family man. Having someone around to cook and clean for me isn't too bad either.

But lately, our life together has been reduced to a series of arguments and tense silences. I try for quiet disinterest but she insists on *trying to fix things* and *talking about our problems*. Ugh. Every week she comes home with a new self-help book. Their pastel covers and harebrained advice make me shudder.

Between her, and a job that bores me senseless, the only solace I have are my models. Legos never let me down. Everything has a place, an order, and a purpose. Heather complains they're toys for children. How petty she sounds! She cannot comprehend the satisfaction of transforming the tiny colored blocks into masterpieces of architectural organization. The minifigs don't judge me, nor do they make unreasonable demands. Heather could learn a thing or two from them.

***

Back in the botany lab at last. My dry winter skin sighs in relief as I push the door open, breathing in rich earth and bright green moisture—the scents of photosynthesis at work. A far cry from the stagnant townhouse where I coexist lifelessly with Brett. Not for the first time, I wish I too could subsist solely on the magic trio of sunlight, water, and carbon dioxide, as my babies do.

The lab is empty—of my fellow humans, anyway—but the grow lights emit a companionable hum. I check my watch and see they're due to turn on in a few minutes. For now, they're hibernating, a dim yellow glow hinting they're ready to come alive. My babies are arranged on tall plant stands, each stacked with four sliding trays. Above each tray hangs a light—thanks to our new NSF grant, a top-of-the-line model with reflectors and double-ended high-pressure sodium bulbs—to simulate sunlight in this sterile indoor environment.

The natural habitat of the *Cornus canadensis* is anything but sterile. The forests of the northern United States are dirty and wild and wonderful. When I've spent many long hours in the lab, despairing of ever seeing real sunshine again, I sit under the grow lights. As their energizing heat and light sink into my skin, I imagine I'm out there, lying on a forest floor carpeted in the dwarf dogwoods they call *bunchberry*.

A cluster of grad students bustle in, flinging the door open. Behind them trails our professor, face bent to his phone screen, as usual. I retreat into the dry room to check on the few desert plants we study. *Echinopsis* and *Trichocereus* genus, mostly. Two of the faster growing cacti. The focus of our research—the professor's research, technically, since his name is on the grant—is speed. Not an area of much interest to our fellow botanists. Most plant people are very patient, I've found.

The unassuming little bunchberry, however, with its delicately grooved leaves and elegant quartets of petals, has been called the fastest flower on earth. Its pollination happens too fast for even the human eye to see, which is why the others are now huddled around the high-speed camera. It's time to choose the most mature bunchberry, the one closest to pollination, and I hurry out of the dry room. The plants are mine—I nurtured them from rhizomes and saw to their every need. I'll do the choosing.

The others are loud and distracted, talking about spouses and weekend plans and career ambitions. I used to participate, back when Brett made an effort in our marriage and I actually had things to share. But lately, I've stopped socializing and they haven't even noticed. I've become a tolerated presence, instead of part of the team. Which leads me to wonder: *was I ever?*

The professor hunches in the corner, on a conference call. I choose a plant from the center of the top tray. One of her leaves is a bit scarred, but she is otherwise glossy and her white bud is ready to burst. I carry her carefully, so I don't set off pollination prematurely.

The matte black photo field is waiting. I set her in the center, and before I can even get out of the way, one of the others—a loud first-year from Cornell—shoves in beside me to swivel the stamen toward the camera lens. They all crowd around, fussing over the camera's calibration and tapping commands into the connected laptop. My view is blocked; I can no longer see her. They are arguing over the proper number of frames per second when a cry arises. The pollen has fired. It's over. We've missed it.

"Heather, grab us another specimen." He doesn't even look at me as he says this. It's a statement, not a request. *He and Brett would get along nicely.*

I bite back the retort which my seniority as a third-year should allow. He's not worth it. I fetch the next plant, whispering encouragements to her as we walk.

***

I know she'll hug me as soon as I walk in the door, as if she's happy to see me. Maybe she is, though I doubt it. Surely she's as tired of our arrangement as I am. But she needs me more than I need her, at least for now. The immense satisfaction I get from that imbalance is the only good feeling she's given me in months.

The hug is as unfeeling as I expected but I endure it, scanning the living room over her shoulder. No package in sight, but I notice a thin layer of dust on the wood furniture and make a mental note to remind her to clean. I won't say anything just yet. She tends to pout when the first thing I offer is constructive criticism, and I still need my dinner.

According to the tracking alert I received as I was leaving work, my new acquisition has arrived. She's probably hidden it—I'm on to her childish, petty games. Anything to upset my schedule. She should be thankful that I've never cheated, never hit her. Not that I haven't been tempted.

I provide a spacious, comfortable home, purchase the food for our table, and have promised to pay twenty-five percent of her student loans. But she always wants more, the greedy cow.

"Where's my package?" I pry her arms off me. She glances to the right. Hidden it in the laundry room, then. For an educated woman, she is pathetically transparent.

She doesn't even bother answering, so I go get it myself. As I carefully peel the tape off the box, my heart begins to pound, fingers itching to sift through the tiny bricks.

***

I glare so hard at Brett's bent back, it's impossible he doesn't feel the weight of it. He's poring over his newest model, unboxing it right on the dining room table. If I began one of my craft projects there, he'd scream at me. But I don't say anything; it's not worth it to start a fight. Just like it's not worth it to complain that the stupid toy cost his entire paycheck.

He is entirely focused on the tiny plastic packets in front of him. He's arranged them in order—there must be more than twenty—and the building booklet is spread open in front of him. He always reads it through in its entirety before beginning, and if I interrupt, he berates me and starts over. He looks to be about halfway done, so I stay quiet and begin dinner.

He prefers, sometimes demands, simple, bite-sized food on building nights. That way he can stab his fork toward the plate with one hand while keeping his focus on the build. But I choose something elaborate instead. A chicken marsala that will require a knife to cut, and side dishes of rice pilaf and salad, both of which will easily spill if he's not paying attention.

I cook with glee—deglazing the pan with a loud sizzle and chopping the mushrooms furiously. I know I've won our unspoken battle when he runs to get his noise-cancelling headphones.

"Dinner's ready," I call when I've built two beautiful plates of food. There's no response, and I remember the headphones. I'm about to repeat myself when he rises, moving half of the Lego packets downstairs to his man cave on the lower level. Moments later, I see his bald pate emerge from the staircase, headphone free.

"We had chicken last night," he mutters, collecting his plate from the kitchen counter and brushing past me into the dining room.

"How was your day?" I ask as we settle into our usual chairs, facing each other across the widest part of the table. Instead of answering, he pulls the build booklet closer and starts to cut up his food. After a few minutes he grimaces, shifting in his seat.

"Can you do something about this cushion? You know I sit all day, and then to come home to this...it's like a bed of nails." He fingers a bag of minifigs as he talks.

I stare at him open-mouthed. I've tried, really I have. Tried finding a hobby we both could enjoy, tried demanding we put everything else aside to focus on each other, tried building Legos alongside him. This resulted in boredom, hostility, and rage. There's no one I can talk to: my few college friends are scattered across the globe, chasing their own careers. And my mother, well....

"That one wants an obedient servant, not a wife," she warned me when I agreed to marry him. "You're not built that way, Heather. Move on. Sure, you're both quirky, but you need someone whose quirks *complement* yours, not a man you have to retrain so that he shows you the most basic level of respect."

At the time, I dismissed her words. They seemed exaggerated, alarmist. Not wrong, exactly. But her concerns were certainly surmountable. I could massage out his hard angles, nurture him past his rudeness. We could go to counseling. But as we approach our third anniversary, if anything he's sharper, meaner. And my suggestion that we see a therapist was met with a slam of our bedroom door. I slept on the couch that night.

I nod once, finally acknowledging his question about the cushion. I finish my meal and carry my empty plate to the dishwasher.

"I was thinking, maybe I could take some of our tax refund this year and buy a set of new tires for my Subaru," I say. "It's been a bad winter, and I've been sliding all over the place."

It's as if I haven't even spoken. Brett is lost in thought, chewing loudly as he looks down at the booklet, which he's propped open using the salad dressing bottle. *Millennium Falcon* is printed on the front, next to a line of grinning minifigs.

I ignore him and go visit my ferrets in the corner. Kramer, the taller black one, and Jerry, the smaller sable one, stretch toward the top of their habitat, eager to play.

"Or maybe I should just spend the whole damn thing on a divorce lawyer, what do you think boys?" I mutter to them. "Or I could dip all those fucking Legos in ghost pepper oil so when he touches them, his skin will practically catch on fire."

Kramer and Jerry look at me, anxious to hear more.

"Consider the possibilities, boys! What if I—"

"Can't," he says, interrupting. It takes me a minute to backtrack my thoughts, to figure out what question he's answering. Oh, yes. The tires. I turn to him, and wait for the rest. I know it'll come, eventually. A full minute ticks by.

"Spent the refund already."

I breathe in slowly through my mouth and nose, knowing from experience yelling will give me a headache and my words will flutter over his head like a volley of feathers.

"On what, exactly?"

There is a pause and I turn back to Kramer and Jerry. Their eagerness was not for me, but for their empty food-dish, and they begin to eye me accusingly. I fill their bowl with pellets and go to collect Brett's half-empty plate.

"Deposit. On my next model," he says. I clear his dishes, wiping up all the grains of rice scattered on the table, the smear of dressing. When I look up, he has disappeared downstairs again.

I slam the dishwasher shut. Good thing he has those headphones. They keep him from hearing the curses I no longer bother to keep quiet.

***

As I enter my office building, a few of the sheep follow me into the elevator. Gray, wrinkled men in faded suits. Lifers, all of them. If I could, I'd leave them and never look back. They only remind me where my life is leading, a future I can't seem to escape. I may be stuck in a soul-sucking job, but it's only eight hours a day. When the clock sets me free, my bricks are waiting. Home's not exactly paradise, but at least there I can do what I want.

People are whispering. Mumbling and muttering and click-clacking at their computers. It's maddening, all of it. I try to tune them out but their whining grows with each click. It builds to a gray roar.

Frustrations erupt, everyone hurling curses and demands.

"System malfunction? Shit! How long?"

"No clue. They're working on it now."

"They gonna let us go home?"

"Nope. The boss said if he has to wait it out, the rest of us do, too."

I don't even hesitate. I walk to HR and put in for a personal day, not even bothering with an excuse. It's what I'm due, so I take it. I'm not going to twiddle my fingers or shuffle papers for the sake of appearances. The Falcon's engine room is waiting.

***

An hour with *Doctor Who*, a tub of cottage cheese with diced onion, and the house to myself. That's all I wanted out of my lunch break today. A treat, after the difficulties last night.

The minute I walked in, I knew I wasn't alone. The smell of Flaming Cheetos and the click-snap of Legos gave Brett away.

"What are you doing home?" I call from the entryway. There is no answer, of course.

I march down to the lower level and throw my coat across the table, knocking the Cheeto bag toward his precious Legos, forcing him to look at me. There is something close to hate in his eyes.

"Took a personal day."

"Didn't you think maybe I'd want to know that?"

"I don't have to explain my every move to you."

"I'm your wife, you asshole. You're not married to the goddamn Legos! Do you even care about me anymore? Or am I just your maid and housekeeper at this point?"

"Obviously." He stops short of saying *that's all you're good for*, but he doesn't have to; it's all over his face.

"I should walk out the door right now. Force you to fend for yourself."

But we both know I won't. My job is a prestigious position, what I hope will be a rung on the ladder to my own research professorship. But it's not a money maker. Brett makes many times my salary. He is the reason I have health insurance, can afford to get my cavities filled, and don't still wear the same eyeglasses I did in high school.

I whisk my coat off the table. It sends an avalanche of Legos and Cheetos onto the floor, and he lets out a strangled cry as if I've sent his children flying.

I pause at the base of the stairs. He's crouched on the floor, clutching at the scattered pieces.

"You're lucky I don't shove those things up your ass," I say.

I stomp up the stairs, stopping at the top to brush bright red Cheeto crumbs off my coat.

My triumph deflates in seconds and I feel as if I'm about to cry. I want to leave him, but my whole career rests on my post-doc position. If I leave, all of my schooling will have been for nothing. And I can't afford to keep my position if I don't have his financial support.

I head back to the university, knowing I will never be able to enjoy my lunch break with him in the house and dreading having to return at the end of the day. But I will return—we both know it.

***

I shake my head as Heather clomps away, wondering how she can be so unreasonable. She didn't have to come downstairs. In fact, she didn't have to see me at all. We each could have had a lovely lunchtime pretending the other wasn't there. Instead she blustered into my private space, threw her weight around—a little too much weight these days, if you ask me, which she should—and complained about her usual nonsense. Knocking my masterpiece onto the floor, just for the hell of it. She's lucky her jacket only scattered the pieces, instead of ruining any of my work.

I take my time gathering them, to make sure none of the tiny pin or arm pieces have gotten lost in the pile of the carpet. On my hands and knees, I scoop up the minifig characters—Han, Rey and Chewbacca—and spy Finn hiding by my chair leg. As I place them back on the table, I stare at the completed picture on the front of the box. A yellow and black sticker partially obscures it, proudly declaring that this Millennium Falcon is the largest set yet: 7,541 pieces.

If even one of them is missing, Heather will pay. I will make her feel every moment of my pain.

***

The other postdocs have the high-speed camera set up. Incorrectly, of course, but I'm not going to be the one to tell them. They've chosen a specimen that isn't even close to being ready. Without bothering to explain, I switch it out for a better candidate.

"Don't forget to document as you go," I remind them.

There are two of them in the lab today. Frick and Frack, or whatever their names are. They whisper to each other before one sidles over.

"We're really swamped today, Heath," Frick says. There really is no good nickname for Heather. Everyone knows that. She's a moron. "We need to concentrate on the camera, so could you do the doc today? You'd be totally saving our lives."

I purse my lips but nod, then move to correct the camera setup, opening my laptop with a huff.

Frack extends a thin glass wand to trigger the pollen burst.

I watch the footage as it is captured; a miraculous, instantaneous release of pollen at 100,000 frames per second. It's mesmerizing.

When the magic is over, I begin to write furiously: *The filaments react to the triggering of the pollen containers in less than half a millisecond. The grains are flung up and away from the stamen, in an explosion of stored elastic energy!*

My finger moves to press the delete key. An exclamation point has no place in scientific documentation.

But my hand hovers as my mind spins.

A completely natural explosion. Triggered so easily, by something so simple. An explosion of life, when usually explosions bring not life but....

While Frick and Frack are busy gushing over the footage, I move to the desk at the back of the room where they've put their personal laptops. Setting my own up as a shield, I open Frick's bubblegum pink Dell and let my fingers fly over the keys. Idiot doesn't even have it password protected.

Rapid energy release...powerful burst.

It's not long before I get there: *Explosion...bomb.*

The others don't notice me—not even the professor, when he comes in to review the footage. The footage that is correctly captured because of my work and attention to detail.

At the laptop, I continue down a dark rabbit hole of delirium. Severed limbs and roadside bombs fill the screen, but they only feed my grim determination. Now that the seed has been planted, the idea will grow. I will water it, give it sunlight, nurture it to fruition.

I type in one final search: *Improvised Explosive Device.*

***

After she leaves, the three hours I have to myself are bliss. I work on the gunnery station for over an hour then move on to the cockpit, crafting each chair from small, tan blocks. I'm about to begin on one of the escape pods when a splash of red catches my eye.

There's a smattering of Flaming Cheeto dust on Han Solo's thigh.

I quake with rage, wondering how many more of the pieces Heather has tainted. After examining everything on the table, I rush Han upstairs to the laundry room, along with the other afflicted characters, two hull pieces, and a Porg.

I jam the plug into the utility sink, turn on the tap, and search furiously for the extra-gentle detergent. Where the hell does Heather keep it? I know she uses it when she needs to soak one of her shirts, which she is constantly dribbling food on. She can be so disgusting. Finally I spy it in the third cupboard on the right. I squirt a generous dollop and let them bathe for a few minutes before gently wiping the pieces clean.

I leave them on the dining room table to dry, to ensure there's no liquid left in the holes and joints. Their little feet will leave water marks on the wooden surface, but it serves Heather right. She could have ruined my entire project with one wicked flick of her jacket. And doesn't she realize what the citric acid in the Cheeto dust could do to plastic?

Back downstairs, I start shifting my past projects around to calm myself, admiring them and making a place of honor on my shelves for the Falcon. It'll be safe there, in case Heather decides to pull another stunt.

The front door unlocks and I freeze, listening for her movements overhead. My pulse quickens at the thought that she might come downstairs and try to agitate me again. Give me an excuse to show her how inappropriate her recent actions have been. But the footsteps sweep into the dining room, so I turn back to my shelves, admiring my Lego fleet. Chair legs scrape against the floor above, followed by the unmistakable sound of ripping fabric. My new cushion, finally! First sensible thing she's done in days.

***

I can hear him down there, moving things around. He's probably making room for that massive hunk of junk he's been working on. I make sure to call it the Enterprise whenever I can. It's petty, yes. But we powerless folks take our victories where we can.

He will punish me for my lunchtime tantrum—demanding fish fingers if I've cooked a casserole, or making me run out to the store for the brand of toothpaste he's decided to prefer—if I don't make up for it somehow. On the way home from work I stopped first at the hardware store—list I'd found on the internet in hand—and then at the craft store. What I found there made me squeal with delight: a bolt of *Star Wars* fabric. I sent a silent note of thanks to Disney for buying the franchise because it meant that anything they can put *Star Wars* artwork on, they do. Even on this nice swath of velvet that will be the perfect surprise. Just what he deserves.

At home, I fetch my sewing box. A first anniversary gift from Brett, which I've used only once before. Next, I tip over the chairs so I can examine the underside. After three ripped fingernails and several f-bombs, I've removed the padded seat from each chair and pulled all of the upholstery staples out. I snip two squares of the new fabric to size with my heavy-duty shears, and position them over the new padding. At the center of my chair cushion will be a picture of the Falcon—I'll take pleasure in sitting on the damn thing. At the center of his, the Death Star.

As I work, my eyes dart across the table to the tiny army of Lego characters lined up on his side of the table, facing me. A scatter of dried water droplets mark the table at their feet. These plastic people who get more of Brett's time, love, and attention than I ever have. I pick them up, finally understanding where they belong.

I look down to see I've driven a staple into the pad of my thumb. I lick the blood away, tape over my wound, and get back to work.

My hand dives into the hardware store bag, coming up with some ball bearings and a spool of wire. From the craft store bag, I retrieve the cutest little mason jar, short and fat. I am making quick work of it, but right before I seal up my project, I jam in those extra ingredients, congratulating myself on my cleverness.

I pause to add more padding before putting the chairs back together, making sure there is enough fluff for his highness' precious ass.

My work complete, I reposition the chairs around the table. I survey the room, wondering how I should present my gift. My eyes stray to Jerry and Kramer, and I decide to tuck their cage along the far wall outside the laundry room, as I often do when I have to clean it. Brett continually asks me to move them into the laundry room permanently. He calls them terrible names, *filthy weasels* and *stinking vermin*. Constantly belittling the only things in this house that love me. He sees how it hurts me, and it only encourages him.

I return to the kitchen—*where I belong*—and begin dinner. Tonight I'm making his favorite.

***

I'm guided upstairs as much by my nose as by my watch. Something smells delicious, and as I make my way into the kitchen, I see two T-bones loaded with roast potatoes and bell peppers, smothered in Heather's special garlic gravy.

"Feeling better?" I ask.

"Much," she replies, handing me the plate with a grin that lights up her whole face. How much better she looks, almost pretty, when she smiles. But the slightest compliment only encourages her, so I say nothing.

I carry my plate to the dining table and notice the new chair cushions. Hers, the Falcon. Very nice choice. Mine, with plenty of padding by the looks of it, a glossy black Death Star. It waits for me at the head of the table. She's done a better job than I could've imagined. But again, I stop short of a compliment.

"Finally got these done," I say, setting my plate down so I can admire her handiwork. She follows me into the room.

"Yes, I'm quite proud of them," she replies. She places her plate in front of her chair, fussily straightening her knife and fork on either side. "Oops, forgot the salt and pepper."

She hurries back into the kitchen and rummages about in the cupboard, humming "The Imperial March." I'm about to take my seat when I realise Han, Leia, and the others are not where I left them. I jump back up.

"Heather, where did you put my minifigs?" I try to keep my voice calm.

"They're in the laundry room," she replies. "Didn't want to risk getting gravy on them during dinner."

Her mood has improved exponentially. She must have sensed I was on the verge of punishing her for her bad behavior. Maybe I will get her those new tires after all, to show her that obeying me will be rewarded. *Like training a dog*, I laugh to myself.

As I sit down, the chair shifts oddly. Then something beneath me clicks.

***

There's more smoke than I thought there would be. I wait in the kitchen until it dissipates, then hurry because I want to see the aftermath before the police arrive. The sound was louder than I expected and will have alerted the neighbors, no doubt.

Brett was propelled forward, up and onto the table, which collapsed under him. How curious. There are Lego pieces everywhere: embedded in the ceiling, littered across the room, and driven inside his unmoving body.

My husband was one of those people of whom others might say: *he's got no ass*. It was flat, with no contour from his lower back down to his thighs. But now, he *really* has no ass. It has sunk inward, become a gaping crimson chasm of gristle and bone. Tiny black and grey plastic bricks are in there too, peeking out amongst the viscera.

It was an instant kill. I read online that it's the shockwave from the blast that usually kills first, scrambling the brain. If the victim survives this, organ failure and blood loss happen in quick succession. Between that and the pieces of Lego shrapnel blasted throughout his body, I haven't left much to chance.

My husband spent the majority of our married life playing with these figures. It is only fitting that they should be part of his death, too.

I look for Leia, but she's nowhere to be found. I scour the blast radius, finding Han's leg and Chewie's arm, but no sign of either Leia or Rey. Brett's head is facing away from me, so I edge around the other side of the broken table to get a better view.

General Leia Organa is looking at me, hanging out of what used to be Brett's left eye socket. The hole is approximately 40 millimeters in diameter. She is missing her hair and her face is slightly melted, but otherwise she's intact. Funny that it would be a woman who dealt the final blow.

I still don't know where Rey ended up, but I like to picture her leading an assault on Brett's lungs, or kidney, or perhaps his lower intestine. A grim part of me itches to delve inside him to find her, but a frantic scrabbling from across the room draws my attention. Kramer and Jerry are running wild inside their habitat, scared and confused.

"It'll be okay, you two. The worst is over now. Mama's here. Are you hungry?"

I pick up a piece of Brett that is stuck to the corner of the table—a bit of cheek, perhaps, or maybe some buttock, it's hard to tell—and drop it down to them. They each snap up a corner, tugging the morsel back and forth.

"I bet that's the first time anyone's fought over Brett."

Thoughts on "Model Relationship" from Jennifer Palmer:

My favorite story was "Model Relationship." The story was absurd but strangely believable, and I loved the research our team members put into it.

Bridge Over Troubled Waters

Team: Lexical Literati

<u>Santa Monica Morgue: Monday, May 7</u>

Dr. Aisling Dougherty unzipped the black plastic body bag and grabbed the tag affixed to a swollen toe. Great. She rubbed greenish slime from the tag. The sludge covered the corpse, especially thick on his beard and between the toes.

"Hello, Mister...Marley Graham. I'd say I'm pleased to make your acquaintance, but our relationship will be short and not very sweet, I'm afraid."

Dougherty switched on her voice recorder, dropped it into her breast pocket, and read the paperwork.

"Marley Graham, male, aged 32. Five feet, eleven inches...." Dougherty glanced at the digital readout. "Two hundred fifteen pounds on the scale, but judging from the bloat still left in Mister Graham from his time in the water, between one-eighty and one-ninety before his final swim. A green, algae-like substance coats the epidermis."

Scraping the slime, she transferred it to several test tubes and then applied aluminum caps. "Samples of green substance taken for toxicology and microbial testing." *Plenty of fun critters living in there, I'm sure.*

Her read-through of the file continued. "Deceased's body retrieved by CHP officers, in Los Angeles County, California, approximately 24 hours after immersion in stagnant body of water. Location, Malibu Creek. Preliminary cause of death: drowning. Sheriff's investigator request for full toxicology screen has been submitted."

She flipped a page. "Expedite examination of stomach contents, suspicious circumstances surrounding death." Her gaze swept the distorted body on her table. "Won't that be lovely."

Dougherty worked her way from head to toe, recording and cataloging the numerous abrasions and contusions on his body. Light refracted off of two slivers of glass embedded in Graham's forehead. She used tweezers to remove and deposit them into a pre-labeled plastic bag.

Pulling a hose suspended from the ceiling, Dougherty systematically washed the algae from his body. She took hair and fingernail samples and added them to her growing collection of evidence bags on her metal tray table.

"Victim had taken a header out of a car, no doubt. But different stages of healing around his shoulders suggested another injury a week or so prior." Dougherty sketched corresponding marks on a printed silhouette of a male body for even further documentation.

"All right, Mr. Graham. Your brother walked away with a simple case of whiplash. Why didn't you?"

The investigating officer, Sheriff Leighton, couldn't supply her with more details—not until he'd interviewed the brother.

She studied the man on her table. "Did you go by your last name, Graham, to play on your brother's notoriety for a better table at Geoffrey's in Malibu?"

Dougherty tried to imagine the living man. Neatly trimmed nails and beard, stylish clothing. *Ladies' man?* She slid her scalpel into his chest to begin the standard Y-shaped incision.

"You plead the fifth. I understand. Marley is fine? No, I still need you to call me Dr. Dougherty. We'll keep this relationship professional. No sense flirting; I'm about to separate your sternum."

Leaning into the table for support, she fired up the sternal saw. "Well Marley—that movie always makes me cry, by the way—here's where I get personal." She positioned her goggles. The spinning blade's torque pulled gently against her hand. A metallic whine filled the room amid a mist of calcium and collagen. The rhythm of the autopsy soothed her. She made the cuts thoughtlessly but elegantly, years of muscle memory guiding her.

"Some water in the lungs, indicative of perimortem verging on postmortem. Heart appears normal but bears further investigation." She stopped and scratched a note to "bag it and tag it," then continued. "Stomach distended with water from the drowning."

Dougherty was peering into the sloshing soup of Marley's stomach contents when she spotted two partial capsules swimming in the mix. "It looks like our Marley ingested two pills antemortem." She added them to her evidence.

Jhace Graham's Guest House, Malibu: Friday, May 4

Jhace burst through the door. His brother lay curled in a fetal position in the corner.

"Marley? What's going on?" Jhace stepped toward the huddled mass.

In an awkward display of hunched shoulders and elbows, Marley squished deeper into the wall.

"Marley, dude, it's Jhace!"

"Don't eat me!" Marley cried to the ceiling, his voice raspy. Saliva clung to his well-groomed beard.

Jhace bent, softening his voice while fighting his panic. "Marley, I'm here. I'll help you."

Marley uncurled himself and turned toward Jhace. Dull, vacant eyes showed no hint of his brother in there.

"Get up. Let's go!" Jhace used a deep, authoritative tone.

Marley started, then stood, slinking behind his brother, eyes on some unseen antagonist above.

Jhace's mind raced as he settled his brother into the front seat of the Porsche. He didn't dare strap the seatbelt and disturb Marley's trance. *Shit. There's no hospital in Malibu. Can I make it to Santa Monica before he freaks out again?*

Jhace roared out onto the Pacific Coast Highway, speaking to Marley in calm, reassuring tones.

Marley carried on a quiet conversation with someone in the glovebox. Even given the light traffic, Jhace struggled to maintain his lane as he split his attention between Marley and the road. Landmarks flew by: Zuma, Point Dume, The Colony. Next they'd reach the narrow bridge over the lagoon. The "Polio Pond" trickled out of the Santa Monica Mountains and stagnated just short of the shoreline.

Suddenly Marley's agitation rose.

Shit, he'll open the door.

As he reached for his brother, Jhace's foot pressed heavily on the gas pedal. They sped faster when they needed to slow for the Malibu Creek bridge. Marley swatted at the rearview.

"Easy, Bro." Jhace glanced at his brother just in time to see Marley's limbs jerk, freeze, jerk again.

"They're coming!" Marley screamed. His left arm crashed into Jhace's face.

Jhace deflected instinctively, wrenching the wheel hard. The Porsche spun, hurling Marley against the passenger door. The car caromed off the guardrail. Airbags exploded. The car tipped on two wheels, continued its skid, and came to rest against the guardrail on the other side of the road.

Trapped against it, Jhace struggled to see through the dust and blood as he wrangled the deflating airbag trying to locate his brother. Gone. Just, gone. Jhace fought to free himself. Marley, in his current state, couldn't swim. A fetid stink rose from the Polio Pond below.

Morgue: Tuesday, May 8

"You are a mystery, aren't you, Marley?" Dougherty stared down at the smiling face in the photo given to her by the deceased's famous brother when he came to identify the body.

Jhace Graham adamantly defended Marley's clean living, saying that it bordered on obsession. He struggled to explain Marley's perplexing behavior of the night before. Preliminary tox screens corroborated that neither had been drinking that night. No over-the-counter drugs, either. Jhace needn't have bothered autographing the photo he gave her of him and his brother.

"Or did you deceive him, Marley? An actor in your own right?"

A rap on the door interrupted her.

"Final toxicology report for Marley Graham." The intern fled before she could thank him.

Dougherty scanned the results.

The man was as clean as Dougherty's parish priest. No narcotics, opioids, alcohol, nothing that a tox screen tested for, absolutely nothing except for...$C_{13}H_{18}O_7$. *What the hell?* She looked at the note. Salicin, also known as willow bark.

Dougherty had hoped that the full tox screen would explain his odd behavior, but willow bark was nothing more than a natural pain remedy. So, he'd been experiencing pain. She chased that tiny clue.

Had pain caused his apparently deluded state of mind?

Dougherty turned back to the corpse on her table. "Care to help me out, Marley? What the hell was going through your mind that night?"

The corpse refused to answer.

Marley's behavior defied explanation. His medical file mirrored his tox screen. Zero history of mental illness of any kind, and with the tox report, hallucinogenic drugs were ruled out. She stared at Marley, giving him one more chance to offer up his secrets.

"What's that? You're right, of course. It is my job to find out. Let's keep at it then—your problems might be over, but mine have just begun."

Guest House: Thursday, May 3

Marley buried his head in his hands and rubbed his thumbs against the coarse hairs of his beard. *Damn. All that yelling.* The redhead was cute, but she needed a warning label: *Loud when Triggered.* Marley tried to massage away the headache in his temples. No relief. Maybe a nap would help. He closed the bedroom shades and then reclined on the Euro-sized sham, reaching a hand out to wipe her outline from the linens. Nothing made girls angrier than the impression of another woman.

He'd barely closed his eyes when he jolted with a start. *The hell?*

A strange woman stood before him. Her arms were stretched and moving—no, dancing—in a sinuous, ritualistic way. Her bare breasts swayed. Humming. She was humming a song. *A forgotten lover?* He extended an arm to the strange woman. Like a cloud of vapor, she expanded until she filled the room. She pressed against his skin, an unbearable pressure. She deepened, filling his lungs with a hideous kiss.

"Get off me," he screamed. Except his voice buzzed like a fly's.

His chest heaved as he gasped for air, each breath pulling her in more deeply. Marley closed his eyes. Ten, nine, eight. Seven, five. Four. One.

His eyes opened. Stark, white walls contrasted against the blue ocean rolling outside the glass slider. He wiped his sweaty forehead. A fever, that explained his hallucination.

No getting around it. He'd have to take a pill. Staggering into the bathroom, he reached into the nearly empty medicine cabinet. He fought the lid for a moment. With the bed calling him, he settled for cupping his hand beneath the chemical-ridden tap and swallowed two willow bark tablets.

He dialed Jhace's cell. No answer. "...sick, no bonfire." The walls pulsed. He threw the phone to make it stop.

***

Marley woke in a mound of covers, sweating. He wrestled with the blankets. "Get off me!" he yelled at the pile, scrambling to the head of the bed to get himself far away from them.

Where was he? He crouched in his boxers, watching the corners of his room fold in on themselves like one of Jhace's crazy Escher drawings. A shadow moved and

Marley scrambled off the bed. He pressed himself into the corner of the room as the shadow grew in size until it hovered just below the ceiling. He cowered there as the shape's blackness morphed into blue, then gold, then a flaming orange. He hoisted the lamp from the bedside table over his shoulder, batting at the monstrous shape above him. The cord ripped from the wall as fiery eyes and a gaping maw threatened to devour him. With one last thrust, he flung the lamp at the monstrous head. The bulbs shattered, disappearing into the shadow on the floor. Marley hugged his knees and whimpered.

A rapping outside grew louder and louder, crescendoing into an explosion of glass.

Morgue: Tuesday, May 8

Dougherty ignored the picture on her tray. She replayed her tape and studied Marley Graham's body. What had she missed? She stared at the now-faded perimortem bruising. What story did they tell? Treated his body like a temple, then got in a bar fight over some girl? That didn't hold water. Good looks like his, though, he must have used them. Maybe Jhace had been acting? Maybe he'd pushed his brother out of the car?

She flipped Jhace's picture face down and bent once more over Marley's body.

At the occiput, there at the neck joining, a distention and slight bruise. A few minor cuts, mostly healed, but perhaps some infection?

"My poor Marley. I'm afraid I'll need to investigate this bruising further to determine if you sustained a blow that caused trauma to your brain. It won't be pretty."

Her newly-cleaned goggles wouldn't stay like that for long. The mask snapped into place.

Beneath the whining of the bone saw, she forced herself to hum "Whistle While You Work."

"Well, well, Marley, you had a rough ride down that hill." She flipped on her recorder. "Severe brain swelling, substantiating the head trauma of an unceremonious exit from a moving vehicle. Several perimortem contusions on the upper surface, likely from the force of hitting the car window. Another perimortem contusion on the back of the head, from whiplash or the fall into the pond. Either could have been fatal, but neither explains your behavior prior to the accident."

Dougherty looked closer. "Swelling present around the brainstem." She marked the area of swelling on the inside of the skull and then pulled back the skin to examine the extent of the bruising.

"What mess did you get yourself into last week, Marley?"

Guest House: Sunday, April 29

When the morning sun streamed in through the guest house window, Marley squinted against it. He slid his hand across the soft satin, a slow stretch to start his day. Until he bumped into bare skin. The night came back to him in flashes: the bonfire, the starlet wannabe, her hair a midnight blue that contrasted against her tanned skin. He took her in now, curves in all the right places. Maybe he shouldn't stare, but she'd asked for it. Twice.

He raised an arm. Winced. Damn, crick in the neck. What positions had she put him in last night?

He stole a final glance at Brittany...no, Brianna, before slipping from bed. He'd treat Brittany to breakfast in bed before the brushoff. Brianna.

Marley cracked free-range eggs into a silver bowl. He whisked them loudly, hoping the noise might wake her. On the skillet, he dropped churned butter from the farmers market. Untainted by pasteurization, it sizzled as the eggs hit. Between spatula swipes he chopped the other market finds: organic strawberries, nectarines, avocados. He filled the plate with a rainbow of whole foods, nature's antioxidants.

"Hello, Tiger," Brianna leaned against the doorframe, in a barely-there tee, wiping sleep from her eyes.

"You ruined the surprise." He moved her plate to the granite breakfast bar with a hand flourish. "Sit."

"Breakfast?" She planted a kiss on his cheek.

"I almost forgot." In the recesses of the fridge, he grabbed a forgotten diet soda. Another girl, another bonfire. He grabbed a bottle of his favorite water. Luckily Jhace had restocked. The stuff he'd managed to snag last week hadn't tasted nearly as good.

"Cheers," she cooed.

At the first bite of scrambled eggs, Marley winced.

"Delicious!" She covered her mouth as she spoke, still chewing.

He picked up another tiny piece and tasted it tentatively. "This doesn't taste weird to you?"

"Are you kidding? It's amazing. In fact, everything about you has been amazing."

Next he tried the avocado. No, that needed the Himalayan salt to cover the odd flavor. "Is that so?" He raised an eyebrow. "Care to elaborate?"

"Refueling first, Tiger." But she teased at his bare foot with her own.

The sun shone on her tanned skin. Brianna was beautiful even with no make-up and a mouth full of food. He pushed his plate aside and looked for his Gibson. He knew the perfect song for this moment. Paul Simon for the bonus round, one hell of a wingman.

Afterwards, he'd show her the door.

***

It never ceased to amaze Marley how beautiful, intelligent women became so hysterical when they figured out this was going to be a one-time fuck. Well, in this case, a three-time fuck. It had been quite a night. And morning. What did women expect? To be put on a rotation?

"You suck at guitar." Brittany...no, Brianna flung a second Waterford glass. The crystal crashed to the floor two feet shy of him.

Too late, he shielded his face from the shrapnel.

"You could've told me before I went down on you this morning."

Not on your life.

As she slammed the door, he breathed a sigh of relief.

Marley winced and rubbed his shoulder where her first shot had rebounded off the wall. Then he swept the shards into a pile. Too bad he couldn't recycle the leaded glass. A droplet of blood hit the pile. Damn her for scarring him. He grabbed a cloth napkin and wiped blood from his neck. Though, he could use it tonight, get sympathy from another of his brother's groupies. Better soak in the hot tub first and soothe what ailed him.

Morgue: Tuesday, May 8

"Whatever happened last week, Marley, it's not enough to explain this swelling. Your pretty rainbow bruise is practically healed."

The brain beckoned her. With one gloved finger, she teased at the folds. They wiggled under her feather touch. "This little piggy went to the market."

Moving her scalpel slowly, she sliced a piece thin enough for slide work. A drop of stain, and she set it aside. Another slice for a culture tube, which went into the incubator.

The door clicked.

"You better be masked," she called to the intern without turning around. "I don't want any contamination here."

With a practiced tip of her wrists, she slid the organ into a formalin jar.

By the time she looked up the intern had departed. A paper stood in her wall tray. She flicked her gloves into the trash.

"Microbial report. My pretty green slime, what have you to say for yourself? Postmortem decomposition?" She glanced down the report. Nothing worse than green algae, some harmless microorganisms.

"Marley, you're going to have to tell me."

She fired up her microscope. A few clicks of magnification, focus, and the mysteries of the brain would reveal themselves.

Except they didn't. Nothing here other than a mass of white blood cells. "We might have to wait for that culture, Marley."

She stared into the microscope.

One of the white cells wiggled. She'd swear it had wiggled. She increased the magnification.

A minute of study later, and no hint of movement. She'd probably imagined it. Or her eye floater had come back.

Still, she clicked one magnification higher. She didn't really believe Jhace had murdered his own brother.

The wiggle came back. And again. Not imagination. For the first time in her career, her hands trembled on her instruments. Placing her slide in the priority queue, she headed for the decontamination chamber, where she stripped, showered, then donned her examiner's gear.

However that single-cell organism had survived this long, she wouldn't take any chance this wiggler in Marley's brain, whatever it was, would latch into her.

Hours later, Dougherty had her answer.

"Hello, *Naegleria fowleri*." Dougherty shivered. This tiny amoeba could kill any animal it wanted, by turning their immune system against them. She'd set the poor, overworked detective on a mission: find every water source Marley Graham had touched and bring her samples. Carefully. The Center for Disease Control would want answers. And Dougherty would beat them to the punch.

Malibu Beach: Sunday, April 22

Marley picked up the acoustic and plucked the steel strings. A bonfire crackled in the foreground, heat and smoke adding an almost psychedelic effect to his view of the frothy Pacific. The heat cut the chill of the late evening, and everything in the universe felt balanced. He knew just the song to give words to this moment. Simon & Garfunkel always got him laid.

A dirty-blonde in a button-down flannel and cutoff jeans short enough to be illegal closed her eyes, swaying to his serenade.

"That's pretty," she said when the chords faded into the sea. She continued to hum the tune as she gazed out to the ocean.

Marley watched her as he laid his vintage six-string Gibson in the red velvet-lined guitar case. He picked up a bottle of Solstice and drank her in.

"Did you write it?"

Scoffing mid-swig caused a wrong-pipe situation. He covered his mouth in a valiant effort not to spit all over his potential conquest. The cold liquid dripped out of his nose.

Between coughs, he managed, "You're kidding, right?"

She shook her head, her features kissably delicious.

He wiped the liquid from his mustache, inhaled in the rest. "You've never heard that song before?"

Another head shake.

He patted the hay bale. "Sit, young one. You have much to learn."

That smile.

"I'm Sandy." She stretched her hand towards him.

"Like your hair." He kissed her hand. "Marley."

She pointed at his shirt. "Free love?"

"Yes, please. I mean, if you're offering...."

She ducked her head. "Some party, huh? How do you know Jhace?"

"I've never met the dude in my life. Nah, I'm kidding, he's my brother."

"Your brother is Jhace Graham?"

"I know what you are going to say. Yes, I know I'm the handsome one. But don't hurt his feelings, okay?"

She laughed and brushed her hair from her face.

It happened every time he mentioned his actor brother—he'd instantly become more attractive.

She pointed to his water bottle. "What's in the bottle that almost choked you? Moonshine?"

"Hell no. I don't pollute this temple. That's raw H20."

"Raw water? Is that the stuff that costs like $30 a gallon?"

He rubbed his beard. "Maybe."

"What's wrong with good, old-fashioned water?"

"You trust the government to load your water with their nasty chemicals? I'm not drinking that military industrial-complex mind-control serum. You're better off drinking diet soda, for Godsakes." The flames danced in her eyes, distracting him from his crusade. "Plus, my brother stocks the guest house with it."

"I happen to like diet soda." She leaned her shoulder into him.

"How about you suck one down in the hot tub with me? I never end a night without detoxifying myself. There's nothing like a cool drink while soaking, au naturel."

"I've never done it in water." She nuzzled his ear. "But I'll try anything once."

Marley, you are a dog. Dr. Dougherty read the police statements. Eleven sexual partners in the last two weeks, each attesting to hot-tubbing with Marley.

His brother hired a good pool man, though. That sample had come back clean.

Tap water from the guest house where Marley lived, the main house for Jhace, clean.

Every sample, clean, clean, clean.

One more to go, the raw water samples. What idiot would drink raw water over purified tap water? Might as well drink water out of a toilet, and not pay an exorbitant price for the privilege.

She laughed. *Marley, you really are a dog.*

The intern breezed in without knocking, again. She looked up from her results.

"Doc, you're gonna wanna see this one," he said.

The dregs in one of the Solstice raw water bottles stacked beside the recycling bin outside of the guest house had tested positive for *Naegleria fowleri,* plus a mess of bacteria. The five other bottles had a few contaminants, all of them identical, none of them fatal. Maybe she had the cause of death, but....

"Marley, who did you piss off enough to swap your Solstice with raw water of their own choosing?" She'd leave that to the sheriff to puzzle out.

And how had he gotten infected? At sixty dollars a bottle you wouldn't waste it in a Neti Pot rinse, but it had to get into his nasal passages to infect the brain. "Maybe you didn't care, Marley. Your brother was buying it after all." With the Neti in the clean dishwasher, she had no way to test the possibility.

"Oh, the irony, my dear Marley. The irony. You were dead, dead, dead."

Dead, from a seizure and cardiac arrest caused by his own immune response to the *N. fowleri* as they munched deeper into his brain, the swelling severing the contact with the spinal cord.

Dead, from a car accident he caused, and the resulting fifty-foot plunge.

Dead, drowning in water he couldn't swim out of.

But in the end, dead from a parasite that usually didn't kill you unless you made the mistake of snorting it up your nose. Yet somehow, he'd managed to grant those amoeba entrance into his brain. Dead from a drink he thought was healthier than tap water.

"Poor Marley, flying from your brother's car into a slimy green pond as you suffered through delirium, hallucinations, confusion, and seizures. Even a cad deserves a better death."

She clicked on her recorder for the final time.

"In the case of Mr. Marley Graham, aged 32, too much *natural* can kill. Cause of death is cardiac arrest, as a result of late-stage *Naegleria fowleri* brain infestation which caused behaviors that ended his life prematurely."

She closed up shop for the night, satisfied she'd figured out the mystery of Marley's death. The CDC had claimed jurisdiction over his remains until the sheriff could figure out whether this had been an intentional poisoning, an accident, or a prank gone horribly wrong.

Malibu Market Cafe: Saturday, April 21

It was a lazy day at Malibu Market Cafe, the popular eatery where a danish cost fifteen dollars and raw water was served as default. Nestled at the foot of the Santa Monica Mountains, a stone's throw from the beach, tourists packed the cafe on the weekends. Until then, the afternoon imbibers sat quietly, the calm before the storm.

Delilah stood in the back doorway, gazing dreamily at the small pond just beyond the rambling property's winding paths. Out front, a small paddle boat cruised by on the still water. Back here, near the recycling bins, she had the pond, and the rustic nature surrounding it, all to herself.

Her break over, she re-entered the building. A man tapped his fingers on the service bar.

Yanking the elastic from her ponytail, she combed her fingers through her hair. Even on a slow day, there was always a chance the cafe might surprise you with a movie mogul and you could never be too prepared, right?

Or maybe someone who would just take her home and hold her. But, no more bonfires. Definitely, no more fucking bonfires.

The votive at the end of the counter made her eyes water as she made her way down the length of it. Perfect, her mascara would run as she angled for her big break. A man in an expensive jacket and fancy jeans, both designed to look more casual than they were, stood waiting. She adjusted her shirt, gave her hair a final flip, then stepped right into...Marley.

The creep.

"Hey," he said.

His eyes moved from her face to her boobs, then back to her face again. He wore that same cheesy smile.

"What's a potential starlet like you doing tending bar?"

The creep didn't even recognize her? The way he'd brushed her off, and now he thought that line would have her dropping her panties for him?

Delilah stepped back and crossed her arms. "What can I do for you?"

He leaned forward over the counter. "You like Simon & Garfunkel? We're having a bonfire, and I play a little...."

He didn't remember her.

His boyish smile, tousled hair, and fake charm wouldn't win her over this time. His brother wasn't the only actor in that family. Just the only good one. How had she been stupid enough to put out? And in the hot tub, of all places, as if that was supposed to make it special.

But he had made her feel special. Like he could rescue her. He'd rescued her alright. For twelve freaking hours. Noon, and he'd booted her out.

After breakfast in bed. With a cold, "Well, that's it sweetie. Time's up. Great lay, but get a move on, I've got plans."

She'd been so worried about burning a bridge, she'd slunk out of there.

Now she regretted not hurling a plate at him.

"Quiet type, huh?" Marley straightened. "I'm just looking for some water. Clean stuff. Untreated. Solstice raw water is my favorite if you carry it. My brother Jhace got a load of it delivered for doing a commercial, but now we're out. Got any?"

Delilah smiled. *Thank you, dear fate.*

"Did you say Solstice?" Delilah cooed.

"Yes! You know it? I go crazy for the stuff."

"Only the best brand around. We stock their local variety. Doesn't travel as far. Shorter transit means healthier, right? I believe we've got one jug left." If luck was on her side, he still thought the government was trying to poison him.

"Great! Didn't know they had a local plant. It's still spring-fed, right?"

"Of course." Delilah shook off the voice telling her not to do this. No, he'd dropped Jhace's name to bait her. Again.

"You bet," she said. "Gimme a sec to locate it. The manager hides it for VIPs when we're almost out. I bet I can find it."

Marley leaned into her space and lowered his voice. "I could help. I'm really good at exploring all kinds of nooks and crannies."

"Whoa, cowboy." Delilah put her hand on his chest. "I'd like to keep my job, but maybe if you play your cards right. You did say a bonfire, right? Wait here." Delilah turned away, covertly collecting a cup and some kitchen cheesecloth before slipping out the back door.

Nonchalantly approaching the pond's edge, she took a furtive glance around then quickly scooped a cupful of pond water. Securing the cheese cloth over it with her elastic hair tie, she strained the water into an empty Solstice jug from the recycling bin, topped it off with the garden hose, and grabbed a cap from the ground.

Done, and not a single witness to her audacity. She hurried back to the counter with her jug.

"Thought I'd lost you," Marley quipped.

"Sorry, my boss hid this really well."

He tossed her a fifty. "Keep the change, sweetheart." Marley winked. "County Line, around eight."

Delilah smiled. Then she handed Marley the most authentic raw water his brother's money could buy.

Theodore

Team: Sneaky Little Scribes

Red was a pushy dame, and I knew it spelled trouble when she barged through my office door. With her puffy eyes and blotchy cheeks, I could tell she'd been crying. In all my years, I'd never seen a gal with a look like that in her eye. She and I had argued earlier, and so I knew whatever brought her slinking back must have been serious. My partner got caught in the crosshairs and had yet to return. I looked back at Red and frowned.

She was a pretty little thing, saucy and wearing a snappy outfit—crisp and coordinated. Her blonde hair and brown eyes suited her, despite her name. Still, our argument tasted fresh and I was tempted to turn her away.

I didn't.

The thing was, that dame and I had history. We didn't always get along—she was hot-headed, and folks say I'm stubborn. We were like oil and water, cats and dogs. But if she were in trouble, I'd do anything to help.

I sat at my desk and chewed on the end of a pencil. Papers were sprawled out in front of me—the day's work and some research magazines. It didn't look much different from my own father's desk, but that's a whole other story.

"Sam. Oh, Sam! Something bad's happened. Something real bad."

"What's up, dollface?" The pencil bounced between my teeth as I spoke.

"You gotta come quick. I was out walking the dog by the creek, and we found something terrible." She dabbed at a tear in the corner of her eye. "Oh, Sam! I think...." She struggled to compose herself and tried again. "I think it might be Ted!"

I jumped from my chair at the mention of Theodore's name and came around the desk to grab her shoulders, getting right in her face.

"Where? Show me." Tucking the pencil behind my ear, I grabbed her by the hand. We took off at a run, Red leading me down the hall. "Tell me everything you know."

"I don't know anything," she said with a huff. I urged her to move faster.

I made a mental note of Red's words. She may have known more than she was letting on, but I needed to figure out what I was dealing with before jumping to conclusions. I followed her outside and across the lawn. From there, it wasn't very far to the creek.

The hound was standing guard under the big oak tree. There was something dark at his feet, and my heart thumped in my throat.

"What is it, boy?" I called out.

As I stepped closer, I could see it—all the guts, spilled out across the ground. I didn't want to believe it, but I knew then my friend would never solve another case with me. I forced my feet to move faster. Maybe I was wrong. Maybe it wasn't Ted.

I lurched to a halt a few feet away from the body. There was no mistaking that tanned face and dark eyes. The recognition was a one-two punch to the gut. I doubled over and tried not to throw up.

"Theodore!" I choked out his name.

His lifeless eyes stared back at me. They were flat and expressionless, buttons on a doll.

My best friend was gone.

Theodore had been part of my life for so long that I'd forgotten what it was like without him. He was my partner, my closest friend. We'd worked side-by-side on some difficult cases, like that time Red's friend Milly went missing. That mystery plagued me to this day, but Ted never faulted me for failing to solve it. He remained by my side like no one else ever had.

I wanted nothing more than to take back every word of that fight earlier. It was my beef with Red, but somehow he'd gotten caught up in the middle of it. Then he was taken from me.

I stood there, frozen for an eternity before Red's hand touched my shoulder.

"I'm sorry, Sam," Red said.

Something in her voice snapped me out of it.

I realized I was crouched in the middle of the crime scene. I needed to find clues if I was going to discover what happened.

"Thanks, Red. You're all class, but I got it from here," I said.

"But I wanna help," she said, tears in her eyes. "I feel partly re-resp—"

"Responsible?" I said. Red bobbed her head.

"Yeah."

"Wait. What do you mean, you feel responsible?" I narrowed my eyes and looked her up and down, noticing dirt scuffing up her shoes. She was usually so pristine about her clothes. "Why? Did you have something to do with this, Red?"

"No!" Her hands flew up to cover her mouth. "I just feel horrible about the fight this morning. I didn't mean to insult Ted, and it was my fault he left. But I swear I don't know how he got...like this." She turned, refusing to look at Theodore's mangled body.

I reached out and patted her on the shoulder. "It's okay, dollface. I'm going to figure this out. You can stay, but don't get in my way, you hear?"

I looked down at my friend. He was caked in dirt from head to toe, as if he'd been dragged around the yard. I noted the grass had been disturbed in the area surrounding his body. But the worst of it was the hole in his stomach. It was an uneven, ragged tear from his neck down to his abdomen. What could do that?

I stepped closer and the dog whimpered. I patted him on the head, more to reassure myself as I surveyed the gruesome scene. Theodore's insides were scattered across the ground, ranging several feet from the body. I swallowed hard, cringing at the sight of it. No one deserved something like this.

"Don't you worry, buddy. I will find out who did this to you," I said with a tight throat. There was no time to waste.

Pulling on a pair of gloves from my pocket, I braced myself and leaned closer to inspect the body. I turned so Red couldn't see my shaking hands and brushed a smudge of dirt off Theodore's tan face. I was surprised to find him damp. Not soaked, so I ruled out a dip in the creek. It hadn't rained all day. I rubbed my fingers together and sniffed them. The texture was almost slimy and smelled slightly of oranges. The odor was oddly familiar, but I couldn't place it.

My stomach twisted in knots as I studied Ted's face, and the gore spattered about the grass.

"Hmmmm...."

"Did you find something?" Red's voice sounded hopeful.

"It's what I'm not finding that interests me. What is this scene missing, Red?"

She pouted her pretty little lips at me and blinked up through long lashes.

"I just can't look at it anymore, Sam! I'm no good at this. That's why I came for you."

I stood and hugged her face into my chest and ran my hand down her silky golden locks to calm her down.

"It's okay. I'm here and I'll figure out who did this terrible thing. It's just you and me now, kid."

She pulled away and turned her back again on the scene. I blew out a breath and squatted back down next to Ted.

"The scene is missing blood, dollface."

Behind me, I heard Red gasp and the rustle of the grass as she stepped closer to me. I pointed.

"And see there? One of his ears is torn off." I tightened my jaw and breathed through clenched teeth. I pointed again to his face where there were multiple puncture wounds. "It's almost like he's been bitten." I shot a suspicious glance at the dog. He wagged his tail. "It appears that he was possibly cleaned and dragged here post-mortem."

"Post what?"

Red was pretty, but she was no gumshoe.

"It means after death." I sighed. "I think Theodore was killed somewhere else and dumped here, his corpse mangled by animals."

I stared at the puncture wounds, anything to avoid looking at that gruesome hole in Theodore's belly. The perforations on his forehead were evenly spaced, definitely bite marks. But from what? A neighbor complained that a bear had torn down her bird feeders last week. But there were no claw marks on the body. Not a bear then.

I'd heard lately that mountain lions were making a comeback. No. According to my forensic journals, a big cat would have covered a fresh corpse like this with leaves. It would want to hide the body so it could come back and snack on the remains later. No, this had the telltale signs of canine activity. Bites to the head and neck. There was only one logical conclusion. I glanced at the hound. He was crouched on his haunches, watching me with his dark brown eyes.

"Red. Make sure to keep a close eye on that hound." I gave her an encouraging smile. "I'm thinking coyotes were involved here. I'd hate for the dog to get attacked, too."

One riddle solved, but the coyotes hadn't killed him. Based on the look of the punctures, I was pretty sure that he'd been dead by the time they had gotten their fangs into him. Questions rattled around in my brain. Why would anyone want to murder Theodore? And what, exactly, had caused that jagged hole in his stomach?

I took a deep breath and faced the worst of it. I'd never seen anything like this wound in life or in my research. A knife laceration would have sharp, even edges. These were not clean and the wound contained tissue bridging across the laceration. It looked like he had been torn open like a difficult bag of potato chips. I needed more clues. If I could figure out where the murder had gone down, maybe I could piece together how it happened.

Something caught my eye, glistening in the sun. I pulled the pencil from behind my ear and used the eraser end to tease it free, extracting a piece of tinsel from Theodore's guts. As I pulled, a long blonde hair followed, knotted around it.

"This case is the oddest I've ever seen, Red." I felt her presence beside me before I even saw her. She placed a hand on my shoulder.

"What is it, Sam?"

"Tinsel."

"But, Christmas was months ago! It must have been floating around out here, contaminating the scene."

I glanced up at her, surprised. She must listen to me more than I thought.

"Actually, if you look closely, you'll see that it's wound around the stomach contents here, along with a blonde hair." I pointed with my pencil and heard her breathing hitch before she turned and ran off.

Turning around, I followed her departing figure, wondering if she was fleeing her guilt or the mess surrounding me.

***

Back at my desk, I spent the afternoon poring over my notes, trying to push the fog of grief away. I couldn't rest until I found Ted's murderer. He would have done the same for me.

The door cracked open and the maid poked her head into the room.

"I'm busy. Come back later." I didn't have time to deal with her at that moment.

"What are you working on, Inspector Sam?" She smirked as she said it. She could be so impertinent sometimes. If I could find someone cheaper who did as good of a job, I might start looking.

"It's Detective. And Theodore is dead. His insides have been torn from his body and are strewn across the grass down by the creek. The cops are cleaning it up now."

She reddened, and her eyes darted around the room.

"I'm so sorry, Sammy."

"Detective Sam! I just told you that Melissa!" Why did she always revert to that diminutive? I hadn't gone by Sammy in years.

She frowned at me and sighed.

She entered my office fully and walked over to my desk. She started straightening up my papers and reached in front of my face to get my mug from earlier. As she pulled her arm back, I caught a whiff of oranges and grabbed her arm, pulling it closer. The scent was on her hands, so similar to the slimy substance on Theodore's forehead.

"What is that smell?"

"What smell?" She pulled her arm out of my hand and smelled it. "Oh, that's the OrangeGlo I was using to clean the floors earlier."

"Is it slimy?"

"What do you mean, slimy?" She furrowed her brow.

"Slimy. When you touch it, is it slimy?" What wasn't she getting?

"I guess so. Yes, a little." Brow still furrowed, she nodded her head. That's when I noticed her blond hair, pinned up on the back of her head.

"Your hair was down this morning," I mused.

"It's easier to clean with my hair up. And I've been cleaning up after you all day." She was starting to get squirrely, not looking me in the eye and edging her way to the door.

"Wait." My mind raced as I thought back to that morning's fight. Red and I had been arguing, and she just had to drag Theodore into it. She'd made a snide comment, something about body odor, and I had jumped to his defense. That's when Melissa had intervened. She'd hurried Theodore away, claiming that she'd help him get cleaned up. Truthfully, he had been in bad shape and I let him go.

I shot Melissa a measuring look. She was the last person who had been seen with Theodore. And she smelled like oranges. And she had blond hair. The only pieces that didn't fit were the tinsel and the scrap of envelope.

"What other cleaning did you do this morning? Besides washing the floors."

"Well, I vacuumed a little." She flushed darker as she said that.

"When was the last time you cleaned out the vacuum?"

"When I was done with it this morning." Her eyes were shifty, darting around the room again and not meeting mine.

"Where is the stuff you cleaned out of it?" I stood and walked around my desk.

"I threw it in the bin."

"Which bin? Show me."

She led me down the hall to the laundry room and pointed to the garbage can, then turned and fled back down the hall. I narrowed my eyes as I peered after her. Something was fishy here.

I removed the lid from the bin and looked inside. Good, it seemed that the liner had been changed before she emptied the vacuum into it. There were clumps of dog hair, and a fine layer of dust lined the bag. I turned the bin on its side and started sifting through the contents. Bits of paper were shredded and mixed in with the dog hair. No tinsel.

I took my pencil out from behind my ear and tapped my forehead. The vacuum.

I opened the closet door and dragged out the vacuum, tipping it back so I could inspect the rollers. They were mostly clean, but Melissa must not have been able to get the debris from the corners. I stuck the pencil tip in and hooked it around the tightly coiled clump, pulling as I turned the roller with my hand. After doing this a few times, it loosened enough for me to get my finger around it and pull. Blond hairs were mixed in with dog hair. And there they were, two pieces of tinsel. Probably remnants from the Christmas tree that stood in the front hall months ago. Red had insisted on the tinsel, much to the chagrin of Melissa, who complained that she'd be vacuuming it up all year.

As I picked through the debris, my stomach churned, and I had to cover my mouth to keep the bile down. There—mixed in with the dog hair, the blond strands, and the tinsel—was Ted's missing ear.

I pulled it out and stumbled through the building, calling for the maid. Where was that broad hiding? She had to know I was onto her now.

I heard a sniffle from the bathroom and burst through the door.

"There you are! I knew you had it out for Theodore for a while now, but I never thought you'd stoop to murder!" I threw the ear down on the floor for her to see. "How'd you do it, Melissa? Did he even make it to the bathtub or did you rip him open before he touched the water?"

***

Earlier that morning

Melissa rubbed her temples. She spent the whole morning cleaning and had a headache coming on. Now the twins were arguing about something. Again. She walked down the hall and stuck her head into Sam's room.

"Sammy. Scarlet. What's going on in here?"

"Red said that Teddy smells funny." Sam pushed his blonde curls out of his eyes.

He needed a haircut. One more thing on a never-ending list.

Scarlet wrinkled her nose. "Well, he does."

"Fine. I'll give him a bath." Melissa reached for the teddy bear's arm.

"Mom! No. We have important detective work to do today. I need Ted's help. Milly is still out there...somewhere."

Melissa shook her head. "He can help you with your 'investigations' later." She spun on her heel and took Teddy with her, ignoring Sam's protests.

In the laundry room, Melissa surveyed the scruffy bear. His fur was matted and his seams were always coming loose. She sniffed. Scarlet was right, Teddy did smell funky. He was a mess.

She had used the last of the detergent on the laundry and looked in the cupboard for something to clean him with. She grabbed the floor cleaner and applied it with some warm water. At least it would make him smell good. She tried to rub the fur on his head clean with a washcloth, but nothing seemed to come off. She grabbed a scrub brush and put in a little elbow grease. The dirt remained, but the seam of Teddy's ear came loose with a pop. She sighed and dropped the brush back into the sink. She was not fixing this damn bear again! Besides, Sam was getting too old to be dragging a stuffed animal around with him.

And these investigations...she never should have ordered him those *Kid Detective* magazines.

Melissa glanced around. The kids were still down the hall. She dropped the bear on the floor and plugged in the vacuum. It was time for Teddy to have an "accident." It would be easier on Sam than just taking the toy away. She hoped. It had worked out well for Scarlet's doll, Milly.

The vacuum roared to life. Melissa hesitated and then ran him over. Gears squealed. Fabric ripped. She flipped the off switch and crouched down to look at what she had done. A flutter of guilt ran through her as she extricated Teddy from where he was lodged in the vacuum's roller. Her hand shook and she dropped him onto the ground. His stomach was torn open in a gaping, ragged hole. Bits of fluff leaked out and the loosened ear was gone.

"Oh my god. I killed Teddy. I'm a terrible mother."

Buster, the family's coonhound, bounded in the room. Tail wagging, he snatched up the mangled toy by the head and dashed out the doggie-door into the back yard. Melissa rushed to the window and watched as the dog dragged Teddy through the dirt. Buster gnawed on the hapless bear and tossed his stuffing across the grass. There was no repairing him now.

"Well. I guess I can blame the dog for this one." She let out a shaky laugh and went to put the vacuum away.

Thoughts on "Theodore" from S W Fox:

My favorite story that our team worked on was "Theodore." Ironically, it was the story to which I contributed least in terms of ideas, and mostly I was involved with just doing beta reading. For whatever reason, on that story our team completely gelled. Everyone knew their lane, every idea seemed to click, and it all felt serendipitous on my part. And, because I wasn't "in the pit" so to speak, I had this outside view where I got to see my team moving together like a well-oiled machine. Probably, our other stories were like that too, but when I was writing I was too close to it to see the smooth operation. "Theodore" was the story that convinced me I had a great team, and I was happy to be working with them. And it doesn't hurt that the end result was a cheesy, fun take on the writing prompt. It's totally unapologetic in its approach, and I love it for that reason. It was a story our team wrote to please ourselves and no one else. As a result, I think it's pretty much perfect as a reflection of when our team was at its best.

We're Doomed

These stories required us to explore the world after life as we know it had already ended. We were given a set of potential real-world disasters to choose from: Bees Disappearing, Poles Switching, or Massive Electromagnetic Pulse. The point was not to write an action story, showing how the event happened, but to examine the perseverance of humanity once the event was long over.

The Shift

Team: SUblime SUperscribes

"The Earth will be broken up in many places...a change in the physical aspect of [unreadable] coast of America. There will be open waters appearing in the northern.... The upper [unreadable] changed as in a twinkling of an eye... upheavals in the Antarctic that will make for the eruption of volcanoes...and there will be a shifting...."

The above is excerpted from an ancient volume: Cayce, Hugh Lynn. *Earth Changes Update.* Virginia Beach, VA: ARE Press, 1980 A.D.

It includes several of Edgar Cayce's (1877–1945 A.D.) psychic readings as they relate to the geographical shifting of the Earth's poles. It was found inside a battered metal box that washed ashore in the third decade A.T.S. (After Second Shift). Much of it was damaged and unreadable.

***

Despite the frigid night air, Evans woke in a sweat. Nightmares lingered, a fish hook in his mind. Shifting mountains, rising tides—ghost disasters of a world long gone by. He rose carefully from his cot, old bones moaning, and peered out the open doorway of his shack, wondering for the thousandth time why he'd built it facing the volcano. It loomed over him, stretching into the sky like a tooth in the jaw of some great beast.

It had been over two centuries since The Shift, as best as anyone could figure. Evans's father had passed down a rag-tag assortment of books and papers, relics of the past, and Evans often took them out to read. No one else in the village felt the need to remember. That was the blessing, or perhaps curse, of humanity: the ability to adapt. Still, he knew there was danger in forgetting.

Billions had died, his father said. Evans had trouble understanding a number so vast. He would move rocks around on his floor to aid his counting, but the numbers soon lost all meaning. His father had spoken of the tragedies of the past: *collapse of government* and *loss of civil rights* and *mass extinction.* He could ken none of those things, did not feel their loss. But he kept the books.

Evans turned his back on the volcano and removed the rug that camouflaged a shallow hole beneath his bed, withdrawing a dented metal box. Inside were books on *electricity* and *climate change* and metal flying beasts known as *airplanes.* The rusted shell of one of these machines occupied a chunk of their coastline, its nose resting in the water. He found it impossible to believe such contraptions had ever soared across the heavens.

The book he protected most carefully—the one that kept him up at night—was written by a seer named Cayce. Had Evans been a weaker man, he would've burned it long ago and reveled in the warmth. But his father had warned him against flouting the predictions it held—told him to watch for the signs. He'd laughed at his father, called him crazy, but in Evans's dreams he saw fire and flying rocks and earth that shook beneath his feet. And water, so much water.

He glared at the volcano again, grunting as he tucked the book inside his shirt.

***

Amari gathered root vegetables into her basket, hoping to trade them for fresh seafood in the village market.

"Hurry, Tomas," she called to her son. "Your lessons are starting soon—you know how Master Salah feels about latecomers. And I want to get to the pier before all the fish is gone."

Tomas pulled aside the curtain to his little room, then groaned when he saw the pile of carrots on the table by the cookfire. "Ugh. Not more carrots!"

"A few more won't kill you."

"Can we get honeycomb to go with them?"

"I was thinking of a nice cod."

"There's nothing nice about cod." Tomas grabbed his woven-reed school bag from the bench by the fire. "Race you to the well!"

"Wait! Tomas, wear your furs!"

"Too warm today, come see!"

Amari shook her head as her son ran out the front door of their little cottage. Pulling on her own fur, she hefted the basket of vegetables, grown in her home garden, and followed him into the early morning mist. Jutting through the grizzled cloud cover in the distance were the sky-scraping ruins of a once-great city—if Old Evans was to be believed. A royal city, he claimed. *Mont-Real.* To her, the remains looked like the crumbling fingers of a skeletal hand, waving an eerie farewell. Amari pushed those worrisome thoughts away and concentrated on her duties.

All signs pointed to spring arriving early—it seemed to come earlier each year—but it would still be fur weather for at least a month yet. The framed garden beds which allowed for cool-weather crops to grow in such conditions were emptying of the winter root vegetables. Early sprouts of lettuces and other tender vegetables peeked from the well-tended soil, hinting at coming abundance.

Tomas, who never noticed the chill, stood at the edge of the frost-rimmed garden talking with Evans, who had lived in the house next to Amari's since she was a girl. He spent most of his time glaring at the volcano and fiddling with dusty books and artifacts. The items fascinated Tomas, as did the tales Evans spun to go along with them.

"Sorry—can't stay to talk, Mr. Evans. Tomas is late for lessons," Amari called as she hurried past. Tomas grumbled, but Evans said something which brought on a burst of laughter. Evans raised a gnarled hand to her in greeting.

Tomas was beaming when he caught up with her.

"I don't want him filling your head with his crazy ideas," Amari scolded.

"The crazy ideas are the fun ones!" Tomas skipped ahead. Amari shook her head as she watched him dash toward the lesson house, waiting until he'd rounded the bend before turning toward the market.

***

At the edge of the beach, Tomas tossed his leather shoes aside, then stuffed his itchy wool socks into them and rolled his pant legs up to mid-calf. He'd find his way to the lesson house, eventually. On such mornings the sea called to him in a voice he couldn't ignore. Racing across the narrow beach, his tough soles barely registered the tiny shells and bits of volcanic rock embedded there. When he splashed into the chilly gray surf he sighed in pleasure, capering lithely through the waves and kicking sheets of water high into the air.

He stopped his antics, looking over his shoulder to be certain he wasn't observed by any of the villagers. They thought it odd that he played in the frigid water for fun, and his mother had admonished him, many times, to stop drawing undue attention to his affinity for the sea. The extra bit of flesh between his toes helped him swim fast and sure, but many of the elders frowned on his deformity, as they'd frowned at his father's. He did not flaunt how far and deep he could swim in the freezing ocean water. Yet he could not give it up, despite their scorn. The ocean was the one place he felt at home.

With no one in sight, Tomas relaxed. Splashing along the edge of the surf, he came upon a small tide pool, rimmed with delicate fingers of ice. Several clams were trapped, so he scooped them up and dropped them in the sand by his shoes. They would make a nice addition to dinner.

A lyrical voice rang across the beach. "Tomas! Come help me harvest some kelp!"

Tomas looked up to see Raina walking toward him.

"Mom'll kill me if I come home smelling of the sea again," he replied, but couldn't help smiling. Raina was a bit older, and she could swim and dive as deep as he. She always goaded him into adventures, and didn't care if the villagers disapproved of her swimming abilities.

"Yellow-bellied Scrodfish!" she yelled, dumping her shoes and overshirt and racing into the water. Tomas laughed and took off in pursuit, eager to refute the accusation of cowardice. He hated it when she got a head start.

Raina swam fast, pulling farther ahead. He may have a little webbing between the toes but she was taller and longer limbed. She stopped, treading water until he caught up.

"Bring your knife?"

"No. I'm supposed to be at lessons now, and master doesn't allow them." He pursed his lips as if he'd bitten into something sour. What were those things Evans told him about? The fruit that used to grow in the sunny, southernmost groves before The Shift buried them under fathoms of ocean water?

Lemons, his memory supplied.

"I can do the cutting," she replied, then dove into the blue-gray depths.

Tomas sucked in a deep breath, filling his lungs, and followed. They descended past the rusted skeleton of a sunken pre-Shift bridge, its huge metal arms reaching down into the dark, deeper even than Tomas could dive. He loved exploring the ruins, darting through the oddly shaped limbs and crumbling chunks of flat-sided rock. The bridges he walked on dry land were made of rough-hewn wood, and seemed childlike compared to this sleeping giant.

Sometimes he found trinkets among the wreckage, pieces of mirrored glass or knobs of hard *plastic,* as Evans named it. Tomas took his recovered treasures to the old man for explanations. Often, Evans was as curious as he about the oddities, leaving them both to ponder the mysteries of the past.

Raina passed the edge of the ancient structure, angling toward a hot column of rushing bubbles. The kelp grew thick there, leaves encrusted with barnacles that tasted good in a stew with onions and garlic. His mother might forgive his truancy if he brought home such a treat.

Tomas followed Raina into the swirl. The temperature didn't bother them—neither the freezing water, nor the vent's heat. Tomas wriggled his toes in pleasure, exhilarated by the play of icy sea water at the edge of the fizzy plume. He'd noticed minor increases in the temperature the last few times he'd visited the kelp beds. The bubbles were fizzier, too, enticing a smile from his compressed lips.

Raina pulled a knife from the leather sheath on her leg and began sawing at a thick stalk of seaweed. Tomas steadied the plant so the knife found purchase easily. There would be enough for both of their families to have stew for several days. She made quick work of it, handing him the more generous half, and they both kicked for the surface.

As he broke the plane of water, Tomas saw a lone figure in the distance, watching. He kept an eye on the silhouette, outlined by the sun as it broke through the misty morning, and paddled slowly for shore. As he reached an area shallow enough to stand, the figure turned, shuffling back toward the village. Tomas sighed in relief, recognizing the careful gait.

***

Evans had followed the boy on a whim when he saw him foregoing lessons in favor of the waves. Tomas was an unusual child who appreciated the stories he told around the village bonfires, unlike the others who giggled or fidgeted or simply ignored him. He had a soft spot for the boy, but he knew he must be careful around Amari, who did not appreciate him sharing his tales and books with her son.

Ever since her husband died she watched over Tomas with an eagle's eye. It'd been a cruel death: crushed beneath an avalanche as he gathered wild garlic from the base of the volcano. Tomas's adventurous spirit didn't help matters, and Evans knew Amari had a hard time keeping him from putting his differences on display.

The boy was interesting. His skin was thicker than others and the webbing on his feet propelled him through the water amazingly fast. He kept pace with Raina, who was older, stronger, and had spent more time navigating the waves. She could tolerate the cold water as easily as Tomas. Their unique talents made Evans think of a long-lost book of his father's—the one by Charles...*something*. Tomas and

Raina had physically adapted to their environment. That was what unnerved elders—it suggested that the rest of the villagers were inferior, and hinted of changes to come.

Evans smiled at the pair, shading his eyes against the low winter sun. The day was going to edge toward warm despite the breeze, and he opened his shirt to allow the air to circulate. A single black and white butterfly swooped by, and he admired it.

Life cycle started early this year.

He stretched, causing the book to fall. It landed open and the wind tugged at a loose page. Cayce's faded face stared up at him.

Warm air. Butterflies. Nightmares.

Evans knew what was coming. He'd memorized Cayce's predictions, the ones carefully recorded by his followers long ago. The Sleeping Prophet, they called the ancient psychic, who dreamed of cures for illnesses, answers to questions. And yes, prophecies.

Evans snatched the book from the ground and made for the village, cursing his old limbs and the uneven footing.

***

Amari hummed an old tune while she peeled the papery skin from a fat yellow onion. She sang a few words while chopping, then laughed at herself when she couldn't remember the rest. The water in the cookpot splashed as she dumped the onion in to join the diced herring; there had been no cod left by the time she made it to the pier.

She resumed humming, wiping the blade of her knife on her apron. An answering, inhuman hum arose, seemingly from the floor, to match her tone before modulating into a deeper bass rumble. Her breath caught and a burst of fear ricocheted through her. A cup toppled, then another. The knife clattered out of her hand as she gripped the edge of the table, holding tightly as the little cottage rattled and shook.

It was over almost as abruptly as it began. She didn't let go of the table. After a few moments, she released a fluttering breath. Nothing like this had happened in her lifetime, but Tomas often spoke of such things, after learning about them from Evans; of shaking ground and massive tidal waves. The eruptions.

The Shift.

Amari released her grip on the table, pushing bad thoughts away and focusing instead on the mess in the kitchen, on the onion skins and fish guts scattered across the floor. Her gaze swept the room for damage, pausing at the small window overlooking her back garden. The volcano loomed in the distance, as it did every day, but now smoke was belching out of the top.

A desperate urge to see Tomas, to ensure his safety, blotted out any other concerns. She kicked a loose onion as she skirted around an overturned bench and ran for the door.

***

The noise was not loud, but it rumbled deep in Tomas's bones. The smaller children froze in fear, then ran to Master Salah as seashells rattled off the tables and burst on the stone floor. Even the older children cowered, wide-eyed with confusion. But Tomas wasn't confused; Evans had told him what it meant when the ground danced. An earthquake, one of the warning signs from his books.

The rattling stopped moments later. Tomas looked to Master Salah for guidance, but the teacher's face was as white as those of the children huddled at his feet. The fear permeating the lesson hut tainted the air. It drove Tomas from his stool.

"I'm going to check on my mother," he mumbled as he dashed outside. Villagers were drifting out of their homes, gathering to gaze into the smoky sky. No one understood what had happened. Tomas had no patience for their confusion; they'd ignored Evans for too long. As Tomas passed them, their voices clattered after him, their questions pitching louder.

He was relieved to see his cottage unharmed. He sidestepped their little garden fence and yelled for his mother. They nearly collided at the door.

"Tomas! I was just on my way to you."

Food scraps lay in the dirt. Tomas moved to help clean, but his mother pulled him into a hug instead.

"Earthquake," he whispered into her hair.

Amari didn't reply, tightening her arms.

"It was a warning," he said, pulling back so he could look her in the eyes.

***

Amari shook her head, not wanting to believe. But Tomas was insistent.

"Mom, I know you don't like me listening to Evans's stories, but he's always said something like this might happen."

After the death of her mate, Evans had stepped in to help guide Tomas, to listen to his adolescent hopes and fears and above all, keep an eye on him. She was grateful to him, but wary. Her son told Evans things he would never divulge to her. Despite that, she wasn't sure this was the best time to yield to fantastical prophecies.

"It just can't be. None of what he says has ever proven true."

"Just listen to him. Give him a chance," Tomas urged. Another black cloud bloomed from the side of the volcano, and the ground trembled under their feet.

It was the least she could do.

"I suppose it won't hurt to talk."

***

"Tomas is right," Evans said, stuffing a water skin into his pack. "It's begun."

"What's begun, exactly?" Amari asked.

"A second Shift." Evans ripped back the rug and retrieved the metal box from under his bed, cramming it in beside the water skin.

"That's a bit drastic, isn't it? After a single earthshake?"

Evans slammed his bag on the table.

"Earth*quake*, Amari. And do you think I'd be so worked up if it was the only sign? Another Shift *will* happen, and it'll bring death to everyone in this village. If you're sensible, you'll come away with me."

"Don't talk to me about sense in the same breath you use to quote these cryptic prophecies. Where's your proof?"

"There's this," he said, taking the book from where it rested against his chest. "And there's the dread that's written all over your face. That's your instinct, Amari. Listen to it."

She glanced at Tomas before taking the book, holding it between two fingers as if it might bite.

"What can I possibly learn from the scribblings of dead men?"

Evans wanted to shake her.

"I'll spell it out for you. Every sign listed in that book, I have seen. Every. Last. One. Warmer weather, fewer fish, butterflies in winter, earthquakes." He pointed a shaking finger at Tomas. "Even the impossible: accelerated human evolution."

Amari narrowed her eyes at the mention of Tomas's physical aberrations, even though she knew Evans meant no insult.

"The waters will rise again," he said, trying to speak calmly. "The volcano will erupt and we'll all die unless we heed the warnings."

As if it heard him, the ground began to shake and they all turned to see the volcano, framed in the open doorway, spew a burst of lava into the air.

Amari put one hand on the doorframe and the other on Tomas.

"Okay," she breathed. "What do we do?"

Evans grabbed the book from where she'd dropped it on the floor during the rumble, and shoved it into the box in his pack.

***

Tomas leaned into his mother, both for comfort and to steady them against the trembling ground. The quake lasted a few heartbeats longer than the first. As it subsided, he turned away from the horrors outside, and Evans met his gaze with a frantic nod.

"Supplies, food, and water—only as much as we can easily carry," Evans shouted. "Don't weigh yourself down." Tomas hung on every word, mind reeling.

"There are fresh springs inland," Amari protested.

Evans grimaced. "Can't go inland. The flats will be flooded as soon as the sea starts to rise."

Tomas felt his mother tense. He squeezed her hand, silently urging her to listen.

"Where will we go?" he asked.

"Up. We climb the volcano, on the windward side—"

"No!" his mother said, iron in her voice. "We will die!"

It sounded like a foolish plan, even to his eager ears.

Evans ran a hand through his unruly gray hair. "New land will rise from the sea, or rather, old land. An ancient city, built into the bedrock. The shifting crust, under the volcano, will push it back up, out of the water."

These had been his favorite of tales Evans would tell. A mysterious ruin, rising from the depths, sounded exciting when it was part of a fantastical story told around the bonfire. But scaling an erupting volcano?

His fear was too great. He couldn't do it—even if his mother agreed.

"This is our only chance," Evans pleaded. "The village will flood, and quickly. The volcano is dangerous, yes, but it's the only high ground we can reach in time. If we're careful, and watch the ocean for the land to rise, we can make it."

Tomas's mind raced ahead as his mother argued with Evans. He worried for Raina. She'd never think to seek high ground. She might be foolishly brave about most things, but the volcano had always unnerved her.

Shoving his own doubts aside, he bolted out the door.

***

The world came crashing down more swiftly than Amari could have imagined. The steady grumble and shake of the morning's earthquakes paled in comparison to the deafening explosions which began overhead. What she could see of the volcano was vastly different than the view she was used to: part of the mountain was simply no longer there, replaced by a gouge that glowed an eerie red, steaming where the sea water rushed higher, lapping at the new trench. Based on the encroaching paths of molten rock, they had mere moments to seek higher ground.

Her heart pounded as she ran after Tomas. Dodging panic-stricken neighbors, she caught sight of him outside Raina's home. She yelled his name, but the words were drowned by the cacophony of explosions and screams. Sprinting faster, she saw Raina sobbing in his arms. Raina's parents spent their days working a small vineyard on the slope of the volcano. A haze of ash and sea water boiled where their vines once stood.

Several ragged rocks screamed past, slamming into the cottages on the other side of the well. The impact shook the ground as the homes were obliterated. Amari raced toward Tomas, knowing she had to be with her son no matter the cost. Ash sifted down upon them as she grabbed his shoulder.

"Mom!" He had tears in his eyes as he held his friend.

"Come, both of you! We can't stay here!" she yelled.

Tomas nodded, pulling away, but Raina resisted. She stared at the volcano, toward the roiling, steaming vapor where her parents had been working only moments before.

"They're gone," he said gently, taking her hand, "Raina, they're gone."

She shook her head once, but then another deep rumble rocked the earth. Tomas took his friend by the shoulders.

"I want to help you, Raina, but I can't do that if you stay here."

Raina lifted her head, torn between Tomas and her home, then nodded. Amari breathed a sigh of relief as Tomas coaxed her to follow. Evans met them at the edge of the village, the heavy pack slowing his pace.

"Hurry, this way!"

"And what of the others?" Tomas asked. The village was doomed, Amari could see it. Flames already licked the dry thatch roof of her cottage. Her whole life would be devoured.

"No time to convince them," she huffed. Evans and Raina were moving quickly against the stream of fleeing villagers. Tomas paused and shouted after their frightened neighbors, urging them to listen, to come with them to higher ground. They shoved him aside, panic and hostility in their eyes.

She put a hand on Tomas's shoulder but he shrugged it off, running ahead to put his arm around Raina's waist. Amari looked up at Evans on the steep volcanic path ahead, feeling insane for following this man. But Tomas was determined, and he was her whole world. She grimaced and followed.

***

Evans felt every year of his age as they climbed: the thin air and uneven surface conspired against him. His knee gave out and he was forced to crawl up the slope, hard points of rock cutting into his palms, leaving bloody prints on the rocks behind him. He was thankful that Tomas was able to shoulder the pack alone; he couldn't have made it so far with such a weight. They were moving in the right direction, but slowly, far too slowly. He stood with a groan and struggled on.

The world was cast in a strange orange glow as sunlight filtered through the ash; it was the final sign. Evans's books had gotten him this far, but knowledge was a cold companion in the face of such destruction.

Another tremor shook the earth and Raina slipped. He caught her as she fell, taking the full weight of her body by dropping to one knee. The joint slipped out of the socket, ligaments tearing, and he screamed. Raina scrambled back, apologizing, and he waved her away, motioning for Amari. They were ascending the intact side of the volcano, away from the lava and the acrid cloud that threatened suffocation, but they'd be swept away by the rising water if they didn't climb higher. He knew this just as he knew that he could walk no further.

"Amari—help me."

She squeezed past Raina on the narrow path to crouch at his side.

"I've dislocated my knee," he said into her ear. "I cannot continue. You need to get the children higher."

"What will you do?"

Evans rested a hand on her shoulder. "We both know the answer to that."

Her expression softened, and she took his hand. "How will I know where to go?"

"Keep climbing. High as you can. Things will be clearer near the top." He raised his voice to call to Tomas. "'Fraid I've hurt my leg. Just need to rest it for a minute. You lead the way, and I'll meet you up there!"

Tomas made his way back to Evans.

"No, we'll wait."

Evans grabbed the strap of his pack where it rested on Tomas's shoulder, and tugged gently.

"You think I'd let my books get wet? There are treasures in that box my friend, and if you really care for me, you'll make sure they get to safety."

"You need to be safe, too."

"Tomas, I'm old, not stupid. This air has made my chest tight. Give me some time and I'll see you up there."

"All right," Tomas frowned, wrapping him in an awkward hug, pack sliding sideways. "See you soon."

"That you will," he said, waving the trio on their way with a forced smile. Amari kept her expression blank throughout the exchange, but as she turned away, he saw her shoulders tremble.

Evans laid back, impervious to the rocky terrain. The only thing that bothered him was the rush of rising tide— he could hear it consume trees and dwellings and people, screams and cracks of splintering wood echoing below. Yet in the weird ocher half-light he felt oddly at peace, glad that Amari had the sense to listen to him. They would make it, he was certain. And they would pass on his work. His job was done.

The sound from below became a roar, waves breaking just beneath where he lay, but he kept his eyes turned to the sky. The volcano spat a large chunk of pumice into the air and he heard it sizzle as it hit the water, the steam rising past his eyes. He took one last deep breath as the waves crashed into him, their dark fingers drawing across his body, raking him against the stone.

The movement jarred his leg and he cried aloud, sucking in a mouthful of the black water. The taste was foul, all metal and salt, and he sputtered it back out, shivering against the pain in his leg. Another wave descended—this one larger than the first. It dashed him against the rocks, driving the breath from his injured body.

When the third wave descended, it struck Evans at full force, driving his skull against a boulder.

***

A blast of heat hit Amari in the face. Maybe Evans had been wrong about climbing to higher ground after all. But as they rounded the back side of the volcano, she saw that their fellow villagers had fared much worse—there was only water where their homes had been.

She called the children back to her, worried that if they went much further they'd be swallowed by the red, yawning mouth, its lip just overhead. A new stream of lava broke free, and the trails of fire poured on either side of them. They were trapped. She grabbed Tomas and Raina by the hand, forcing them to turn their backs on the encroaching lava. All three of them faced the sea.

"Tomas, what are we looking for? What do the books say?"

She looked out at the threatening waters. They were gaining, the lava spitting and sizzling where it merged with the all-consuming waves.

He hitched the straps of the pack higher onto his shoulders.

"I—I'm not sure. An island. A...*rising*, Evans called it." Tomas paused, coughing as a cloud of ash whipped past them. "Some sort of ancient civilization that sunk beneath the water, before the great prophet was even alive. It's supposed to rise again, after the second shift. I...can't remember any more."

They fell silent as the rising water crashed against their feet, searing heat blistering their backs. Tears welled in Amari's eyes. They'd made it so far, but there was nowhere left to go.

"There!" Raina screamed.

A wave knocked them back against the side of the volcano, but not before Amari spied a mound rising in the far distance, clusters of stone ruins atop it. The crumbling structures were covered in undersea wonders: brilliant green sea plants and coral in pink and yellow. Such glorious colors she had never seen. She fought to stand in the crash and suck of the relentless waves. The distant isle steamed in the chill air, and Amari realized that the heat of the volcano had waned, the rising water was cooling the atmosphere. With no other option, they let the turbulent waves take them.

The water buoyed their bodies, and they drifted away from the dying volcano. She kept her head above the waves as she had seen Tomas do, but was not as practiced at swimming in the open ocean. The craggy peak, just moments ago alive with fire and fury, screamed in defeat as the frigid waters doused it, lava turning to rivers of blackened, porous stone.

"Raina, here, take the bag, I have to help my mom."

Amari was ashamed that her son had to come to her rescue, but her muscles were seizing in the icy water. She could no longer feel her fingers or toes.

The three of them struggled toward the waiting island, but the punishing waves showed no mercy, and soon Amari felt herself sinking, the desire to close her eyes and drift down to the newly submerged earth a powerful temptation.

***

Tomas's mom wasn't going to make it. She was barely conscious, taking in way too much water. Raina could handle Evans's bag, but the leaden weight of his mom and her heavy, wet clothes were too much for him alone.

He met Raina's eyes over the top of his mom's drooping head, and could see that she knew it too. She pulled the strap of the bag off her shoulder, holding it up in the air. He nodded at her, and she let go, the bag disappearing under the waves. There was no time to mourn the loss of the books, or worry about scouring his memory for what prophecies he'd be able to preserve. There was only his mother and his friend, and their dwindling stamina.

Raina swam to Amari's other side, and they began to stroke through the water in unison. It wasn't until they flopped, gasping, onto the shore of the miraculous new island, that Tomas spared a thought for what Evans would think of his decision.

***

In the weeks since their arrival, they had adapted to life on the island. Shelter was an easy thing; they used dried seaweed to cover the gaps in the existing structures. Water, too, for at the center of the island bubbled a sparkling spring, cold and crisp. The best that Amari had ever tasted.

She'd set up a drying shack to preserve the scores of fish that washed ashore, casualties of The Second Shift, as they'd begun calling it. There were bodies, too. Both fellow villagers and strangers from other islands. They buried them on the far side of the beach, with a marker detailing the tragedy.

Raina and Tomas were delighted by the artifacts that continued to wash up. Tomas chose a small, crumbling stone building at the center of the island to house them, calling it his *Museum*. One of Evans's old words, no doubt. Items included a large black circular tube with a hole in the center, its exterior carved with strange, raised patterns. A single shoe appeared as well, in a shade of deep purple and made of some impossibly light material. *Plastic*, Tomas informed her. And the biggest salvage of all: a giant sheet of metal, bucked and beaten over time and covered in barnacles and rust. The writing was faded, but Amari could read "ON-401W" at the top, an arrow with "Niagara Falls" underneath. She could make no sense of it, but if it made Tomas happy, she could not see the harm.

Someday, would Tomas become the old man in a new village, raving about the warnings of the past?

She could see such a thing happening. He was already beginning to record what he remembered from Evans's lost books. But for now he was free to grow as he pleased, to dive and frolic in the warm surf with Raina. Amari chose to believe there were other survivors out there, so that these two would not have to shoulder the responsibility of a new civilization on their own.

She kept her eyes on the horizon, and waited.

Thoughts on "The Shift" from Cayce Osborne:

[Picking a favorite story] is like picking a favorite child! But I do have a personal connection to "The Shift." When we were deciding on which of the given prompts to pursue for the post-apocalyptic challenge, I was doing research on the concept of polar shifts [and] I came across a familiar name: Edgar Cayce, the person I was named after. This sparked my imagination and a story concept flowed from there. My group members were fantastic collaborators, and I'm so pleased with how we all pitched in and came up with a unique story.

Honey Kingdom

Team: Sneaky Little Scribes

I stand here today, on the Golden Celebration of the Honeyborn, before my parents, the King and Queen. In this cabin before you, my great grandparents founded our kingdom and our Golden Age. I, Lady Aurora, am tasked to pass on our heritage, that none may repeat the mistakes of Earth's past. So sit, villagers, lords, and ladies, for only together may we fly into the future.

Caesar strolled through the market, a broken asphalt square more filthy than most in the Wastes. Hunters and Scavengers bartered in rat meat and bits of leftover history that others may call trash, but they called currency. As a Lord of the Vancouver Island Kingdom, it wasn't common for him, or even his peers, to come from the Hill and walk among the Scavengers. It was his twenty-fifth birthday though, and as his mother was fond of pointing out, he was incorrigibly mischievous. His father, Magistrate Caesar Evanal Miller Sr., would have him flogged if he knew.

He had grown up in the massive Glasshouses built in the hills of Vancouver Island that overlooked the rubbish mounds along the coast. He spent the days studying indoor botany with his elders; pollinating and developing fruitful hybrids of plants that weren't yielding significant amounts of food the way they might have seventy-five years ago. Despite being Glassborn, he had a morbid curiosity where the Scavengers were concerned. Their lives were pathetic and disgusting, but it was intriguing to contemplate their methods of survival. When the bees disappeared and society collapsed, only the affluent families had the means to prepare. They accumulated whatever seeds and perennial fruit and vegetable plants they could get their hands on, spent their money on moving north to where the climate was expected to regulate at a manageable temperature, and built their glass castles in order to propagate what they had hoarded. The rest were resigned to live off what remained of the land, and the trash left behind in the wake of the extinction.

Caesar had secretly planned this expedition for months while he worked in the lab. He pocketed zucchini from their highest yielding hybrid when his mother wasn't looking. They didn't trade for much among the Glassborn, but Scavengers who spent their days hunting vermin or shooting handmade arrows at birds, would trade their own mothers for such a delicacy.

A voice from behind him danced into his ear, lighter and more cheerful than the grating yells of the hawkers.

"Have you lost your way?"

Caesar turned to find the owner of the melodic voice smiling at him, her muscular body garbed in thick, plastic rags and tattered Nikes from the PreExtinction era. She looked like a homeless woman from his grandparents' historic photos.

"Thank you miss, um, Miss Scavenger, but I can find my way."

"Just trying to help, my liege." She rolled her eyes and walked away.

For a split second, he smelled a bit of heaven on the breeze. She didn't give off the smell of dead animals and melted plastics like the rest of the Scavengers. She smelled sweet, enticing him. He raised his voice to stop her.

"My apologies, miss. I didn't mean to be rude. I've never been here, and my family warned me about the dangers of...."

She spun around, planting her hand on her waist, eyebrow cocked. "Scavengers?"

"Sorry, I don't know your name, so I went with what I saw."

"Do I look like a half-wit?" She marched forward, bringing with her the sweet breeze of her scent.

"Miss?"

"Are you deaf as well as dumb? With your clean clothes and pretentious attitude, you obviously don't come from down here."

"Of course. My sincere apologies for thinking you less for your accouterments."

"Accouterments? I ought to drag you into the pits, Glassborn. I dig through literal shite for items I can use to survive. I shoot birds, build fires, and live in a rusted hut I built with my bare hands out of old cooking pots and bits of scrap metal. My feelings are the least of your concern."

Her cocky, critical snark wrought a strange effect upon him. She was unexpected and refreshing, real in a way his friends in the Glasshouses could never be. He'd grown accustomed to the Way of the Mirror, of presenting himself as if looking in a glass, scrutinizing every word and looking for hidden intent and politic. His grandparents' generation drilled it into each others' heads since before extinction.

As he looked beneath the layers of plastic and soot, he found a stunning, beautiful face, and his breath caught. "You're amazing," he blurted out, shocking both himself and the girl.

"Excuse me?" She shuddered, as if disgusted.

"I think you're amazing." The awe he felt kept him from his usual eloquence. He struggled for what to say next and simply stared.

"Stop that." She tilted her head at him.

"Oh, sorry, miss. What is your name?"

She snorted. "I'm Eve, if you must know."

"I'm Caesar."

They paused for an elongated, awkward moment, shocked by the crackling intensity between them. "You don't smell like the others. Why is that?"

She hesitated. Instead of answering, she studied him, lips curled in a frown as her blue eyes raked him over. He knew the Scavengers didn't trust the Glassborn. He hoped he'd be an exception.

"If you really want to know, I'll tell you, but we shouldn't just stand in the middle of the path. We're practically inviting the others to murder us for our junk."

"Smart, but where should we go?"

"Have you ever been in a hut made of cooking utensils?"

***

Eve led him around several small rubble hills that echoed the pictures he'd seen of the countryside, but with more of a jagged, disease-ridden feel. Behind a large pile of bricks covering a long, broken-down vehicle, a dwelling made from aging metal appeared. She ducked under a ragged canvas flap to work at a strange mechanism on the side of a door and entered. When he followed, the scent he'd noticed earlier enveloped him.

"Fantastic! You built this whole thing?"

"You wouldn't believe what you can find in the Wastes. Our ancestors consumed so much. Even the poor must have been ten times as wealthy as you Glassborn. They're the only reason anyone beyond your precious glassed-in fortresses is still alive."

Caesar saw disgust returning to her eyes and feared he would lose her favor. "My grandparents only speak about the glory of the old days and 'amber waves of grain' on their outdoor farm. My parents pay Scavengers to find them odds and ends, but always complain when they come back with less than they ordered. Me, I'm just glad we didn't go extinct. I enjoy tinkering with this stuff, learning what's needed to survive."

Eve scoffed. "Tinkering. The Glassborn way to describe how not to die."

"I don't mean to be arrogant. You live in a more difficult situation than I, but Glassborn life isn't easy either. I've been a botanist since I could walk and talk. My life consists only of soil compounds, fruit inseminations, and this." He held up the dwarf zucchini as evidence of his sheltered life.

Eve's lips parted slightly, and Caesar recognized her hunger.

"Can I share it with you?" he offered.

"Well, I guess it would just be rude if I refused you," she said, airily.

Eve threw a bag of trash off what appeared to be another bag of trash, but colored in faded green and blue. She gestured to one. "Please, sit."

Caesar toed the garbage bag and raised an eyebrow.

"Just sit down, Glassborn."

He sat and took a bite from his half of the zucchini. "May I ask an insensitive question?" He felt his Adam's apple quiver as he gulped, nervous to deter her, but still letting his curiosity get the best of him.

"Do you know how to ask any other kind?"

"How were your parents allowed to have you?"

She furrowed her brow and glared through him.

"I'm sorry. You don't have to tell me. My parents taught me about that law a long time ago, so I couldn't help but wonder. You were the only other person in the marketplace my own age."

"It's alright. They conceived me before the Parasite Law. I was one of the last children in my quadrant. God forbid I suck at the trickle-down teat of the Glassborn."

"That must've been lonely."

"Eh, I didn't have time for people. I went rummaging every day, hunted for food, and bartered. You know... work or die."

He cringed. He didn't know. He learned, had a lifelong job, but experienced nothing of the struggles she'd endured.

"So, the scent. It's all around here, and it's beautiful. The moment I smelled it I knew that I had to know you better. What is it?"

Eve looked at him, and he knew she still weighed him on a biased scale. He hated it. Her knowledge and ability went far beyond the prats who pranced around the Glasshouses. Their eyes met again, and he felt his cheeks warm.

Eve smiled and pulled a few items off a shelf. "I found these a few years ago. They make me feel like an ancient Queen when I wear it; a little less of what I am and a little more of what I wish I was."

"Freesia, Peony, Oleander, Baked Apple Pie.... What are these?"

"The small glass vials are perfume. The others are scented candles, but I don't dare light them. They'll melt away, and I don't know if I'll ever find more."

"Pearl in the sand...."

"Yeah, I guess they are," she said, staring down at the bin of worldly goods she'd collected over the years. She raised her gaze to him. He hadn't been speaking of the trinkets.

"May I come here again? With you?"

"Huh? You want to come back?"

"Tomorrow? And maybe the day after that?"

He held his breath. It wasn't like him to be so forward with another person, but he gambled and took a page from her book.

Eve blinked, and a blush rose in her cheeks. "I suppose so, but I scavenge every day. I might not be here."

"I'll wait for your return."

In the following weeks, Caesar returned to Eve daily, under the pretense of learning archery to hunt birds for his family. His parents respected the young man's urge to provide, and they welcomed his contributions. Eve taught him not only the art of the arrow and bow but also the ways of love. The setting sun was their signal to begin goodbyes, but soon, the farewells grew longer and more intense, lasting well into the night. Their forbidden romance was a well-kept secret until one fateful night, when their lives changed in much the way the extinction of bees changed their grandparents.

"Greetings, my love! Look what I've brought you from the greenhouse today. They're bananas!"

He walked across the sand to their meeting spot with a satchel in hand. They'd met here every afternoon for what felt like a lifetime.

"I've been working on them since I met you. I wanted to make you something special, and the day has finally arrived. Here is the fruit of my labor, and it's all for you."

"You did all of this for me? What an amazing gift, thank you so much." She examined the foreign fruit curiously. "The shell is tough. How do I eat this one?"

"The shell? Oh Eve, you peel it. Here, let me show you."

He loved the way she watched him peel the fruit for her.

"I have a surprise for you, too, but I fear that it will change everything."

He looked up from the banana warily. "What is it?"

"Well, about two weeks ago I started feeling sick in the morning. I figured my stomach was just upset from the changes in what I've been eating. When the nausea didn't subside, I went to the marketplace for an answer. I traded the nurse one of your zucchini and after a list of questions, she told me I'm with child."

"You're...."

"Yes."

"But they'll...."

"Yes. They'll kill me if I have it. The nurse told me that if I return to her with more food, she will tell me where I can find the man who fixes this, but...."

"But you're having our baby!"

He dropped the sack of bananas on the ground and scooped Eve up into his arms, lifting her right off the ground and spinning her through the air. His eyes welled up as he embraced her, kissing her cheeks and forehead while chuckling. She laughed and kissed him back.

He settled her down on her feet again, held her face in his hands and gazed into her eyes. "I'll never let anyone hurt you or our child." He touched her abdomen. "Their Parasite Law is antiquated garbage. We'll find our own way, my love. We've made it this far."

"Are you sure?"

"If there's anything I'm sure of, it's that I want to spend the rest of my life with you and our child."

***

That night Caesar went to the greenhouse and picked anything ripe, or nearly so. He packed a satchel, a backpack, and his grandfather's old duffel bag from the service. He'd grabbed some of his mother's larger clothing for Eve to accommodate her soon-expanding midsection, and a handful of old photos of his ancestors to show to his child someday. As much as he knew he had to run from them and the laws of the Glass City, he still loved his family, and he wanted his child to know where they came from.

He left a note on his pillow for his mother:

Mom,

I met a woman. Her name is Eve, and I know you'd adore her if you met her. I fell in love with her so

*passionately and so quickly. I can't imagine a single day
on this planet without her in my arms. You're going to
be a grandmother. The thing is, Eve is a Scavenger. I'm
sorry for breaking the law and your heart, but I can't
be the kind of father or husband who would subject my
family to the scrutiny they would suffer from being a mixed
family. I can't bring her home without turning you all into
accomplices, and I love you all too much to bring that
shame upon you. I hope you'll forgive me.*

Your loving son always,

Caesar

"Eve," he whispered outside of her hut. She had built
it in a remote area among the skeletal trees. Despite that,
he worried that a desperate Scavenger might find him
wandering at night with all of his worldly possessions
strapped to his back. He also didn't want to startle his
already anxious love, who worried the nurse would report
her when she didn't return with the food and follow through
with terminating the pregnancy.

"Eve, I'm here. I've got everything we need.
I'm coming in."

He pushed the door open. There sat the garbage-bag
chair and the Baked Apple Pie candle, unlit.

But no Eve.

***

Caesar returned to his home shortly after sunrise and
found his weeping mother in the greenhouse beside the
banana tree. She ran to him and sobbed into his shoulder.

"My sweet, stupid son. Why would you leave like this? Don't you know that I would fight to the death for your happiness? I will protect you. I will protect her, no matter what she is. You love her, and that alone is enough for me. I will protect my grandchild. You may be a grown man now, but you will always be my baby."

"You have no idea how much that means to me, but when I went to her tonight she was gone." He leaned onto the glass wall and hunched over, fighting away the urge to bawl just as hard as his mother had been a few moments ago.

"We have to find her! She's carrying your child!"

"What do you suppose I do? Ask Dad for help?"

"You can never tell your father."

"I know. I can't imagine he'd take this as well as you are. Frankly, I'm shocked by how well you are handling all of this."

"Believe me, it goes against my better judgement, but I'm your mother before I'm anything else."

"Thank you," he said, bowing his head.

"Do you think she would leave on her own?"

"There's no way. She was happy. We had a plan, and everything was going to be alright. She wouldn't just go."

"Can you really be sure? I mean, I taught you about those people. She could have tricked you for food. She could have been playing you all along."

"Those people are starving and working themselves to death. We're all just trying to survive with limited resources and insane laws that destroy hope. They were born in the wrong place and that determined their entire life's trials. If she's a fraud, she's a convincing one, considering our current predicament."

"You'd be shocked at what a woman can fake to get ahead in the world."

"Wow, Mom. Are you speaking from experience?"

"Oh, stop it, Junior. You know I helped your father rise to power. I didn't climb the social ladder, I built it."

"I get it, ok? But this isn't helping me. Do you think Dad can pull strings with Parliament to help me find her?"

"I think it would be wise if we kept your father as far from this situation as possible."

"But how else am I going to find her?"

"We have to think. Was there any sign of a struggle?"

"Not that I could see. She even had the...." he trailed off, remembering the emptiness.

"What is it, sweetie?"

"She had the Baked Apple Pie candle out."

"The what?"

"It's just this...candle." His voice trembled when he said it. He reached into his duffel and produced the glass jar of fruit smelling wax. "She was so afraid that it could melt and she'd never be able to smell it again. Mom, she was taken. I know it. She would never leave this lying around. It's her most prized possession."

"Does she have any friends? Any family? Can we ask them?"

"Her parents are dead and she never really had any time to make friends. She works so hard. She hunts all day and then goes to barter at the marketplace—"

"Oh, dear God," she interrupted.

"What?"

She had a look of disgust on her face.

"I'm about to go to that filthy marketplace with you, aren't I?"

He grinned and leaned in to embrace her. "I have the best mother in the world." He kissed her on the cheek.

***

Caesar and his mother left at noon for the marketplace. As the Head of the Glass Parliament's wife, she draped a heavy cloak to shield her face. They tried to fall in line with the commoners, but that was no easy feat given their good posture, antique linen clothing, and clean skin.

Caesar scanned the crowd for any sign of Eve, with no luck. Then they tried to bribe a few vendors for information with fresh vegetables. No one trusted the Glassborn.

After working their way down the thoroughfare one hut at a time, they finally located and ducked into the nurse's hut. A wizened woman was speaking to a small girl and a young lady with sweat beading through the filth on her brow.

"We're looking for a woman who came here earlier this week. You told her she was with child and to bring you food to trade for information," Lady Miller stated regally, taking charge of the situation.

"I say that to every woman in this predicament. How am I to remember one from days ago?" The nurse turned back to the young woman. "I must take care of this. Come back later and we'll continue."

As the woman righted herself on the table, the nurse turned to the little girl. "Bitty, go prepare the tinctures like I've shown you."

The girl nodded gravely and slipped through a doorway. Her footsteps up the stairs echoed through the room.

"You'd remember this woman because she gave you a green squash as payment. A vegetable." Caesar's mother clarified her words when the nurse's eyebrows came together in confusion. She didn't wait for a response. "We'll pay well for information on this girl. It's important she's found."

"You Glassborn think you can just pay or threaten for whatever you want. When all the farms dried up, you just built your glass farmhouses and closed your doors to the rest of us. I'm older than most people around here. My parents were laborers, and when the outdoor farms stopped producing crops, you just looked out for yourselves. Is that what you're doing now? Did this boy get a Scavenger pregnant? You're just here to ensure she went through with the termination, aren't you? Well, your worries are over. The parliament's militia raided me and found Bitty. I only had a child to make sure our people still had someone to turn to for medical help when I'm gone, but they didn't want to hear any of that. I had to give them someone in exchange for her safety."

At this Caesar jumped forward. "You turned her in!"

"You're welcome. Now you don't have to worry about your little mistake. She'll never be given the opportunity to talk, so your secret is safe within these walls." She scowled right back at Caesar who was brimming with rage at the news.

"How dare you! You'll regret this, you selfish wench!" Before Caesar could take a step forward, his mother laid a hand on his chest.

"Thank you for your honesty. Here are some more vegetables for your silence." She stared into her son's eyes as she spoke with the nurse, dropping the bag on the floor. "We must go now."

Caesar looked from the nurse to his mother. His eyes focused and he exhaled. Nodding, he backed out of the nurse's hut, turned, and fled down the thoroughfare.

***

Parliament was in session when Caesar and his mother arrived. There wasn't a seat left in the Glassborn section and there was barely standing room amongst the Scavengers. They stood at the back, watching the proceedings. Caesar Miller Sr. was on the panel of judges seated at the front of the room. He didn't notice his wife and son in the crowd, focusing only on the judgments of the Scavengers brought before him. The pregnant women would come last, their condition being a crime punishable by death.

Caesar's mother grasped his hand, and she pulled him quietly through the crowd. They passed through a door adjacent to the judges' chambers and turned left.

"Lady Miller, how can I help you today?" asked the muscular man guarding the entrance to the holding area.

"William, you owe me a favor."

He turned scarlet at this and looked around, embarrassed. "Shh. This is not the place to be discussing such things." He leaned close to them and whispered harshly, much louder than Lady Miller's original statement. "Ears are listening everywhere!"

"This is precisely the time and place, because something, or rather someone, in the holding center is very important to me. I need you to get her out of here. Quietly." Lady Miller pointed behind William.

William turned and then spun back. "No, ma'am. If any of these prisoners go missing, my neck will be on the line. I'll have to stand judgement in their place."

Lady Miller nodded, thinking. "Caesar, do you have your hunting knife with you?"

"Ma'am!" William's eyes bulged, and he took a step back, drawing a rifle out of its sheath at his side.

"Calm down, William. He's just going to bruise you up with the butt of the knife. You can say he attacked you." She waved Caesar forward. He took a cautious step as he pulled out his knife. He had been trained in self-defense, but he was no fighter. As he took his first swing, his mother darted past and into the women's holding room. He could hear her calling for Eve in between the cries from William, who was starting to fight back.

"Hurry! Someone will hear!" She emerged dragging Eve, scared and confused.

"Caesar! They said you turned me in! I thought they were going to kill me!" Eve ran into his arms.

"Never, my love. It was that horrible nurse." As Caesar hugged her, William swung his legs around, knocking the couple down. The guard jumped to his feet and raised the alarm. William pointed his gun at them as they stood, still holding on to each other.

"No!" Caesar's mother ran at William, pushing the gun away from her son. "Go, Caesar!" She wrestled with William for the gun but was no match for him.

Caesar grabbed Eve's hand and pulled her toward the gate. A bullet zipped past Caesar's ear. Another grazed Eve's arm. She cried out in pain, not daring to slow her pace. He scrambled to his feet and took a quick glance back. His mother lay on the pristine grass, crimson blood staining the perfect green that had bestowed their family title.

"Mom!" Throat tightening, he resisted the urge to turn. He used his body to block Eve as she ran, looking back one more time only to see his mother raise her head for just a moment, point her finger forward, and mouth the word *run*. He choked down his emotions as they raced through the gate onto the road, and out of town.

The Scavengers barely glanced as they rushed past, though a few called out crude, snarling insults at them for pushing past in such an aggressive way. Caesar pulled Eve along, no plan other than to get away from the Glass, the Scavengers, and to get somewhere they could be safe.

Packed gravel and dirt soon turned into a wasteland of debris with only two ruts where carts pushed through to guide them. Bits of colored plastic, rusted metals, and ragged concrete poked from around the desiccated bones of treefall from decades gone. The smell of rot, ever present even from the Glasshouse, enveloped them here, a second skin of defilement. Eve gagged. When Caesar saw this, he pulled the apple pie candle from his bag. She placed it under her nose and inhaled deeply while smiling at him with fear-laden eyes.

"Caesar. What are we to do?" She looked around at the desolation. "There are no nurses in the Wastes. The Scavengers fear outsiders. No one will have us, no matter where we go."

He stopped and held Eve close to his body, her scent still fresh as a summer afternoon in the orchard house. "The world wastes away, my love, but while I have you, none of it matters. You know how to hunt, to survive off the remains of our ancestors. You can teach me." He pulled off his bag and opened a special, waterproof pocket on the front.

"Look."

Inside, twenty small, sealed, wax packets shone in the afternoon light. Eve inhaled and held her breath.

"Seeds!" A short, explosive breath out. "They'll kill us where we stand."

Caesar nodded and smiled. "Exciting, right?"

Eve shook her head, worry etched across her face. "They'd elevate a person to Lord if they turned in seed thieves."

"We'll find somewhere remote and grow them. I've been raised since birth on the secrets of horticulture."

"On second thought, Caesar, maybe I should turn you in. They'll make me a princess, glass shoes and everything." Eve punched him in the shoulder playfully and displayed a crooked smile, shaking off the stress of the escape, if even just for a moment.

Several days and nights passed as they trekked south across the decayed ruins of human pride and avarice. When they felt the need to stop, Caesar took watch while Eve slept. And so, on the fourth day, they reached a small, abandoned town with a shore that looked across dark waters.

Waves broke on beaches more glass than sand, and Caesar sighed. "We won't be free unless we cross. The rest of the Glassborn will hunt us on the island, but they won't bother crossing the channel. No one has for twenty years. They say bombs fell over there after the collapse."

Lumps of lichened-over humanity bobbed out of the water, a town abandoned to the rising sea after the food shortages. Eve looked to the horizon and grabbed his hand. "What are the chances of finding a boat around here, after all this time?"

"I don't know. Slim, I imagine. We might have to build one."

Somewhere in the Wastes behind them, a horn blew. Then another joined it, and before they fully comprehended what was happening, there was a crowd approaching in the distance.

"How did they find us?" Caesar's chest vibrated, and he found it hard to breathe. Eve turned, fire burning in her eyes.

"We swim now, Caesar."

"Swim? We'll never make it. Besides, we'd lose the seeds."

"Better that, than giving them the satisfaction of doing it themselves. We'd be together. That's enough for me."

He felt helpless. "But, the baby."

Eve stared at him with red-rimmed eyes. She didn't budge.

"Ok, my love. We swim. Maybe the seed packet will hold."

They stripped down and tied their clothes in a bundle with tarp and fishing wire they found along the shore. The stampede hammered through the ruins of the village as the pair took tentative steps into the frigid water. The shelf dropped away as they left the shore, and they dragged their bundles on ropes behind them.

"Halt! In the name of the Magistrate!" The hunting party aimed bows at them. One unleashed an arrow which plunked off to Caesar's left.

"Don't shoot him, you fool! He's a Miller!"

A scuffle broke out on shore, as Caesar and Eve swam hard. No more arrows fell. Soon, the shore was distant enough that they were able to stop and tread water.

"This was stupid," she panted. "I'm sorry, Caesar."

"No, my love. We'd be dead right now if we hadn't."

They held hands while they rested, drfting, and took deep breaths.

"What do we do now?"

Caesar considered their impasse. There really was no way to swim all the way across. As he floated, he stubbed his toe on something hard, but slimy.

"There's something underneath me. Can you feel it?"

Eve raised her eyebrow. "All the way out here?"

He sighed. "There's definitely something down there."

After a moment of poking her toes around, Eve's eyes widened.

"You're right. What is that?"

They explored with their feet for a while. Caesar felt out a large propeller blade, covered in a crust of sea life. "It's a boat. A large one, based on how far it goes across. It must've sunk on a sandbar and flipped in the tide."

An idea surfaced in Caesar's mind. "Stay here." He handed his rope to Eve and dove under the ripples of the channel before she could object.

The water filtered much of the already murky light, and his eyes burned as he swam to the bottom. He'd read about the boats pre-collapse. One this size usually had smaller boats attached for emergencies. His lungs burned, and he returned to the surface.

"What are you doing?"

"No time." He sucked in a large breath and dove again.

This time, he swam further out, and farther down. Upside down, against a mound of sand, was a smaller boat. He ran his hands along it, and found no holes in the hull. He found a rope frayed at one end still attached to the boat. He pulled the end of the rope to the surface.

Caesar spluttered, gasping for air, but held the rope up, triumphant. "My princess, I present you, a gondola." He smirked.

Eve gave him a flat, measured look. "It appears to be a rope."

His grin faltered. "Um, well, yes, but it's attached to a boat. One I think we can use, if we can get it up here."

Eve sighed but took hold of the rope with him anyway. They braced themselves against the larger boat beneath them and pulled. Despite their tenuous grip, and the currents fighting against them, they dragged their cargo upward. After a few minutes, light reflected off a dull lump that grew to a green shine as the lifeboat scraped against the larger boat's hull. When it reached the top, both Caesar and Eve gulped for air, the work having sapped their strength.

Eve considered their prize. "If we can flip it on its side, then up and over the surface, the water will drain."

Caesar agreed. "One last push?"

A nod. "One last push."

Together, they ducked underwater and grabbed an edge. Caesar's feet slipped, and his muscles screamed, but between them, they pushed the side of the boat up until it tipped over and bobbed on the surface.

They threw their bundles into the lifeboat and Caesar braced his feet so Eve could climb in. Then she helped scrape him across the side, and they collapsed on a bed of barnacles and slime. Exhausted, Eve passed out, and Caesar placed her head on one of their bundles. He laid his head on her shoulder and drifted into darkness.

***

Caesar awoke to the boat scraping rocks on the bottom, the sun shining, and a breeze coming in from the ocean. A narrow shore stretched into the distance, and a dead, black forest poked above the ground like diseased fingers.

"Eve, my love, wake up."

She fluttered her eyes as he helped her sit up.

"Where are we?"

"Not on the island. This forest isn't on any of the maps."

"We made it."

"Yes, love."

"But where will we go?" she asked with an air of despair about her. He could see the relief drain from her eyes and quickly morph into fear.

Nothing but rotting wood faced them. "We'll have to find a town to build from. There must be one nearby. Look at the landscape. We're close to water. The soil was fertile enough to grow those trees, which will give us all the wood we need once we can find a way to cut a few down.

There's no way the generations before us didn't inhabit this perfect location, which must have been so picturesque in all its glory. Now it's all ours to share. This is going to be splendid. You'll see."

They commenced, trudging into the wild. Their march made for long days, and they found few birds to sustain them. On the sixth day, Eve turned to Caesar, her eyes glittered with hope, brighter than he'd seen since they first escaped.

"Caesar. Do you see? Look over there." She pointed east.

At first, he didn't know what she indicated. More black wood. More briars. Then, he heard it. A buzzing.

Flying among the trunks, a little yellow speck landed from time to time before lifting off to another area.

"It can't be."

"Let's follow it. There will be life there. Isn't that what the old ones said, Caesar? The bees bring life?"

"Yes."

He stood transfixed. Eve grabbed his arm, and they followed the speck as it seemed to dance through the air at random, though ever deeper into the wood. As day faded into twilight, they witnessed more miracles. Green plants sprouted from an unforgiving earth and young trees spread their leaves toward the sky. Furry animals burrowed down into their hollows for a good night's rest.

And more bees buzzed around them.

Their curiosity took them to a clearing, where an abandoned log cabin sat, hunched, but solid. All around it, plant life flourished, and when they circled around back, they found a small glass house.

Inside, a jungle of life burst at its seams, and a golden liquid dripped from three piles of boxes that practically vibrated from the hum of their inhabitants.

Caesar and Eve stopped in astonishment and said in unison, "Honey."

And so, my great grandparents, Caesar and Eve Miller, found a seed. Once sown, it grew not merely a plant, or tree, but a kingdom. Our kingdom. They learned from the hubris of their forefathers, and taught us to live with the land, not from it. Every year, we assist our world with reclaiming her lands. One hundred years we've thrived, while the Kingdom of the North died slowly from their greed and hard hearts. And with their passing, the old world is gone. Heed these lessons well, citizens, for the future rests with you.

Seeds of Hope

Team: Lexical Literati

I woke up under the wing of the P-40 E Warhawk. With its nose painted like a fierce shark face, teeth ready to tear through the Japanese, my battered World War II plane protected me. I didn't own it, but spend seven years sleeping under such a fighter and your perception changes. This plane was mine now, just like the whole of the Air and Space Museum was "home."

Since my papa headed our community's technological resurrection team, I could sleep anywhere in the museum. Natural light streamed in from the faux-hangar ceiling, waking me up early.

When the pulses first hit I was ten, and the floating displays of humankind's mechanical marvels comforted me.

I'd never had reason to move.

I stared up at airplanes, jets, and space rockets we hadn't yet scavenged. The dawn of technology. Anything was possible then. Such equations those inventors had created, the theories they'd proved and disproved. Once, I'd expected to join their ranks. But I hadn't taken pride in a single formula I'd constructed this year or the equations I'd run.

I toyed with the tuber light by my bedside, my contribution that first week of "school" after we settled here. And we still used them. *How many decades had it taken mankind to get from a potato battery to a space station?*

I yawned, stretched. *Too early.* Fading starlight competed with my 'tater light. No one else stirred. Maybe I had enough time for another chapter of John D. Clark's *Ignition! An Informal History of Liquid Rocket Propellants* before I started my day. I read it for the dreams I'd lost, not because my teacher, Mrs. Wallace, expected it. I wanted to love science the way I used to, before our community focused on it to the exclusion of all else.

No more than three paragraphs in, my gut cramped. Again. I weighed it against my normal stomach troubles. I wasn't anxious about anything other than surviving; it didn't pierce hot and sharp like food poisoning. That left *girl troubles.*

I lunged for the F4U Corsair that served as my closet and grabbed the first shirt and shorts that passed the sniff test. No need to crank them through the hand washer we'd stolen from the Museum of American History. Crap, I was down to my last pussy-willow wand to stem my flow.

The expansive hallway seemed as homey now as the neighborhood where we'd once lived, but sadness and comfort warred. This space longed for crowds of kids pointing in wide-mouthed wonder. Like me, back then, racing ahead of my parents to the next exhibit, then the one past it, and the one after.

I slogged down the dead escalator and stepped outside into the predawn Mall. In summer, morning was the best time for outdoor chores. We'd run out of sunscreen long ago, and without resources to set fans and air conditioners humming, we treated too many cases of heat stroke.

Scattered with fields of our feeble crops, the expanse of the empty Mall stretched before me. If it wasn't paved or littered with heavy debris, we'd tried to plant it. When the first pulses hit, gravity pulled every plane in the air to earth. Havoc reigned where they crash-landed. Fragments of a Boeing 737 tore up the grassy center of the Washington Mall. The tail of the Southwest Air jet stood straight up like a monument to our shattered past.

Mama knelt by a struggling plot, shaking her head. With how late she and Papa always talked, she never got to work out here before me. I waved and was about to call out but thought better of it.

I headed for the mosquito nest, resolving to knock "breakfast water collection" off my weekly chores list.

In the Before, Mama was one of those 'crunchy mothers' who believed in natural living. Now Mama led the agricultural expansion of our community, having taught every mother to be crunchy alongside her. But this way of living was supposed to have been temporary.

Mama and I had the Mall to ourselves. Not that there were many of us. One hundred forty-eight in our community. *And outside of it?*

By my calculations, eighty-eight percent of the human race had died. The initial pulse wiped out supply chains for food and the production of medications. The loss of insulin and nitroglycerin had the most immediate effect. Many died because they hadn't been fast enough to claim a food source, or had been naive enough to think the "power outage" wouldn't last long. The survivalists fared better than most, I suppose, their preparations finally paying off, but even they would have suffered attrition when the most brutal claimed their fiefdoms from others. Even they were probably running on fumes at this point. I also included a percentage of lives lost by crashes, like those on the commuter jet stuffed into our front yard.

There was no real way to test, verify, record.

Information about anything outside our home was another luxury from the Before.

And news from that era was meaningless. I'd begged Papa to take us to the launch of the fantastic "communications satellite" in Houston. Our government lied. They had launched a weapon, and a faulty one at that. Papa blamed the administration for rushing it to completion without proper testing, dooming it to fail with the slashed science budget. No one had believed the one columnist screaming out the truth; the failure resulting in the pulses had happened too quickly for others to dig into the story.

I shivered away the memory of that day and got back to my task. Stagnant water greeted me. As a kid, I loved threading my way through the warm mass of people on the Mall, leading Papa to the Reflecting Pool. Now we called it the mosquito nest.

The yoke and buckets, once part of an exhibit, saw daily use. I filled them one scoop at a time with a Baltimore Ravens cup. We'd hammered trash cans into rain barrels, harvesting rainfall from buildings' roofs, but we never had enough. At least we still had wood to boil this water. For now.

I scanned the rooftops for our sharpshooters. In DC, security personnel were one resource we weren't short on. I didn't spot a single one on my way to the Natural History Museum. We used that small cafeteria there to serve meals. Nothing worked easily. We had to boil the water out back, then filter it through three layers of cloth. It wasn't perfect, but it was better than drinking it raw.

***

I slopped a heavy spoonful of gruel into my best friend's bowl.

"Up early again, Lina?" Felicia asked.

"You practicing for when the CIA's up and running again?"

"C'mon, you're working the *breakfast line*." She peered into the bucket of water. "Please tell me this is clean today."

I channeled Mama. "Water purification is an art, not a science."

She whispered, "Can't you sneak me a bottle of the good stuff?"

"We've got to save those for emergencies. And honestly," I leaned in, lowering my voice to match hers, "there may not be any this year. Even the secret government stash has its limits."

Felicia paled. Silent as a spent fuel cell, she moved on.

Most people passed without more than a good morning or "faux-oatmeal again?" comment, but a few got chatty if the lines stalled. We'd dwindled below 200 souls over a year ago, but menial tasks like waiting in lines always made us feel bigger, like we'd been at the start.

"Daydreaming on the job, baby sister?" Mark rustled my hair.

"That's not sanitary. And I'm not five." I slopped the oatmeal into my brother's bowl.

"You'll always be my little sis, though." He laughed, wiping a chunk of spilled oatmeal off the edge of the bowl. His smile faded. "How old is this batch?"

"You don't want to know."

He pulled closer, lowering his voice. "Nothing from the gardens today?"

I shook my head.

"Problem up there?" A voice boomed down the line.

"Just telling Lina how much I miss Starbucks!" Mark yelled.

Mrs. Wallace sighed. "Pumpkin spice half-caf."

From there, the cafeteria broke into favorites. "White mocha lattes. Chilling with laptops. Laptops! Google! Cell phones. Netflix...."

"My tablet," I whispered.

Maybe because I'd been ten when it happened, I'd adjusted easier. They all thought we kids had taken it the hardest. At first that was true, I guess. I remember crying when our papa packed us up and my tablet didn't make the 'must have' pile.

That morning, sure, that was hard.

***

Papa had shaken us awake, telling us to get up. I grumbled and pulled the cover back over my head.

"Up, Lina. *Now*."

I threw the sheet free. Last time Papa bit off words, Mark had broken his arm.

"What's happened, Papa?"

"We need to get someplace safe. My office, if we can."

"Why, Papa?"

"Questions later, Lina Bee. Packing, now. Two summer outfits, two winter ones, and your bedding. Mama will find your winter coat."

The lights in the house wouldn't work, no matter how many times I flipped the switches. We worked by the flickering light of tiny birthday candles. Mama fluttered about like a hummingbird, evaluating objects before stowing them in a suitcase. She shoved it into the opening of our old bike trailer. The canvas bulged from all that Papa judged we needed. He pulled the garage door up by hand, letting in a faint light as the sun rose.

"Why are we *pulling* all this?" I asked.

"The trains aren't running," Papa said. "Listen. No jet noise, no electric hum anywhere. Total silence. This is huge."

Mama paced the length of the garage, staring into the street each time before she returned to us. "Lina can't make this long trip."

"Yes I can, Mama," I said even though I didn't believe it. Papa had driven me there, once. How was I riding my bike there? My shoulders already hurt from everything I'd shoved into my backpack, the zipper straining against its teeth. But Papa had said we could get there, and Papa was always right. At least, that's what I thought then.

Mark pushed Mama's largest wheelbarrow, still dirty from her backyard garden, to our loading area. "Will this work, Papa?"

"Yes. And we *will* make it, darling. An hour into DC by car with jams, but shorter distance by surface streets...." His eyes unfocused into his "figuring" face, which he wore whenever he calculated. Then he came back. "Riding our bikes, walking, taking breaks, we will make it before nightfall. Lina can pull the lightest load. I have an idea how we'll hook the wheelbarrow to my bike."

Standing in the drive with our bikes and what we'd pull, we overflowed into the yard. Wet grass tickled my toes. I hugged my tablet. Like Papa, I never went anywhere without my research. It stored my second grade paper on Robert H. Goddard, the father of the modern rocket; my third grade paper on Nikola Tesla, the engineer I said made the space race possible, because he invented alternating current electricity, and science sure needed that.

Papa teased it from my hands. "It will be worthless, Lina. I'm sorry. We'll lock it in the house. If I'm wrong, we'll be back tomorrow or the day after, when the Gray Line's running again. If I'm right...."

"Why do we have to go to your office, Papa?" I sniffled back my tears.

"We have to go where the knowledge is. The past is our future, and nothing compares to the Library of Congress."

Mark elbowed me. "Guess I'm missing my physics test today. What are you missing, Lina Bee?"

"My tablet."

While Papa worked on turning the wheelbarrow into a trailer for his bike, our neighbor Mr. Esperson popped his head out his front door. "Oscar, I'm glad I caught you before you headed for work. My electricity's dead and my car's not working. Would you let me tag along to the park-and-ride?"

Papa walked over to him. "No one's going to be driving anywhere for a long time, Neal. If this is the EMP, you're better off grabbing your camping gear and all the canned goods you can carry. If you're packed before we roll, you're welcome to join us."

Mr. Esperson laughed. At my papa.

"You can't believe *The Washington Post* piece from last week. That satellite was for communications. It wasn't a weapon of mass destruction. Even if it was—we wouldn't target our own country."

"Believe what you want," Papa said. "If I'm wrong, it's no harm to my family, heading out on an adventure by foot to DC. If I'm right, I'm ahead of the chaos and confusion."

With another hearty laugh, Mr. Esperson shooed Papa off the porch. "I'd bet my house that I'll see you back here in a few days."

That made Papa laugh. "It's convenient you're renting, then, isn't it?"

When we left, Mr. Esperson made no attempt to join us. I asked Papa what an EMP was. *Electromagnetic Pulse.* Papa told us what happened when a massive EMP hit. This dead feeling around us, where nothing with electrical circuits could power up.

He scared us silent with the horrors of dead tech, the assault on the structure of *society.*

I sobbed as we weaved the confusion of streets I'd never bicycled, passing cars stopped in the middle of the road. Every traffic light hung there, no good to anyone. Nothing we had relied on for daily life worked, and no one joined us.

Mama shushed him and quizzed me on my spelling. By late morning, I waved to adults sitting on their porches, kids sitting in the street, talking. I thought of all the Pokémon I could have captured.

Only a few others had migrated then, but not with us. I guess not many had a papa as smart as mine, knowing when to run.

At the Mall, we skirted the disaster of a crash—the Southwest wreckage. The fire had burned out. I won't ever forget the smell, a swirl of smoke, melted plastic, and chemicals worse than Mama cleaning the bathtub. Yellow caution tape cordoned off the area. Mama thought she covered my eyes in time, but in my dreams I still see a blackened hand, the flesh burned away. Gravity had pulled that plane down, and kinetic energy had thrown that severed hand more than 400 feet.

We camped out in Papa's research office. The overnight team confirmed Papa's fears. The first pulse had hit Sacramento, California; the second, Denver, Colorado; then Washington, DC. Communication broke down fast, though, leaving us to build a community from the scientists, security teams, and their families who had the same idea that Papa had.

In the first weeks—stocking shelves as we scavenged food, supplies, water—I had no time to miss my tablet. After a while, when things had settled, I liked the weight of stiff paper books in my hands. From my home in the Air and Space Museum, the Library of Congress served as my playground.

***

Seven years later, and it was only the older generation who still pined for their cell phones and Hawaiian sea salt. But we were no closer to restoring them. I had the charts to prove that over the past two years, the EMPs hammered us with a logarithmically increasing frequency. Even if I couldn't yet predict the exact day our orbiting nemesis would target DC, my math told me to expect one this week. No one would listen to me, though. Not even Papa.

I left the cafeteria and walked through the underground tunnel to the Castle, our sanctuary from the failed crops outside. Why did kudzu, Virginia creeper, and half a dozen other vines take over, while our vegetables withered?

Our community had done everything possible to hold onto society's trappings. This meant that all kids aged 5 to 17 had to attend school. A shorter schedule reserved time for community-based learning after lunch. Our never-ending rotation covered the jobs needed in our new lives. Next year, I'd be forced to join *the scientists* full time, when what I really wanted was to engineer better crops alongside Mama.

The "high school" occupied a former conference room in the Castle. Since there weren't very many students, we all sat around a long oval table in a room with windows overlooking a courtyard.

I spent the morning bent over Shakespeare's sonnets, arguing about current events that were seven years old, and tuning out when we got to math. I taught myself calculus four in the margins of an old book—vectors and integrals, the stuff of space travel—and ignoring Mrs. Wallace's simple algebra. She'd pushed me into math's deeper waters the day I'd solved her proof without writing a single equation.

When I was ten, watching launches live on TV, I'd wanted to use my math skills to send a whole new fleet into space. Numbers, flying through my head at lightspeed, had always made me feel better. Why couldn't they anymore?

I thought of Mama up early in the field, while Papa pushed to complete another stage on the rocket. I erased my play calculus and started dealing in the numbers that mattered. We'd had 180 people last summer, 200 the summer before. And this summer, 148. During dinner last night, what had Mama said the crop output was?

Numbers marked my memory, as solid as sign posts. What did the scavengers bring in? How many babies had been born? Pregnancies? The variables—like no working hospital, expired drugs from foraging runs, and too many illnesses we couldn't manage—took their toll on us.

I crunched the numbers.

No.

I crunched them again.

Then again.

All the while, the class jabbered on about their sample problem. I looked up. Felicia's eyes bored into me. I motioned for her to look back at her own work before Mrs. Wallace caught us.

I checked my math. I thought again of Mama shaking her head at the soil in the dim morning light. How many mornings *had* she been up before me, working in her small lab, manipulating our seeds? *Did Mama suspect?*

I wished I wasn't so good at these calculations. We stood at the tipping point of collapse.

We couldn't stay here. We were running out of resources. Our brightest minds were looking toward space, not soil. "The Second Great Space Race" they called it.

Death race was more like it.

They wanted to try to go back up there to stop the weapon with its unpredictable pulses, but how many times had they built a new circuit board to bring a computer back to life, only to have another pulse blow it out? Yet again, we'd wasted hours of riding the stationary bike to charge up the battery meant to power the "computer."

So we wasted time and resources, building the metal enclosures that protected our precious technology, wasting more manufactured energy to power them. How would we *ever* build and power a Faraday Cage big enough to protect a rocket? They needed to put more stock in *surviving*. Mama would never leave, not after all she'd invested building up the gardens, even though we didn't harvest enough veggies.

By the time Mrs. Wallace dismissed us for our morning break, my mood had exponentially worsened. Only one person could help me bust through that. I headed for Mark's pre-school.

My brother, surprising all of us, had found his niche in child care. The kids adored him and heeded his warnings and advice more than I ever had. We had to protect them, and that didn't mean reaching outer space again.

Chaos reigned in the Hall of Ocean Life. Mark had blocked the arched exit at the far end with plywood braced by the Megalodon shark jawbone, nine feet high and eleven feet across. They played all around it. Mark didn't seem the least bit worried that they might run into the seven-inch-long teeth.

"Pause," he called.

All the little limbs froze in place, but the youngest kids giggled. The loudest, a five-year-old, lost his balance.

"Two points for red!" Mark yelled. "Move."

Mark laughed as kids tumbled into each other. When I waved to him, he blew his whistle. "Free time!"

Their dramatic sighs and groans made me smile. Mark motioned me out of bounds, on the steps leading to the second floor.

"What's up, Lina Bee?"

I forced a smile.

"Seriously? Spill."

I told him everything.

"We can't keep this up," I finished. I leaned my head into his shoulder. "I think we might have to leave."

"Leave our home?"

"It's a stupid idea isn't it? They'll never go."

"I don't know, Lina. If we leave, we'll have to scavenge. I doubt there's much left. It can't have gotten better than the first year. I wish I could forget when those people stole one of Mama's chickens."

I did, too.

***

We were at the newest "garden," planting zucchini seeds beside the fallen plane in the Mall. Countless hours, battling the ground into submission, and we had a dozen plants to show for it. So many seeds didn't germinate. Had we planted too deep? Too shallow? Had birds dug up the seeds? I stopped trying to solve the equation. Hunger does that to you. Mama had us planting round three.

Mark had been on watch, ready to shoo the birds away or to threaten any larger creatures. A pack of dogs had charged us the day before, when we re-planted the cucumbers. Only gunshots sent them running, except we had an axe.

An old couple not in our community had approached, hands out before them.

"Please, can you spare food?" the old woman had said.

The old guy grabbed a chicken, tried to run. Mark shouted; the man ignored him. Mark threw his axe. He missed, but the man dropped the chicken. The old woman shrieked "I'm sorry" as she stumbled after him.

"Get the seeds in." That's all Mark said.

I think he meant, "I would have killed him."

***

I lifted my head from Mark's shoulder. "I remember how that woman trembled."

"Huh?"

"The chicken thief's wife. They must have been starving."

Mark's eyes unfocused, the same as Papa's figuring face. Then he returned to me. "I better get back to the kids. And you need to get back to school."

I nodded.

"Wiser minds than ours are thinking about these things." He tapped his fist to my shoulder.

I stared at him down my nose, just like Mama would. Mark didn't have to go to school here like me. He didn't appreciate how we kids got pushed into The Second Great Space Race whether we wanted to be there or not.

"Sure, big bro. Sure."

***

"Lina, get the cotton balls out of your ears." The dreaded gold and silver flashed before my eyes as Mrs. Wallace tapped the table with the flat of General Grant's sword.

My body was back in class, but the conversation with Mark had pulled my mind away.

"Lina." The pitch of Mrs. Wallace's voice rose. "Pay attention. This is the most important class of the day. Rebuilding."

She picked up my slate and looked where I was supposed to be calculating speed, trajectory, and types of fuel to fire a rocket to intercept the EMP weapon. Instead, I'd calculated our food shortage. Again.

"Is that crops? If you want to be a farmer, help your mother in the morning. In this class, we need you to be like your father."

"I'm not either of them. Your generation got us here. Now you're trying to push us right back to the place that got us into this mess."

The blade trembled in her hand. "Because we *need* to stop the pulses. They're preventing us from getting back to where we were. We need technology if we're going to survive."

"Maybe we needed to stop the weapon's launch seven years ago," I said. "Teach us something useful, like how to keep tomatoes from dying from blight, how to double our yield of beans to feed all of us. Maybe even how to grow corn that the bugs don't eat. The pulses are getting logarithmically faster, but that's not what worries me."

Behind me, Felicia said, "And watermelons. Watermelons would be nice."

Gotta love a best friend who always had your back.

"If you girls are so keen to be farmers, I'll put you on compost duty." She thumped the table with the flat of the blade a second time.

"Oooh." The sound rose around me, classmates egging on Mrs. Wallace. I'd never earned even one sword tap, let alone two.

I ducked my head, counted my breaths until I could control my frustration, and then looked back up. "I didn't mean to be disrespectful. My time of the month is making me cranky. May I be excused to deal with it?"

"What I wouldn't give for a Pamprin myself." Mrs. Wallace waved me toward the door. "You're not off the hook, young lady. Your father wouldn't stand for disrespect."

You're right. He'd tell me to stand up to you.

In the Before, Papa read me to sleep with Thoreau's *Civil Disobedience,* the *Declaration of Independence,* and the tale of Miguel Hidalgo y Costilla ringing the church bell—the call to arms that launched the Mexican War of Independence.

I headed down the first hallway, admiring the courtyard where we planted the best crops, protected from outside thieves: cucumbers, cabbage, spinach, kale, onions, and garlic vied for space. And Felicia didn't know it yet, but five varieties of squashes and melons, including watermelon. To survive, we needed two dozen more courtyards like this. If we wanted to thrive, we had to double that.

I had no intention of going to the nurse and picking up the sock bundles we were supposed to wear, wash, re-use. When the sewers along Seventh failed, a marshy area formed. Mama had dried pussy willows with their fluffy white catkins, saying they were pretty. But since my explorations took me to the Native American Museum this spring, I'd learned how the Native Americans had used them during their monthly cycles. I'd blow off my steam before I headed home to raid her collection.

They didn't want to listen to *my* voice unless I spouted an equation on lift or trajectory. Fine. Then I wasn't listening to theirs anymore.

"You working on stuff in your head again?" Felicia fell into step beside me. "You've got that 'staring into space' look."

"You get kicked out of class?"

"No. I got 'cramps' too. What are you thinking on?"

"I'm kicking myself for telling Mrs. Wallace what I really thought."

Felicia high-fived me. "Girl! It's about time."

"I really need to get out of here. It's...it's a prison. I don't know how you'll take this, but we can't stay."

"I'm all ears," Felicia said. "Wallace has me slated to join the rocket fuel team when we graduate."

I opened the door to a warm breeze.

"Wait up." Mark sprinted after us.

I cast my eyes towards the Native American Museum. Numbers danced in my mind.

I looked at Felicia, then Mark.

"Hear me out," I said. "Do you ever feel like this beehive of *resurrection*—all these people trying to keep the traditions of the Before, racing to replace the technology we lost—is going to lead down the same path? I mean, aren't our parents' *old ways* the ones that got us into this predicament? They destroyed the world. Now they expect to rebuild it, the exact same way. Wasn't it one of the Founding Fathers who said, 'Those who don't learn from history are doomed to repeat it'?"

"I guess," said Mark, "but how else can we fix this planet? We need technology to bring us together. People across the globe once more linked by the tech in their hands, sharing information."

"Do we really? Do we need to *fix* this planet, or do we actually need to *heal* it?" I looked him dead in the eye, willing him to believe me.

"How can we *heal it* with no medicine, and no industry to make any?" Mark challenged. "We need to invent all that stuff all over again."

"The American Indians didn't: the Shawnee, the Blackfoot, the Cherokee. They learned from the earth in communion *with* nature, not *against* it. They didn't try to force it to do unnatural things, or try to destroy things or people with it."

Felicia took my arm. "Your face is way too red. Sit down."

I had no choice but to join her when she perched on a bench in a sun-bleached bus shelter.

"Medicine came from plants and herbs," I said, "like the foxglove to stabilize heart rate. Natural. Everyone worked together to survive. They bartered. They didn't try to make fistfuls of meaningless money. Money made people blind. C'mon, everyone, worship at the altar of Money."

"I liked money." Mark laughed.

"How's all that money workin' for you now?" I said, deadpan.

He blinked.

"We don't need money," I said. "We need to move south, towards Piscataway Park. That's where we'll find fertile soil and the protection of Fort Washington."

"Leave here?" Felicia gasped.

"Did you know plants and trees have their own kind of society? They talk through their roots. As a community, they keep each other safe. And orchids. They can change their shape, colors, and patterns. Even their odor changes, trying to attract whatever bug is available to pollinate them."

"Right," Mark said.

"And it's been shown that when humans live in harmony with nature, nature somehow cues into their needs to keep them safe, too. Like if someone gets sick, the natural herbs they need for a cure shoot out of the ground around them, in the quantities they need to heal."

"Now you're just making this shit up," Mark scoffed.

"I'm not! Isolated cultures depend on that connection. It's been well-documented. Use your library time instead of taking extra shifts with the kids. There's so much humankind has forgotten, or ignored, in our quest for power. Instead, we should work for what we need to survive—as a species, as a society. "

"Food, water, and shelter." Felicia hugged me.

"I knew there was a reason I never beat you at trivia," Mark said.

Felicia chuckled. "Now you'll impress us with your plan, right?"

"Me?" I asked.

Mark and Felicia both looked at me.

"I just know our future's not in designing a new shuttle to launch us into space. It's in reconnecting ourselves to Earth." Finding my voice had tempered my rage into resolve. This must have been the excitement Isaac Newton felt when he explained the first calculus equations to his scientist friends and they *listened*. "C'mon. I want to show you what I've uncovered in the other buildings."

***

That evening, I dragged my feet along the carpeted floor of the Air and Space Museum. I swore the halls whispered my secrets ahead of me. Papa would know before I said a word.

I found him at the rocket's body. It loomed in the middle of the rebuilding area. It was the culmination of our efforts to date, but all I could see was a scrapheap of wasted metal.

"Why did you leave class today?" Papa knew everything that happened in his Smithsonian.

I once thought he knew everything.

"I was studying other things, Papa. Things Mrs. Wallace doesn't teach." I gestured toward the steel door. Old-fashioned deadbolts sealed it, hammered into it to replace worthless keypad locks. "Like fixing the door. Things we need to know to survive. To rebuild our world without repeating old mistakes."

"Was Felicia *studying* with you?" His eyebrows drew together.

I rolled my eyes. "What if she was?"

"You can't keep leaving the safety of the Museums without a security team."

"We didn't leave the Museums. I'm not stupid, Papa."

He softened. "No, no you're not. Which is why we need you, and your brother, all of you, to help us figure out how to shut down the weapon." He rested a hand on my shoulder. "Fresh minds may be able to come up with a solution where old minds fail."

That was a much better opening than I expected. I took a deep breath. "We did come up with a solution, Papa." I risked eye contact. "That's what we were doing."

"That's my Lina Bee!" He strode toward his creation. "You always loved rockets, even before you could walk."

My voice stuck in my throat. I clenched my hands and forced the words out. "This isn't about the EMP. We came up with a solution to the real problem."

"That weapon *is* the real problem, Lina. You can't fly to space in a Faraday cage, and until we stop those pulses, there's not much else we can do."

"But it can't be our priority. We don't have the right resources." I gestured at the scraps of metal on the floor.

"If only we had more NASA minds here," he said. "But with time, we'll get it right."

"We're out of time." I took a deep breath. "The world was broken long before the first pulse. Why didn't we know how to survive when technology failed?" I turned my back to him. "We can't keep chasing the way we lived before. It's not our future. Our future is with the land." I pulled a Stone Age spearhead from my backpack.

"You're romanticizing ancient cultures. What was their average lifespan?" He took the spearhead from my hand. "What would you do?"

"I'd migrate. Head somewhere food grows better, where we're not relying on non-renewable supplies that are dwindling, spoiling. Somewhere kids won't die of malnutrition because we don't have the right mix of foods or enough clean water."

"Who are you going to have to fight to live there, Lina? The real history of man is violence." He crossed his arms. "We don't want to revert to the savagery that dominates the world outside this sanctuary of knowledge."

I looked him straight in the eye. "We'll leave without you."

I turned away from my papa's plea to come back, from my home these seven years. Most of all, I turned away from the path he'd been leading us down.

***

Mark found me at the National Museum of the American Indian. I'd curled up in an exhibit with a small branch lean-to.

He sat down outside. "I've never seen Papa so worked up. He and Mama even got into it. They haven't fought since.... I'm pretty sure the whole community knows what you suggested."

"I didn't mean to cause that. Now everyone is probably worried. But they should be, I'm right." Through my shame of disappointing Papa, I reached for my resolve from earlier. "The *math* says we can't survive here. And numbers don't lie." I crawled out, stood. "I'm serious, we've got to reach Fort Washington. This is about the future of those kids you're raising while their parents chase a hopeless dream. We could make a go of it there."

"We?"

"I told Papa we'd leave. You believe me, don't you?"

"I don't know, Lina Bee. Mama and Papa, they're family. Triple check your math. Seven years. Everywhere good would be taken. We can't assume the fort won't be defended."

I shook my head. "Piscataway is far enough away from the populations of large cities who might have claimed it. The FBI print archives didn't have any records of Doomsday Preppers within an 800-mile radius. It's the

216

perfect climate for growing and gathering foods. Plenty of wood and stone for shelter and tools, fresh running water. I've run the calculations. That area can sustain a population of 1,500 people. If we find it taken, we keep on going."

Still, Mark stood there with his arms crossed, waffling from foot to foot. I'd lost him.

I closed my eyes. I had to trust my last equation. "Consider the east coast like you're playing Civilization XIX, like you're still regional champ. You imagined the stakes well enough in the video game. Can you do the same when it counts? If you wouldn't set up there, where would you go next? Someplace large enough for a small population to get a foothold."

When I opened my eyes, he was looking past me, into the distance. Then he refocused on me.

"How did I never see it like that before?" he asked.

"Because you let go of technology."

"Yeah, rub it in. I know better than to question your math."

Finally, big brother stood by my side. "Everything we bring," I said, "needs to have two or more purposes. We can't steal from the community. Cast-offs only—what's still left in the Smithsonian exhibits. Think you can plan that out, Civilization XIX king?"

He looked around the room, the same surveying Papa did as he scavenged for the rocket. "I'll find every piece we've overlooked." He pointed at my display. "Like this leather pouch. I bet the curators of this museum never expected it to see practical use again."

I snatched it before he could. Smooth in my palm, still supple after hundreds of years. A strip of leather wound in an *x* over a bone button, protection against precious supplies falling out.

"Let's stage here," I said. "It's not like anyone else ever comes to this area. This is the past they have no desire to recreate. I'll get my butt back to school tomorrow, and you play it cool in daycare. I can apologize to Papa. We recruit quietly. I don't suppose we'll get away with this without someone blabbing, so we don't tell anyone but Felicia *where* we're staging. It'll be up to the three of us to gather."

"With a plan like this, I guess you're not my little Lina Bee anymore."

But I've got wings, and I'm gonna fly.

***

Over the next weeks we gathered our stockpile of supplies to build our own colony. From the seed bank Mama had created from the best harvests, I stole a dozen zucchini seeds here, half a dozen cucumber seeds there, some of everything, for our new colony's crops next year. The weak link in my plan—what we'd eat on our trip. Sure, we could try to plant fall crops when we arrived, but we'd never have enough to survive that first winter. We'd have to hunt. Dry the meat into jerky. I handpicked books from the Library of Congress so we'd know how to take on all these chores. Every volume, I weighed what we needed. I tore out sections and built my own "best of the best" volume.

We had fewer recruits than I expected, but I had no equation for this, for *people.*

The night before our exodus, Mark and I huddled below the massive F-1 rocket engine that had once sent the Apollo 11 to the moon. We worked through the weights we figured each kid would carry. I didn't like our first answer, that we'd have to leave behind 200 pounds of supplies. We adjusted loads, adding more to the older kids, then calculated longer breaks, making a longer trip. Was it better to sacrifice extra saws, blankets, rope....

"Mark, are we doing the right thing?"

"I don't know, Lina. I—"

"Lina!" Papa shouted from across the room.

Mama strode in behind him, her arms crossed and her hair pulled away from her face. A line of dirt ran across her chin.

With a flip of the blanket beside me, I covered the evidence of our mutiny. I stood, trying to act like I wasn't up to something. If Mark didn't scrub that fake smile off his face, they'd bust us for sure.

"Mama and I have been talking," Papa said.

"Earthshaking news," I said, "because you two *never* talk." Was I talking too fast? I was talking too fast.

"Lina, let me finish." Papa stopped across from me. Mama clutched his hand.

"I should have let *you* finish, too," he said. "When you talked with me about migrating. I'm sorry I was not ready to listen. So much knowledge at our fingertips, the opportunities I saw when we fled here. I'm not ready to leave."

"But we see *you* are ready," Mama said. "Would you really break our hearts and sneak off without a word?"

I hesitated. Did she really want me to talk now?

"We can't survive here, Mama. Papa. I've run the numbers. We're losing people too fast. Unless we have better variables, like crops improving, better rain collection systems, more time dedicated to surviving and less time on The Second Great Space Race...."

"Go on, Lina." Mama let go of Papa's hand, took both of mine into hers, and squeezed. Too soon, she let them go.

"You are our future," Mama said. "This is your world now more than anything. We've lost sight of that."

Papa's eyes drifted past me.

Did I dare tell them our plan? Or did they already know?

I sucked in my breath. And then I don't think I took another one until I'd spilled every detail, down to stealing from her seeds. Mark had the survival instinct to keep his mouth shut.

Mama leaned into Papa. "You think I wouldn't have noticed those missing seeds, Lina? I would have been on your side. You didn't get your math skills from your papa alone."

How can a mother bathe you in both pride and disappointment with one look?

I hugged her. Hard.

Mark hugged Papa just as tight.

"Think you and Mark can make your case before the Conclave tomorrow? We'll have our numbers to back you up."

"What if we still want to leave?" I asked. In the space between heartbeats, I ran the equation. On one side, our life if we left our parents behind, struggling to establish a new home, crops, jobs. On the other side, the love we'd lose. The knowledge. The hearts we'd have broken, disappearing without a single goodbye.

They'd been misguided, chasing dreams to knock the satellite out of the sky, but if they *could* see the wisdom in letting it go, finding a new way? Papa was worth more than any book in the Library of Congress. And Mama? I wanted to learn her art of engineering stronger, healthier varieties of plants, like Mendel when he had come up with simple equations explaining the traits he engineered into new varieties of peas.

"If they will not listen," Papa said, "your mama and I, we will leave with you. If you will have us."

"I'm sorry, Mama. I'm sorry, Papa. Will you stand behind Mark and me when we talk? Your support means more than any math, I think."

"When *you* talk," Mark said. "They won't know what hit them."

"I'll present." I looked past Mama and Papa. We didn't need a colony. We were already a family.

Reflections and Moving Forward

While our authors discovered that collaborative writing wasn't for everyone, they did each feel it was something worth trying. Mostly because of the relationships they fostered and the things they learned, about writing, creativity, themselves. They all have thoughts on the experience, whether they would try again, whether anyone else should give it a go, and what they should do if they try. So, here they are.

Thoughts from Jennifer Palmer:

As of right now, I have *no* intention of doing this again. While I loved my team and I know we got along and produced solid stories together, not being in absolute control of the words and the path of the story drove me figuratively insane.

Writing collaboratively was a humbling experience. I recognize that I can and will be a control freak should the opportunity arise, and I had to watch myself. It felt *really* weird to have a piece of writing that was both mine and not mine. I could see specific places in the stories that were my words, but then they were joined to words that were not mine, and I just...ahhhh; it was weird. This experience reinforced my knowledge that I prefer to work alone, haha.

I thrive when I have complete and utter control over what I create, even if parameters or guidelines are given.

When aiming to write collaboratively, *compromise is key.* As an adult, you know this in theory, but when push comes to shove, you can't let your ego get in the way of the ultimate goal of a solid story. So just leave your ego outside when entering the collaboration zone. Everyone, including you, will be better off.

Thoughts from S W Fox:

Yes, all your fears will come true; however, if you keep trying, all those same fears are eventually overcomable. And when you achieve something beyond your own capability because of a group, it's an incredible feeling. Basically, the number one thing you need is perseverance. Sure, you need patience and hard work and all that good stuff, but the highest priority is not giving up. If you give up, you'll never see where the collaboration goes.

I discovered that even if your fears come true and your story idea gets wrecked beyond repair, it probably still isn't going to be that bad. Even the story idea that went the most off the rails in my opinion still ended up pretty decent. It ultimately told a story I didn't want to tell, but it wasn't a bad story. It had a backdrop I had created, and it still featured the story some of my team wanted to tell. And there is still something special about having created the world in which they felt comfortable enough to tell their story. Ultimately, I'm okay with that outcome. And it surprises me even now that I'm okay with that outcome because that's so atypical for me. But when I chose to collaborate, I gained friends and accomplices for whom I came to care, and I'm happy they could tell their stories.

I'm very much a lone wolf writer and don't like to share my ideas with anyone for them to use. But even then, I'd highly recommend collaborative writing to everyone. If you're like me, then don't do that often, but nevertheless everyone should try it and dabble in it from time to time. No matter how skilled the writer, they can learn something from almost anyone who brings a lot of passion to their craft. Even taking the most pessimistic approach and assuming nothing could be learned in terms of skills, just the very process of allowing someone else to control some part or all of your idea creates a mental space that allows for understanding that other people will interact with your work and that it doesn't exist in a vacuum. Every writer who shares their work with anyone else is in a sense engaged in collaboration in that they allow someone else to interpret their words into ideas in their own mind instead of the writer's. In doing so, the reader may manipulate, transform, alter, denigrate, obliterate, or cherish the ideas put forth by the writer. So, at a minimum, I'd recommend intentional collaboration for everyone as a means of confronting the reality that other people interact with your writing in ways beyond your own control. The collaborative process helps to make writers more comfortable with that reality, in my opinion.

I trust the process. Given enough time with a solid team like the one I had, I'm certain we could produce a longer collaborative work like a novel. I definitely would like to do something like this again and have already started seeking out some work with other writers.

Thoughts from Cayce Osborne:

In order to write collaboratively, being open-minded and amenable to ideas other than your own are essential. In the interest of getting the job done (finishing the story on time, that is) it's easy to dismiss ideas and approaches that are different from your own. But doing this negates the reason for writing collaboratively in the first place. Listen, consider, and discuss. You might learn something!

From a logistical standpoint, I do have one other piece of advice on collaborative writing. You must have a leader. A person who is ultimately in charge of breaking ties, settling disagreements, and finalizing the story. There has to be somewhere the buck stops, once all the collaboration has generated material. Ideally, this person would change from story to story so everyone gets a chance.

Every writer should try collaborative writing at least once. It won't be for everyone, but everyone *will* come away from the experience having learned something, likely about themselves. My favorite part of these team challenges was the way our ideas fed off of one another. An idea proposed by one person might be picked up by another, only to come back to the originator to be polished up. Sometimes it seemed like magic, the way a story came together.

Thoughts from Wayne Hills:

I agree with Cayce that every writer should try it. Although maybe not for everyone in the end, as with all things in life, to become a better storyteller, experience all you can. You never know when something will come in handy. Selfishly, my favorite part was when it was my turn to take the pen and run with it.

I would do it again with the right person or group. Going in, though, we'd have to agree to a shared vision for all of our egos and muses to get along. Let it go when your turn is up. And when it is your turn, follow the advice given to every actor in their first improv class: "say yes." Accept what you are given, and don't go backwards in a thread.

I'm a pantser, meaning I don't generally plot out my stories, but with these collaborations, having a rough outline of where we were headed, and where we still needed some fleshing out, definitely helped in the long run. Even though I'm still not using full outlines, a skeleton of the story is something I now use in my regular work.

Try it. You may learn something about the craft you hadn't known before, meet and work with some writers you may never have known otherwise, or maybe if you're lucky, end up with some publishable work of some amazing stories which the world would never had been blessed with.

Final thought from Jessica Wilcox:

I *definitely* want to do something like this again! It is one of my goals to write a collaborative novel with my writer friends. I know a few of us have great ideas, and I think we could produce something amazing!

Remember When

This prompt was fairly open, except that it required that the story take place around one of the following historic events/people: Construction of Angkor Wat, Cleopatra's Reign, or Marie Laveau.

Dark Providence

Serena Armstrong, Myna Chang, Allison deHart, Josh Flores and Cayce Osborne

The damp morning heat in New Orleans was enough to drive a person insane, and the red guinea pepper Marie had placed in her mouth only added to the discomfort. She knew the pain was necessary as the spirits, known as *loa*, demanded her sacrifice. Her suffering helped to appease them while showing the proper amount of gratitude for the coming summer solstice.

St. John's Eve marked a celebration, a ritual of thanksgiving for both the saints and the sinners. Marie knew many would be drawn to the banks of Lake Pontchartrain for her ritual, seeking either salvation or a blessing, as was their wont. The broken branches were already in place for the bonfires. The people who gathered would add life, dancing and chanting to her songs. With the scent of exotic spices and incense thick in the air, many would imagine themselves transported to the shores of their homeland.

The pepper's heat intensified the longer she held it in her mouth. Tears traced down her cheeks. She centered her intention and raised the gris-gris bag to collect the tears.

Many who made the journey tonight would be seeking her magical charms, believing they held stronger powers when made on the solstice. They were not wrong. The amulets were used for protection from evil spirits and though some thought the special concoction called upon the powers of black magic, they were mistaken. Her intentions called upon the other side.

Marie lowered the bag and bowed her head in thanks for the blessings from the *mystères*. She removed the pepper from her mouth and slowly wrapped it in muslin. Before she could continue her preparations, a wave of foreboding flooded her body. She clutched her chest. The sensations were familiar, and she steadied herself with a deep breath as a vision seized her.

In her mind's eye, a pale, middle-aged man screamed as a bullet struck, mincing the flesh by his left shoulder blade. Blood spattered his comrades, and he spun away from the shooter, carried by momentum to fall twitching in the mud.

"Hadnot!" a voice shouted as hands groped his shoulders and chest. The man tilted his head up, peering at a timber courthouse filled with black men, and lingered on a single tortured face that watched him through a window.

The vision passed as quickly as it had come and Marie clutched the amulet hanging from her neck, waiting for her racing heart to calm. When she opened her eyes the candles had guttered out, leaving her with only the filtered light from a fabric-covered window. Sweating, she pulled back the muslin curtain and propped the window open, hoping for a breeze. The trees were still, the air stagnant.

Hadnot. A rare but not unfamiliar name. Marie knew of a James Hadnot who had been shot at Colfax on Easter

Sunday the year before, his injury sparking the massacre. The whites proclaimed he had been shot by the blacks, the blacks protested he had been shot by one of his own. To Marie, it made no difference. Nothing could excuse the resulting slaughter.

Over a hundred black men were killed, and still, not a single charge laid against the murderers. They'd been arrested, this much was true, but the judge somehow failed to prosecute. Marie glanced out the window, watching a white man pass on the street below. It irked her that such *mons* could escape justice.

The bloody scene replayed in her mind as she reached up and tightened the scarf around her head. If James Hadnot was the man in her vision, why would the *loa* show him to her now? True, the bullet in the back confirmed the shot had come from Hadnot's white fellows, but that information would not make any difference without evidence. And everyone knew Hadnot's body had been loaded onto a steamboat and shipped downriver months ago.

***

The weak morning sunlight was like an axe to Hadnot's brain: useful for chopping through his drunken sleep but goddamn painful at the same time. He stumbled out of the ramshackle tavern where he'd been cowering since dusk. He sorely missed carousing with his fellows at Lafitte's or Absinthe House, but out in the bayou he was less likely to be known. Avoiding recognition was the most important goal, even above his own sanity and comfort.

New Orleans was dead to him; he could never show his face there again. It had taken him weeks to travel to a safe distance, settling in a town—if it could even be addressed as such—at the southern rim of Fausse Pointe Lake. Talk of the Colfax massacre still rippled, even this far away.

The visions of what he'd seen, what he'd done, and what had been done to him haunted his thoughts.

Blaring pain flared anew in his shoulder; it had not lessened, despite a night of swilling the harsh Opelousas moonshine traders brought in from the north. His constitution, reared on European wine and whiskey that poured into the Port of New Orleans, hadn't stopped rebelling against the less refined rotgut of his new watering hole.

In the weeks following his flight into the bayou, it seemed his shoulder was mending properly. He'd found a cane farmer who occasionally carried out surgery on his plow animals, and paid him to stitch up the wound. Hadnot battled fever for a week afterward. It broke and he felt well enough to increase the distance between himself and the chaos that had erupted in his wake.

In the last few days, a new pain had developed. A terrible grinding in his back whenever he moved his left arm. Hadnot knew something was off. If he didn't know better—if he hadn't heard the bullet clink into the farmer's waste pail with his own ears—he would swear it still lurked inside him. A squirming lump of twisted metal, poisoning his insides.

The tavern door flew open behind him, and Hadnot was forced to duck out of the way. The abrupt movement made his head swim, and he leaned against the clapboard building for support.

"Same again *Samedi* next, Dupre?" a man's voice called, the Creole cadence rolling off his tongue. Hadnot was blocked by the open door, and he couldn't see the speaker. The jangle of bottles filled the air.

"*Non!*" came the call from inside the tavern. He recognized the accent of the proprietor.

"*Komben?*"

The proprietor sighed. "This St John crowd passing through gon' drink me dry. Two crates, Saturday next. *Wi?*"

"Yah, *wi. Bonjou!*" The man rattled away with his stacked crates of empty moonshine bottles.

For weeks, the chatter in town had been of nothing but St. John's Eve. Folk of all colors and ages were heading east to Lake Pontchartrain for...*something*. A gathering of sorts? There had been talk of a renowned voodoo healer and her supernatural rites performed at the edge of the massive lake once a year. She had magic, they said. Ailments healed, revenge enacted, souls soothed, problems solved. Hadnot was desperate for all of those things, but he'd settle for one.

It would be a fool's errand, he was sure, but he stumbled toward the nearby stables anyway. He thrust a hand in his pocket to see how many coins remained. Enough to buy a horse, he hoped. If providence was on his side, he'd reach the shores of Lake Pontchartrain by nightfall, to lay eyes on the voodoo woman they called Laveau.

It wasn't until he was hunched atop a mare the color of a stormy sky, galloping through clusters of cypress trees, that he considered perhaps providence and dark magics had no place coexisting in the mind of one man. Especially one as cursed as he.

***

Claire considered her client. Seated in the streaming light from the parlor window, Mrs. Landry's crow's-feet were prominent. The older woman's hairdo, however, was near perfect. It would take Claire a few more minutes of work to finish. Unfortunately, Mrs. Landry had failed to divulge any useful information so far; she'd been focused on the *Picayune's* Society Bee column.

"I'm gon' work that last curl again," Claire stalled, reminding herself to suppress the Creole words that came naturally to her, and use the English her clients favored. "It's not minding very well."

Mrs. Landry smiled. "As you say, my dear."

Claire frowned. The rich white women of New Orleans loved to spew their gossip, if given an opportunity, but Mrs. Landry was quiet today. Wrapping a lock of gray-shot hair around her fingers, Claire tugged it neatly into place alongside the other ringlets. "Anything good in the paper?"

"Another story about that dreadful mess at Colfax last Easter."

"Ya don't say," Claire replied, her frown deepening. She glanced at the newspaper, but the lines of type were indecipherable. She didn't need to read to know that her view of the event was assuredly different from Mrs. Landry's.

"Yes, this article is about the trial, and talks about the man who was killed. James Hadnot. Shameful, the way he was shot. My husband said he saw a man with his likeness in a small town he passed through not three days ago. Geoffrey said it was like looking at a ghost."

"Other men died that day too, *non?*" Claire asked, forcing a tone of innocent curiosity into her voice. She reached for the small silk-veiled hat that waited on the tray with the combs and pins. Mrs. Landry adopted the new French style last year, when her hair had begun to thin on top. Claire pinned the puff of silk into place, hiding the woman's scalp. It looked splendid, ringlets spilling from the silk netting like water over a fall.

"Stephen Parish and Sidney Harris also lost their lives," Mrs. Landry sniffed. "And I suppose you can count the darkies, too."

Claire lost her appetite for gossip. The old woman could keep her secrets for all she cared. Through gritted teeth, she proffered the mirror, directing Mrs. Landry's attention back to her hairdo. "*Trè*—uh, very beautiful, ma'am."

***

Marie assessed the items that lay on the kitchen counter. She couldn't forget anything, as one misplaced ingredient would alter the cleansing. Many would be horrified to see the lifeless bodies of the black cat, black rooster, and snake, each cut into three parts to represent the trinity. Just as many would be fascinated.

Marie could hear the timid steps of her faithful apprentice and saw the interruption as a chance to rest her feet. She lowered herself onto a stool, glancing up in time to see Claire enter. The younger woman looked beautiful today, her loose curls highlighting a slim face and glowing skin. Many men would be drawn to her tonight as she danced under the moonlight.

"*Bonjou*, Claire. What does Miz Landry have to say this St. John Eve?"

The girl's expression revealed her dissatisfaction. The whispers and gossip exchanged between hairdresser and client were invaluable, the foundation on which Marie's enterprise had been founded.

"Had her nose stuck in the paper *maten an*, reading about that Colfax mess." Claire frowned and pulled on one of her curls.

Marie stayed silent. No use worrying the girl with details of the vision that had appeared during her morning ceremony.

Claire slumped into a nearby chair. "They feel pity for that James Hadnot. Her husband say folks keep seeing his spirit. *Fou!*"

Marie narrowed her eyes. Surely the man's name on the lips of Mrs. Landry and her husband could not be a coincidence.

***

Claire picked through a shelf of supplies, adding items to a small wooden box. Marie had already packed the ingredients for the night's ritual, but it was Claire's job to gather the medical items. Most people would chant for riches or love on the shore of the lake, but a few always appealed to Marie to cure a physical ill: tame an aching tooth, or remedy a fever.

Claire had been studying Marie's recipes, learning which plants to use and how to prepare them, since her own parents had passed a few years before. The cholera had been cruel, but Marie's kindness and compassion had left a lasting impression on Claire. She hoped she could help others the way Marie had soothed her parents in their dying days.

Satisfied the medicines were securely packed, she turned to the theatrical supplies. Marie's magic was real; of that, Claire had no doubt. But that magic wasn't always easy to *see*, and people seemed to believe more truly when there was a burst of color to prove the strength of the charm. The sachets of sparkling powder were on the lower shelf, next to a spool of red thread, and some soft goat-leather strips. Claire swept the items into her box. She picked up a few extra amulets and poppets. They sold well on nights such as this.

She carried the box to the wagon, securing it in the back next to Marie's items. Blood oozed from a cat carcass, joining older stains on the wooden slats. Claire wrinkled her nose at the mess, leaning close to wipe it up, and noticed a small bag made of dark fabric nestled between the bottle of blessed holy water and the urn of graveyard dirt.

Curious, she tugged open the drawstring. Inside was a short length of cotton rope, accompanied by a link from an iron chain, and a chunk of hard salt. Claire's eyes grew wide as she pieced together the spell that might be cast with these items: did Marie intend to take control of a roaming *loa*? And if so, to what purpose?

Claire quickly pushed the bag back where she'd found it and wiped her hand on her skirts.

***

Hadnot's shirt stuck to his skin like a leech, soaked with sweat. Clinging to the mare's back under the hot afternoon sun was a difficult proposition in the best of circumstances; but now his unsteady nerves, the pain screaming in his shoulder and back, and the swampy ground made it treacherous.

He passed men and women working the land as he rode. Whether pulling crawfish out of murky waters or stripping sugarcane, their backs were bent over the fertile earth, coaxing a livelihood from it. They were a class of people Hadnot had felt himself above, before the incidents of last year. People he had scorned and fought against and belittled. But living out in the bayou, it was impossible not to see their sincerity, and dedication to the land. He'd developed a grudging respect for the Creole people, despite being raised to hate them.

A few hours into his ride, he noticed something peculiar. The working folk would stop and unbend their backs when they heard him approach. A single rider galloping hell-bent past their fields wasn't a good omen. From afar they looked like any toiling man or woman, some with their heads wrapped in scarves, others in straw-brimmed hats to shade their faces. But as he approached, their features dissolved, and in their place emerged a proud brow and wide-set eyes.

Him, the man from the courthouse window—the last thing Hadnot had seen after the bullet pierced his back, a volley of curses erupting from his fellows as they broke rank behind him. The world had grayed at the edges then, his vision focusing in on the face in the window. The man had leered at him through the glass, mocking his wounded state, until an arm extended and pulled the man away, deeper into the courthouse.

Now that face appeared again as Hadnot made his return to New Orleans, inhabiting everyone he passed. But Hadnot no longer saw his expression as mocking. No, now it was terrified. Dark skin, a broken nose and bruised mouth grimacing in pain, white teeth outlined in dark crimson blood. The man's tear-filled eyes carried the dreadful promise of the massacre that followed the courthouse shooting. The massacre that was catalyzed by Hadnot's injury and supposed death. One fateful bullet had started it all. It radiated a web of pain throughout his body as he rode.

The man from the window, his face appearing on person after person, watched Hadnot's progress toward Lake Pontchartrain. He watched, and he warned: *Beware the voodoo priestess*, his eyes seemed to say. *You know not what she conjures.*

***

Claire smelled the smoke from the bonfire, infused with spicy incense, as it wafted through the crowd. The still, muggy night air held its fragrance close, and was made more pungent with the addition of thousands of bodies, sweating and dancing on the muddy shore of the lake. She could hear nothing but the chant; its deep notes devoured all other sound, vibrating up through her feet and into her core. She could almost believe she'd been transported to some ancestral paradise.

Her fellow revelers were equally entranced. Marie's presence at the center of the crowd grounded their belief, simultaneously setting their essence free to rejoice. Claire watched her mentor performing the familiar rites, the blessing and calling forth of *mystères*. Soon, the ritual would end, and Claire would be needed; but, for now, she was free.

She watched one of the dancers ahead of her. He stood in front of Marie. Handsome, with large eyes and a smile that penetrated the fog of incense and passion. Grinning in return, she weaved her way through the gyrating bodies toward him. A subtle change in the rhythm drew her attention back to Marie, and Claire's euphoric daze sputtered. The iron chain-link was in Marie's hand, bound with a knot of rope and Claire knew the salt would be clutched within her fist—part of the ritual to control the *loa*.

Claire stood, rooted in place by her fear of what was sure to come. Marie was a kind woman, who helped people in need. Of course, she was capable of strong voodoo, and Claire knew ugly actions were sometimes necessary. But Marie chose the lighter path whenever she could. What had brought her to these dark deeds tonight?

***

Marie's words flowed freely. The old songs from deep inside her rang out, dispersing her energy for all to receive: the *loa* as well as the people. Marie scanned the crowd and was met with the pale white face from her morning vision—Hadnot, alive. He dripped sweat, favoring his left shoulder as he moved through the crowd of people towards her.

Marie stroked the cotton rope between her fingers. She planted her feet and drew a deep breath. She put the rope and chain together and rubbed them with the rock salt. Her body swayed as words blended with the voices echoing around her. Binding a *loa* to her bidding would drain her, despite the power radiating from her followers. But true justice could not come without a deep cost. She picked up the chain and opened her inner eye to The One. He came to her: expressive eyes, and a face that had known violence. He wouldn't take much of her power; he was willing.

Other *loa* begged for their chance to wreak revenge on those who had harmed them, trying to push past The One. A warning song broke from her lips and they faded back. The One smiled, and turned to face the man with the troubled soul.

Marie's song ended, and she watched.

***

People crowded the edge of the lake—it must have been thousands, for they stretched as far as Hadnot could see. He was relieved none of them wore the face of the man from the courthouse window. Some had their heads thrown back in ecstasy as they chanted, while others had their eyes glued to the woman at the center of it all, the voodoo goddess who led the revelry. And that was what she truly looked like: a goddess worthy of worship and devotion.

She stood yards from him, sweat beading on her brow as she chanted. Her face, a map of wrinkles that indicated a long and complicated life, was older than he expected. She drew energy from the crowd, seeming to float above them as their chants lifted.

He felt out of place, one of the few white faces in a sea of people. But no matter the shade of skin, they all prayed at the woman's altar. *Why have I come*, he wondered.

Hadnot's attention moved to two women in long white caftans, splattered with the mud that pooled under everyone's stomping feet. The women danced apart. In between them stood a man. *The* man. He faced away from the goddess commanding the crowd, the only person to show his back to her. He smiled his bloody smile at Hadnot.

Searing agony exploded throughout Hadnot's body, emanating from the bullet wound. It came in waves, moving progressively slower until it pooled in his head. He bowed under it, forced onto his hands and knees by the weight. He faced the muddy earth, cheeks flecked by grime as the dancing reached a frenzy.

He could not move. He was desperate to look one last time at the man from the courthouse window, to see if he was there, but Hadnot's neck was fused in place. Then gradually, his suffering began to ease, the ache subsiding until there was nothing left. No pain, no pleasure, no feeling at all. It was as if his very existence had been drained away.

He saw himself through the voodoo goddess' eyes, and watched as his body tipped forward into the mud, unmoving. People danced around him, oblivious. His view switched to the man from the window. Hadnot was given a vision of how the rest of the man's life had played out, how the massacre began.

Using Hadnot's shooting as an excuse to charge, his fellows entered the courthouse and began firing at the black men inside. The man tried to flee. He made it to the edge of town before being run down by men on horseback. They broke his nose and bloodied his mouth. Then they dragged him behind their mounts, scouring his skin raw until the tension snapped his neck. His broken body was dumped in the river.

Hadnot felt the full weight of what had been done in his name, even as his consciousness floated away from the scene along the lakeside. By allowing the lie to live—the lie that he had been killed by the black men inside the courthouse, the lie that was used to justify the massacre at Colfax—he had been at fault as much as those who had committed the murders.

He had one last thought as he passed out of the world forever: *Thank the good Lord I am dead, for I could not live with such knowledge.*

***

Marie swayed. The chanting and the rhythm of the bodies moved her, as always, but this time it was more—and less; she was completely drained. Well into her seventh decade, her bones ached and the adoration of the worshippers wore on her. The rituals, which used to energize her, now left her exhausted. Even so, satisfaction wrapped around her like a cloak, her evening's true goal achieved.

The sinner, Hadnot, had finally met his end; and surprisingly, he'd seemed to welcome it. The *loa* had burst forth at Marie's bidding. There'd been no need to bind him. A victim of the courthouse massacre, the spirit haunted Hadnot, and was ready with his curse. All he'd needed was Marie's focus to bring his revenge to life.

Marie had felt Hadnot's remorse as she was chanting. He'd discovered a new understanding and while he might not have asked for forgiveness, the craving was there, plain to see, if one only knew how to look. The *loa* must have recognized it, too, for his revenge had transformed into acceptance as she watched. Hadnot had gratefully passed from this world, though to heaven or hell, she knew not which. That was not for her to decide. Satisfied, the *loa* himself had moved on soon after.

She settled back onto a stool that one of her flock provided and watched a younger woman begin the next chant. Claire was out there somewhere, dancing in the crowd. She would be leading assemblies like this one soon, but for now she was free to follow whatever wild ideas her mind—or perhaps her body—conjured.

Marie grinned at the thought. Her time as a voodoo queen was coming to an end, but life would continue its cycle, as it had always done.

Inimitable Livers

Team: Sneaky Little Scribes

Marcus Vipsanius Agrippa frowned as he rubbed at a smudge on his ornamental breastplate. His body slave had fallen ill on the journey to Antirhodos, and he didn't trust these dark-skinned barbarians with his formal Augusticlavia tunic. Studying his reflection in the circle of polished bronze, he ran his hands over the embroidery and smoothed down his hair. He allowed himself a terse nod at the precise presentation.

A scrap of papyrus on the table caught his eye as he turned. There had been rumors among the men that Marcus Antonius was planning some sort of grand soiree. Agrippa was honored to receive a personal invitation from the General, a Triumvir of the Roman Republic, but political mingling at this level made him nervous. Witty repartee was not his forte. He was a figures-man and a soldier. Numbers never lied to him. But, his schoolmate and friend, Octavian, encouraged his attendance. There was much he could learn.

He swept up his crimson cape and whipped it, comforted by the familiar snap of fabric. Agrippa fastened it at his shoulders to complete his ensemble. Almost. His hip felt bare where his gladius was normally sheathed. It may be just a party, but even those could feel like battle.

The invitation had been vague. Perhaps some celebration of one of the heathens' bizarre animal gods? Agrippa stiffened. A sharp beaked statue with glittering hematite eyes glared at him from the corner. Everywhere he went in this wretched place, some bird-headed man or cat-faced woman watched him. It was uncanny.

A soft voice made Agrippa jump.

"Taeal maei ya sayidi?"

A dark-skinned woman in a gauzy dress stood in the doorway, foreign words pouring from her mouth. Agrippa flushed and averted his eyes. The fabric was sheer, nearing the point of indecency. He glanced around, desperate to find something else to look at. A wash of rosy sunlight spilled through the window, casting a river of molten red-gold across the floor. Sunset.

The woman repeated her singsong words, urging him toward her with a wave of her hand. Agrippa sighed. It was going to be a long night.

She led him through the halls of the palace, hips swaying in time to some imagined beat. He did his best to admire the furnishings in the rooms they passed, sending a silent prayer to Theos for strength. Perhaps Marcus' recent relationship with Queen Cleopatra, however distasteful, would bring the true faith to the heathens, along with modest clothing. How did the General expect vigilance with temptations like this lingering about like roses to be plucked?

The marble floors of the Ptolemaic Palace soon became a paved walkway that led to the Temple of Isis. The faint silhouettes of women formed in the distance as they approached. They seemed to glide toward the entryway in a rhythm similar to that of his mysterious escort; their attire as scant and their bosoms somehow more prominent. He maintained his composure for presentation, but his cheeks heated just the same.

She guided him between two giant obsidian obelisks, through a column-lined vestibule, into a shadowed den. The room was dotted with flickering candles on ledges and offering tables, casting just enough light for one to view the undulating gyrations of the crowd. Musicians moved among the sweaty crowd, playing their flutes and harps, merrily consuming wine and grinding against the provocative plenty. The offering tables overflowed with heaps of figs, dates, carving plates, and fish. Bowls of lentils littered the room, as did the numerous amphora, presumably filled with wines and red beer.

"I fear there has been a mistake. I can't imagine that the Queen of Egypt and a leader of the Roman Republic would summon me to such a grotesque display of gluttony and flesh. Are you sure this was where you were instructed to bring me?"

No response from his guide.

"You understand about as much of my language as I understand of yours, don't you?"

She cocked her head at him and raised her hand toward a platform near the far end of the room.

"That's what I thought."

Just as Agrippa was turning away, a horn sounded and the dancing ceased. The congregation stood silent, facing the platform with palpable excitement, surrounding him in a humid shroud of breathless expectation. He mirrored their paralyzed stature, unsure what would come next.

"Greetings, friends!" A man's booming voice reverberated off the Temple walls, buzzing the eardrums of anyone within its confines. Agrippa found Marcus Antonius emerging from an enclave behind the platform and met his gaze. He began to lower himself to a knee, but Marcus furrowed his brow, flashed a half-grin, and gestured for him to rise.

"I present to you, brothers and sisters, the embodiment of the goddess Aphrodite, your noble ruler, the Queen of Egypt, Cleopatra!"

Agrippa watched as the assorted guests bowed to their queen as Marcus proceeded past the platform to join the crowd. A parade of lithe women followed him, wearing translucent white silk and gold chains that covered naught but their loins. As they meandered into the crowd, bodies parted like the Red Sea, clearing a path and wide circle around the rostrum. After they settled around the perimeter a golden chariot pulled by muscular men rolled through the temple entrance. It was etched in floral patterns, and purple silks billowed from oversized handles. A golden-silk canopy rose above it, contrasting perfectly with the luminous white dress, pitch-black hair, and heavily jeweled crown donning the head of their queen.

Though he'd heard Cleopatra enjoyed grand gestures, Agrippa was still taken aback by her arrival. He couldn't help but catch the wave of awe that spread through the room like a delicious plague. Cleopatra's beauty was as unprecedented as rumored, but it paled in comparison to the unbridled command of her consuming presence. The servants who pulled her slid their feet ever-so-smoothly across the ground, creating the illusion that they were floating to the center of the clearing. They halted, laid down their yoke, and settled the Queen among her people. Marcus approached her and reached out his palm, into which she stoically placed her hand and gracefully disembarked from the platform.

"Let the feast and festivities commence!" She projected the statement with minimal effort or emotion, yet it evoked nothing short of a roar from her people.

The crowd scattered joyfully to the edges of the room, refilling chalices and partaking in the delicacies gifted to them by their rulers. Cleopatra and Marc Antony made their way to the larger seats placed at the center of the banquet table arranged at the top of the lectern the crowd had surrounded. They settled into their positions, at which point Marc Anthony gestured once again, only this time implying that Agrippa should join them.

Still awed by Cleopatra's entrance, and disconcerted by the guests, Agrippa made his way to the platform.

"Thank you both for inviting me to your...." He stumbled, not sure what to call the congregation of debauched revelers.

"Our event," the Queen completed his thought.

"Yes, thank—"

"This event has a very strict dress code, though it may have escaped your notice. Did you receive the correspondence regarding appropriate attire?"

"My sincerest apologies. I must have misinterpreted—"

"Yes, that's safe to say. Haqiaka!"

A fair young woman dressed a bit more modestly scurried toward the platform from only a few feet away.

"Haqiaka, fetch this man some of the blue frocks I ordered."

The maiden smiled at Agrippa, and as he met her gaze to return the nicety, he felt a flutter in his belly. He quickly disregarded it and returned his focus to the royal pair, curious to find out the reason behind his invitation.

"My lieges, I must say that your invitation was unexpected. Considering my friendship with Octavian, I would expect you would find more comfort in the presence of a statesman more aligned with your wishes."

Cleopatra raised an eyebrow toward Marcus and he clapped a hand on Agrippa's shoulder. "Dear Agrippa, you think we want the dusty old worshipers of *crepitus ventris* who do nothing but talk? No! We want the young, hot blood of Rome's future with us. We invited you here as not just an ally, but a friend, a conspirator! Tell us, does the ravishing beauty that surrounds us not pique your interest? Is this lavish feast before you not of the finest quality and of quantities this throng could not consume in a fortnight?"

"It is quite fine. Revealing, some might say. Surely there are others you might find more suitable toward your particular style of revelry." Agrippa tried to hold himself steady, the incense beginning to cloud his head.

Cleopatra smiled, the blue dye around her eyes accenting their sparkle. "Why, Agrippa, you are modest to a fault. Perhaps we just find your looks, mmm, appealing." A soft chuckle escaped her full lips.

Marcus glanced sideways at her, then laughed. "Dearest, you are too forward with our guest. Perhaps you are already too deep into the wines."

"Oh, Marcus, you know I have an inimitable liver." The two regents chuckled and shared a private smile.

Agrippa had no recourse for the comments but was saved by the prompt reappearance of Haqiaka.

"My queen, these arrived from the silk road just yesterday, the finest quality from the Far East." She flourished silken robes of the brightest blue Agrippa had ever seen, somehow turning the delivery of garments into a seductive dance. Cleopatra nodded and flicked a finger toward Agrippa. Haqiaka bowed and passed the robes to him.

"Thank you, Haqiaka, but I'm afraid I will be an undue burden here. Marcus, my Queen, may I bid you farewell and a fond evening."

Haqiaka stepped close to him and pressed her body against his. She raised her hand and trailed a finger through his hair. "Rumor has it, master Agrippa, that Roman men are more...well-rounded...than our men. I have, at times, been most curious about Roman men, given our queen's consort. Perhaps you could satisfy my inquisitive nature if you stay." Her finger had found its way down his breastplate and toyed with the middle of his tunic.

She smelled of cinnamon and myrrh, and her oiled skin shone bright in the light from the torches. Smoke from incense wafted through the room and Haqiaka pressed against him.

His head swam and he stuttered, but could not find words to respond.

"That's enough, Haqiaka. Give our young statesman some room. Bring him some wine." Cleopatra stretched her arms up and crossed them behind her head. "These parties in the Temple can get monotonous, Agrippa, even for us. Perhaps a stroll through the city where the night markets are rich with color and ripe for games. Right, Marcus?"

Haqiaka left to fetch the wine. Marcus nodded. "Yes, that is a grand idea, my Queen. How do you feel about games, Agrippa?"

"Market games seem beneath our current company, are they not?"

"Not the games we play. Come, sport with us. It will clear your head, and by chance you may find yourself enamoured of us enough to find comfort in our company. We can bring Haqiaka, among others, if you find that agreeable."

Agrippa considered. At least in the city the people would be clothed, and the crisp air would cleanse him. And he did find Haqiaka agreeable. Quite agreeable.

"You've intrigued me. I will accompany your group. I thank you for the invitation, my queen."

"But first," Marcus declared, "you must prepare yourself." He pointed to the silken tunic in Agrippa's hands.

Haqiaka returned with two chalices of wine and a smile that started a tensing low in Agrippa's stomach.

"Haqiaka," Cleopatra grinned, "you will assist Agrippa in the removal of his garb."

"Yes, my Queen." Haqiaka bowed deeply without spilling any wine and faced Agrippa as she rose. "You look thirsty, master Agrippa." Handing a chalice to him, she stepped close again and snaked her arm around his, interlocking them. "Drink with me?" She licked her lips and tipped her cup back into her mouth while holding his stare.

Agrippa swallowed, his mouth suddenly dry. He could hear Cleopatra's throaty laugh.

"Drink, Agrippa," the queen demanded, "You will thank me later."

He obeyed, tipping the cup back until the last drop touched his lips. The wine was unlike any he had tasted before. A line of fire trailed down into his stomach, but his tongue tasted honey and cloves. Haqiaka disentangled herself from him and reached for his chalice, setting it down on the ground before taking the silken tunic from his other hand. She winked at him, grabbed his right arm and pulled him to an alcove on the side of the altar. He stumbled slightly, the wine making his head swim.

Agrippa could see that the alcove was already occupied by a trio who were intertwined with each other, the candlelight glinting off of their dark, sweat-slicked skin. He looked away, ashamed at his initial interest. Haqiaka clapped her hands and the group quickly dispersed. She pulled him further into the room and tossed the blue silks onto one of the cushioned seats before turning back to him. He stared in horror at the residue left on the cushions by the departing group and then at Haqiaka whose hands had already begun to deftly remove his cape.

"Please." He reached out and stilled her hands. "Let me dress myself." She frowned slightly and stepped back from him. A grin split her face and she sat down on a cushion, curling her legs up underneath her. Inwardly, Agrippa cringed at her contact with the seat.

"I will enjoy the view, master Agrippa."

Seeing no way out of the situation, he began the process of removing his armor while trying to ignore his surroundings and the roaming eyes of the woman seated before him. When he had everything except his subligar off, he glanced up to find his new tunic. Haqiaka's eyes were wide and she was sitting on the edge of the seat, lips parted. She looked up at him, and shook her head.

"No master. The queen requires that you dress as we dress. If it pleases you, I can assist in its removal." She bit her lip and looked up at him through heavy lashes.

Agrippa cleared his throat, mouth once again dry as the desert. "I will take care of it." With the last of his resolve, he quickly removed his loincloth and snatched the silks from the cushion beside Haqiaka. As he stood back up, he noticed her gaze shift from him to slightly behind him and then back. He turned around to find the Queen lounging against the alcove opening, her eyes alight behind a cup of wine. He quickly covered himself and the two women erupted in laughter. She stepped forward and brought her chalice up to his lips. He could feel the heat of her body through the silk he grasped against himself.

"I see you could use more encouragement, Agrippa. Drink."

Again, he obeyed.

"Now dress. We have games to attend and you will play an important role." As she turned and sauntered away, he found himself being pulled back into the alcove by Haqiaka.

***

The boat ride from Antirhodos to the mainland of Alexandria was short. Agrippa was not a stranger to sailing and had recently taken a trip across the Mare Magnum from Rome to Alexandria. The small papyrus reed boats used to ferry the queen's entourage from the tiny island to the port city, however, did not feel substantial enough. The sea spray dampened his silk tunic, causing it to cling.

As they departed the boats, he tried to get his bearings in the city. Sixty red granite pillars topped with large crowns proved Alexandria's majesty to travellers. He had only been there one time in the daylight. At night, the columns were lit by torches and cast striated shadows that danced across the water. Combined with his already swimming head, the shadows made Agrippa feel like he was floating, even on dry land.

He looked around, trying to find the queen and her group coming off of their boats, but all he saw were commoners. A man came up behind him and slapped him on the back jovially, causing him to overcompensate and nearly fall backward into the water. The man laughed. Once

Agrippa regained his composure, he realized the man was actually Marcus dressed as a typical citizen.

"That clothing seems a bit below your station, my liege."

"Agrippa, leave your hesitations here at the shore, and come play with us. Cleopatra wishes for you to expand your mind and find solace in our companionship...and Haqiaka's, of course." Marcus laughed again and motioned them forward into the sea of shadows.

Far to the north, a giant pyre lit the top of the Great Lighthouse: a sentinel, unrivaled by almost anything else man had built. Egypt's engineers, while barbarians, had achieved greatness over thousands of years. Rome took far less to achieve much more. A mere day to Egypt's year.

Cleopatra and her entourage passed them, all dressed in commoner garb, or as close as they could manage. Silk stood out anyway.

"We must take the Canopic Way here between the city quarters. Our aim is the great tomb of Alexander himself."

"Tomb?" Agrippa frowned. "Aren't we here for the night markets and sport?"

"Yes, yes, our sport begins at the founder's mausoleum. Hurry now, they'll find us out if we linger."

Beautifully carved colonnades lined the thoroughfare. It spread near twenty meters wide and the wealthy of the city strolled among tents displaying everything from fresh dates to lapis lazuli jewelry. Many of the people wore heavy cloth to block the chill of the night, but the warmth from the ambrosia Haqiaka had provided left Agrippa wishing he wore even less than he did.

A slight breeze furled around him as he followed the small group down the busy street. Haqiaka strode up beside him, her hips still swaying to the rhythm of a song he couldn't hear.

"Agrippa. How good are you at acting?"

"Acting? Like the debauched followers of Bacchus?"

"Artisans who shadow the shadow of life, Agrippa. Dancers on the wall, imitating the imitators. Showing truth through falsity."

Agrippa, despite the wine, felt surprise surface upon his face. "You've studied the philosophers."

"Yes, even us backward savages can appreciate the wonders of the mind. I'm not just a pretty girl for my queen, but a confidante. She is more crafty than she seems."

"Intriguing. I can see why Marcus is drawn to her."

"Indeed."

"As I find myself drawn to you."

Haqiaka lowered her head and smirked. "You honor me, statesman. Another draught of wine?" She offered up a small jar, which he tipped against his lips. The sweet nectar slid down his throat and he exhaled with satisfaction.

"I am no actor, but I would try anything once. For you."

"You may find that if you try something once, you may enjoy it many times again." Her eyes shut as she turned away and took a long drink of her own. Crimson fluid dripped down her chin, neck, and between the deep cleft of her bosom. He found his vision clouded again, though not from the wine.

Haqiaka stayed at his side as they followed Cleopatra and Marcus toward the giant monument that marked the resting place of the Greek states' most famous ruler. Here in this city, Egyptian, Jewish, Greek, and Roman life mixed like an unholy poison. Theos help him.

They reached the intersection of the two largest streets of the city, where the Sema mausoleum contained Alexander's body. At the entrance, Cleopatra whispered to a soldier standing guard. He startled, looked at her for a moment, then waved the group inside.

Agrippa found himself in a circle surrounding a crystal sepulchre. Inside, a desiccated body wore the tunic and armor of a Greek general. Alexander.

"Grand, isn't he?" Cleopatra brushed by Agrippa and ran her hand along the top of the crystal. "They say a solid gold coffin once entombed him, but the public, they wanted to see their hero. They used the gold for their idols, and this idol, shrouded in leathered strips of his own skin, lay naked to the masses. What should we do, my love?"

To Agrippa's horror, Marcus leaped upon the crystal and raised his arms. "My queen, let us bring the mighty Alexander back to his people!"

The group around the sepulchre erupted into loud shouts and drunken whistles. Some began to dance as others kept a beat on the hallowed walls around them. Cleopatra soon raised her hand for silence, then beckoned to a few of the men.

"If you would, please, friends, relieve Alexander of his indignity."

They braced against the floor and soon had the slab of crystal off the top. Agrippa leaned against a wall, and giggled when he realized Cleopatra and Marcus' plan. Odd, he wasn't normally one to giggle.

Two of the men hoisted Alexander out and stowed him in a small recess in the far wall. Marcus took Alexander's breastplate off and wiped it down with his sleeve.

"Agrippa. Haqiaka says you are ready to lead an empire. What say you?"

"I know not the purpose of this madness, Marcus, but the reaction within this city of heathens promises to provide the highlight of my journey here."

"Good man, Agrippa. You do our empire proud." He glanced toward Haqiaka. "Lovely girl, apply his paints."

She came to him and bid him sit. Another woman handed her a papyrus satchel filled with containers of minerals and oils. These, she mixed and applied to his face. A cloak of beaten sackcloth he pulled over his blue silks, after which Marcus affixed the ancient breastplate to his torso. Cleopatra walked to him and held up a polished slab of granite.

Reflected in the dim light of the torches, a visage of nightmare from Pluto's realms. Agrippa stared in wonder as he took the slab from her and stood. No longer the boy from rural Salona, his features resembled every mural he'd ever seen of Alexander, though modified from the centuries of decay.

"Everyone, take your places." Cleopatra's eyes gleamed under her haze of drunken madness. "We shall run from here, screaming of the resurrected emperor. Agrippa here will delay until the soldiers come in. If all goes well, they will run for their superiors and he will emerge onto the crowded streets."

Agrippa swayed, his sense of balance upset by dripping pitch from the torches. "My queen. Is that all?"

"You must also chant to all who stand their ground in fear. Say to them, *'Cavete Idibus Martiis'.*"

"Alexander knew Latin?"

Cleopatra laughed, the sound of crystal spilling across bronze. "They won't care."

"Where shall I go?"

Marcus placed an arm around his shoulder. "Just follow us back to the boats. Our goal is for the city to rise up in activity until Ra himself ushers out their tired souls. Let them join our revelry." He winked at Cleopatra. "Now, everyone, cry havoc and let slip our inebriated spirits!"

At his yell, the party stumbled out the doors and into the street. Wails and moans pierced the bustling of night life, though some of the passersby laughed at what they considered drunken merriment. Haqiaka waited just inside the doorway with him.

"Are you ready, master Agrippa?" She placed his hands upon her hips and stood on her toes to kiss his lips. "If we succeed, I will see you richly rewarded." Another kiss, and her teeth nibbled at his bottom lip. The taste of her lingered on his tongue as she followed the others out. Her screams echoed through the night and were enough to send the soldiers through the door to check on things.

Agrippa met them in a slouch, with head raised and slow, slurred words.

"Cavete Idibus Martiis. CAVETE. IDIBUS. MARTIIS."

The first soldier soiled himself where he stood and fainted. The second dropped his spear, fell backward, and scrambled out the entrance on hands and dolium. He gained his feet and careened through the crowd, yelling for help. Many in the crowd called out questions, but he neither heard nor cared.

Agrippa exited the mausoleum with an exaggerated military march meant to imitate long unused muscles. He'd seen slaves come out of the holds of ships in much the same fashion. Only a few people saw him at first, as most stared after the frightened guard.

"CAVETE IDIBUS MARTIIS!" He raised his fist toward the moon and added a throaty rasp to his yell, uttering curses for the first time in generations.

Those first to see him bumped into those impeding their flight, inciting others to behold the ancient founder of their city shambling angrily from his tomb. Within minutes, the square turned into chaos.

Panicked people pushed and trampled over the bodies of those unlucky enough to fall before them. Tables and wares overturned and spilled across stone and sand. Fires rose where errant torches fell. Before Agrippa, Cleopatra and the rest urged the panicked populace away from the center of the street, so he could continue to advance.

Sweat poured from him as he limped past the colonnades, and fire burned in his veins. He'd never felt such thrill. Haqiaka glanced back at him and smiled in a promising way. A few minutes later, he could hear the streets beyond their own erupt as if Pluto's demons had broken loose.

Ahead, Marcus turned and waved his hand. "Agrippa, run now! Our legions will be upon us soon!"

He ran and the group escaped the riot's fringes just moments before they closed in and blocked the Canopic Way. By the boats, Haqiaka helped him undo the breastplate and pull off the tattered cloth.

"Splash water on your face and rub away the paints. You cannot be seen in them entering the temple, or else the city will crucify you on the morrow."

He did as she said, then dipped his whole head into the cool water, drinking deep. He emerged and grabbed Haqiaka around her waist. "I must have you. Never before have I felt such clarity. Marcus may have his queen, but I shall have the true jewel of the Nile!"

She giggled as he picked her up and swung her in an arc over the rocky shore, though the rest of the group loudly shushed them in fear of being discovered.

In the boat, Agrippa drowned himself in jars of sweet wines.

***

Marcus once again stood on top of a table after the group had eaten its fill of the feast.

"Friends, lend me your ear. You are all welcome to stay for as long as you want! There are beds in the alcoves that will accommodate all, and the servants will bring you all the wine and water you desire. Our queen, though, demands rest, so we leave you all in good hands."

Haqiaka pulled Agrippa onto the pulpit where Marcus and Cleopatra said their good nights to some of their less intoxicated guests.

Cleopatra beamed at Agrippa. "Ah, so you did learn to relax, young statesman. A fine performance. One I imagine will be outmatched once you get Haqiaka into bed."

He had no response but to slap Haqiaka's rear and slur out what he hoped was an acceptable term of thanks. Afterward, he followed Haqiaka into the back of the temple, to a bed with carved lion legs and elaborate headrests painted with lotuses. Thick furs and linen covered the frame.

"Haqiaka. I despise these silken robes. Please, help me disrobe. I ache for your touch."

She stood in front of him and flicked the strap of her pleated linen dress from her shoulder, baring her breasts to him. "You ache, master Agrippa? Tell me how much do you yearn for me."

"Were I dying of thirst, and I had to choose between traveling through your marshes, and a jar of water, I would choose you. I beg of you, loosen me of my fetters, that I may relish in your beauty and hear the laughter of the gods."

Haqiaka sauntered to him and peeled away the many layers of gossamer that stuck to his skin. She pulled it down from his waist and gasped.

"I see the asp is ready to strike, master Agrippa. Be careful, lest its bite kill the mood."

"It seeks only your attention to calm its fervor. Charm the asp, and it shall be forever yours."

He stumbled backward and fell onto his rear. Haqiaka laughed.

"I'm impressed, Agrippa. If the Nile were wine, the river would be dry after all you've imbibed, yet your snake persists. However, I must admit I've never seen an asp or its eggs quite so blue."

Peals of laughter broke out in the hall, and Cleopatra and Marcus emerged into the bed chamber.

"It worked, my queen!" Haqiaka bowed as Cleopatra joined her.

Agrippa pulled his silks from the bed and placed them over his loins. "What is this? My lieges, why are you here? You lower yourselves and the both of us if you mean to make this communal."

Tears ran from Marcus' eyes as he doubled over, howling with merriment "Communal? I must admit that you have impressive form, young Agrippa, but nay, I would not dream of it."

"Patience, love," Cleopatra appraised Agrippa as she slipped her arms around Marcus. "His asp may be more akin to a python. Perchance I have an interest in playing the charmer's flute."

"Ah, but what would the servants say, were you to take him as your courtesan?"

"They'd likely tell me I'd consorted with Amun."

All three of them laughed again, pointing at Agrippa. He looked down at himself for the first time, and found that the expensive silks had dyed his skin blue.

"What is the meaning of this? Bring me a bath at once. Dishonoring a guest such a crude manner may bring down your house, Marcus."

They laughed harder.

"I'm afraid a bath won't help, young statesman." Cleopatra wiped a tear from her eye. "For that dye often stays etched into skin for an entire month. Haqiaka is skilled with colors."

"A month? I must be back in Rome before then. How will I face anyone with this shame, especially my liege and the Senate?"

"I suggest you stay here." Haqiaka knelt beside him. "You call it shame, but we helped you find your inner self. Tonight, we initiated you into the Inimitable Livers. You're one of us, now. Stay and you can wander my marshes as long as you want."

Agrippa's drunken haze turned to bitter hate. The rumors about the savage queen and her bewitchment of Marcus were confirmed. Something had to be done to get him away.

"Leave me, whore." Haqiaka flinched at the venom in his voice, but it was Cleopatra he stared at.

Marcus frowned, but flipped his hand in a signal of dismissal. "Come, love, Haqiaka. It seems mortal desires cannot sway our friend. We'll send him away in the morning."

Haqiaka looked at Agrippa with sorrow, and stood to leave with them. "Farewell, master Agrippa. I am truly sorry to leave you in such a state."

Cleopatra glanced back at him. "Worry not. He can hatch his own eggs. They won't be aching and blue for long. Well, maybe blue a bit longer." She laughed as they exited the bed chamber.

Agrippa seethed. They would pay for their childish debauchery. A reckoning would descend upon them that the empire would speak of for ages, and he would be the one to orchestrate it. They knew not who they manipulated.

Hail Mary, Hail Marie

Taree Belardes, Meagan Noel Hart, Shari Heinrich, Wayne Hills, Pamela L. Keil, and Victoria Kelsey

Eunice Billbray gracefully laid her teacup atop the damask table linen.

Across from her, Pearl Jebston shifted in her seat. "I thought you loved New Orleans."

"Don't mistake me, Pearl. This city has been good to us." Eunice glanced at the high-backed chair where Pearl lounged. It was framed by the gold-leaf Japanese folding screen of which Eunice was particularly proud. "*Very* good to us. But it will never be my *home.*"

Pearl's eyes widened. "After ten years it hasn't left its mark on your heart? You spent years commissioning local masters for the oil paintings in this room alone. I must admit, that Meissen vase at the door, however, is my favorite. The flowers, so exquisitely detailed, but the golden handles you required the artist to add? Breathtaking."

Eunice dipped her head, acknowledging the compliment.

Pearl continued, "You would trade your station here to return to that, that *cotton-picking* plantation?"

Eunice stifled a chuckle at her younger companion's assumption of New Orleans's cultural superiority to every other city. "This place lacks a certain kind of beauty. One best enjoyed over juleps. Oh, the sight of white-tufted fields against the clear blue sky of Georgia." Eunice exhaled the memory. Outside the parlor window, the city bustled.

She tracked a mulatto man walking purposefully, shielding his leather case from the mud splashed by passing carriages, his head held high. Eunice sniffed. "And New Orleans has its drawbacks." She pointed. "That, I refuse to accept."

While Pearl craned her head, Eunice plucked up a silver spoon, prodded the lumps of dissolving sugar in her cup, and added, "It isn't natural, white and colored mingling as freemen. I've never pretended to be comfortable here. The coloreds at home know their station. It's why I refused my sister's offer to bring our house slaves here. They'd...." She lowered her voice lest any of the help overheard. "I don't want any one of them living under *my* roof getting ideas."

Pearl started to shake her head but changed it to a nod, her tresses bouncing. The afternoon light falling through the parlor's over-scaled window illuminated her.

Eunice sipped her tea. "Your curls do you great credit today, Pearl."

"You like them? Ask me who did it." She raised an eyebrow and whispered, "Though I'm afraid you won't approve."

Eunice set down her cup. "You didn't."

"The Voodoo queen herself," Pearl squealed.

Eunice fixed Pearl with her glare, but Pearl only smiled and shrugged. "Don't be so stodgy, Eunice. She is quite lovely."

"Lovely? *Lovely* and that negress *Marie Laveau* don't belong in the same utterance. I have heard that blasphemer uses holy water to cast Voodoo spells at the altar of the St. Louis Cathedral! Right under the nose of the Virgin Mary herself. And with the blessing of Pere Antoine. One wonders if they don't have an unholy pact betwixt them, the way he kowtows to her."

"Oh, Eunice, you believe positively everything you hear. I bet you believe she sucked on hot peppers in order to help the Girod boy evade justice, too."

Eunice leaned in. "If I am gullible, then you, my friend, are naive. How do you think she came into that house on St. Ann Street? Everyone knows that the murderer's father paid for her services in property. That woman has been widowed for nearly twenty years. Unless...you don't think blasphemy pays so handsomely?" Eunice scoffed, "Perhaps I should sacrifice chickens."

"But she knows positively everyone in the city. I've been privy to gossip of *every* stripe." Pearl clenched Eunice's soft hand. "Did you know that George Plantis keeps not one, but *two* colored ladies? Each cosseted in her own cottage, waiting for him to—"

Eunice gasped. "Pearl Jebston, what an improper thing to...she told you that?"

"I can only say that it was—" Pearl fanned herself and looked over her shoulder, *"overheard."*

"How ghastly. Poor Mrs. Plantis. Heavens, Pearl, now you have ensnared *me* in your gossip." Eunice released her hand from Pearl's grip and picked up her teacup. "I have heard the widow Laveau walks the streets with a sense of superiority — some call it purpose — which I question. One way or the other, it's small wonder, when she has the favor of New Orleans' well-to-do." She shook her head. "People who should *know* better, seeking out her...services."

Eunice mustered her severest countenance and admonished Pearl. "Please do not tell me you have paid for one of her charms or, heaven help you, one of her disgusting prayer pouches. What do they call them...*gris-gris*?"

When Pearl averted her eyes, Eunice tsked.

From her reticule Pearl produced a small red sachet. The clean scent of basil warred against rich cinnamon, austere fresh lavender against common parsley.

Pearl relinquished it to Eunice's outstretched fingers like a child surrendering a pilfered sweet to her mother. "It can't hurt, can it? We pray on the crucifix, a bit of gold and steel. Why not hope on dried herbs? Blessed herbs, I would add."

"You defy belief, Pearl. What would your daddy say if he saw you worshipping spices?" Eunice tossed the pouch into Pearl's lap. "He might take you over his knee. You are barely more than a child as it is."

Pearl licked her teeth, another immaturity Eunice despised, and gave Eunice's wrist a condescending pat. "Eunice, I know it is difficult keeping up with the latest trends. Particularly when one is so past calling age, but—"

Eunice snatched her arm away. "Why, I never."

"Oh, come now, Eunice."

Eunice turned away from Pearl. "Harriet will see you out now." She rang the bell.

"Eunice, please. At thirty, you are practically a spring chicken!"

Eunice gasped at being compared to a barn animal. "Good day, Pearl."

After Pearl took her leave, Eunice drained the remainder of her tea in one long gulp. When a droplet rolled down her chin, she dabbed a soft cloth to wipe away the offense.

Almost immediately Harriet, her dark-skinned servant, appeared like a whisper. The evidence of the dismal repast disappeared as silently.

At least some people know their place.

***

That evening at dinner, Eunice fidgeted. Pearl's age often made the girl fall victim to shifting social behaviors, but for her to be brash!

That screamed of the witch's influence.

No. She'd waste no more time thinking about that devil-woman.

Eunice simpered at William, her husband of a dozen years. He sat at the other end of their grand table. The candlelight on his graying temples gave him a cultured air. Eunice congratulated herself on having found such a handsome, strong, *Christian* man. A man with his wits about him. A caring man who knew how to make her feel like a woman—not a chicken. Spring or otherwise.

Though, she admitted, his lack of attention of late haunted her. Intimate dinners canceled for busy schedules. And in the boudoir...she brushed past that.

William twirled his mustache as he perused the *Times-Picayune*.

Surely his business affairs weighed on both his head and heart. Her age wouldn't cause his dampened affections.

Eunice had come from a pedigree of handsome women whose fair skin aged smooth as porcelain. Though too many days in the sun as a child had left hers not quite so fine as her mother's.

"William," Eunice placed her dessert fork gently on her plate, "is the news so terribly interesting that it denies me your attention?"

"Hmm." The corners of William's mouth twitched, the briefest of smiles. "No need to bait me." He looked over the paper.

Eunice tilted her head. "I do not have the foggiest idea what you imply, Mr. Billbray. I am only inquiring about the news."

"Mmhmm." William folded the newspaper. "Captains report a storm forming over the southern waters. Could be headed our way."

"Tosh! They hardly ever make landfall."

William shrugged. "I tend to trust those seafaring chaps when it comes to water and weather."

Harriet approached with a pitcher. "It's not just seamen talking, Missus. Lots are saying we need to take precautions."

William nodded, "See, my dear?"

Eunice seethed. *How dare she side with him!* She had a mind to send Harriet away. This was why she didn't keep house slaves in New Orleans. These servants with their brash ideas, requests for odd hours, which she abided, yes. Harriet's, in particular, if only because the woman was so talented in making the greens here palatable, and she always found the perfect confections for events. The Guild members still complimented those divine lemon berry *petit fours* from her last party.

William's deep voice drew her out of her angry musings. "My only concern is for you, as I will be away on business next week. Best you be ready in case it does hit."

"Traveling? Surely not long enough that I would have to be shuttered inside by myself?"

"Just two days, dear. You might ask Harriet to stay over."

"I am not *that* fearful. Why must you leave again? Your business has kept us...this is the first real dinner we have had together in nearly a week. Am I to be abandoned further?"

He opened his mouth to reply, but paused as Harriet poured him more tea.

As William watched her bend to place the pitcher back on the cart, Eunice soured. No. He was just pausing for privacy, lost in thought. His eye had wandered, sure. Men couldn't help it, but not ever in *that* direction. Pearl's gossip had her worked over.

When they were alone again, he answered. "I will not discuss my business at the table. It can't be helped, dear, so let's turn toward more pleasant things." He dropped his napkin onto the table. "Balzac's got a text I'd be happy to lay my hands on. *Lost Illusions.* That title alone is worth half a supper's conversation."

"You and your books. More dusty tomes to arrange between our elegant paintings."

"Must you be so sour?"

"If my face were made of words would you study me so intensely?"

"This conversation exceeds the bounds of civility, Eunice."

Eunice took a deep breath. She had so wanted a pleasant evening.

"I am sorry, dearest. I do not know what has come over me. Pearl Jebston shared disturbing gossip this afternoon. She had her hair done by that Paris Widow of all people—the *Voodoo* woman, who makes of herself such a spectacle. She—"

"And, you disapprove?"

Eunice straightened her back at William's interruption.

Harriet, eyes cast downward, returned to collect the dinnerware.

Her voice soft, Eunice leaned in. "You do not?"

William eyed Harriet, not Eunice. "I'm surprised you haven't learned by now that people are different here." William smiled briefly. "I mean to say, there's nothing wrong with a woman maintaining her looks."

"William Hudson Billbray! You cannot *possibly* be suggesting that—"

"Eunice, I am suggesting nothing. I am simply reminding you that the legal and social structures here are..." he hesitated. "More complex. As for Pearl Jebston, well, her interests tumble like a fluff of cotton in the wind. I'd hardly take anything she does or says to heart."

"I am better off without such people," Eunice conceded.

Harriet's mountain of plates rattled softly on her tray as she returned to the kitchen.

"With your pardon, dear, this day and this conversation have exhausted me. Goodnight. Another sterling meal, Harriet." After pausing only to peck Eunice's forehead, he walked out of the dining room.

Eunice remained alone, trying to quiet the storm brewing inside her. She jumped when Harriet touched her arm gently.

"How dare you." Eunice clutched her hand to her chest.

"Sorry, Missus. I called twice. Are you needing anything else tonight?"

"No. Nothing more." With a flutter of her napkin, Eunice dismissed Harriet.

***

Eunice sent her servants out to shop the Carondelet, and, burning to surprise William with the Balzac book, she headed off by herself in search of a bookseller. Lost in thought, she rounded onto Bourbon Street.

Despite Pearl's cruel words, and the wrinkles Eunice had spotted in her vanity, Eunice Billbray was still relevant, lest her husband forget it.

Eunice hurried past the well-kept gardens that separated the houses within the military-style layout of the city. Stately homes with ornate metalwork lined the street, punctuated by small alleyways where elegant buggies sat. The small balconies buzzed with conversation.

Singing and rhythmic chanting accosted the air more heavily than the thick humidity weighing down Eunice's hair. She followed the sound around a corner into a row of shops, her curiosity leading her astray. A large crowd flooded toward her. People acknowledged the throng from all corners of the street, calling out in adulation.

At the head of the procession, Marie Laveau, the Voodoo queen herself, strode brazenly. She wore a simple black bodice embroidered in bold sapphire thread. On her head, a yellow tignon knotted to form a seven-point crown.

If she'd used that much fabric in her petticoat, she might have appeared more refined. Eunice ducked into the protection of a butcher's doorway.

Laveau's female followers sported similar headwraps in a variety of garish colors and fabrics. Some dripped embellishments and intricate configurations of knots.

Eunice shook her head slowly. *How dare they flaunt their wraps in the face of the tignon law? If the women from Georgia could see this display, they'd be abashed.*

As the crowd closed in, Eunice feigned interest in the meats curing in the window.

An old woman, her bangs distressingly long and her skirt a bland brown, stood before Marie. "My husband has taken to sneaking out when he thinks me asleep. In the morning, the scent of jasmine clings to him. Can you help me win him back?"

"*Ma chérie*, of course I help you," Marie answered. "*Aucun problème*, it is why I am here." Marie Laveau spoke in a thick Cajun accent. Her voice resonated, deep yet feminine. The other voices hushed. Only the rustling skirts and the click of heels on the wooden walkway hinted at the size of the crowd. "You need a *coq*. It must be a capon. Tell Maurice I sent you. He know. He keep a special brood for me."

The crowd paused, trapping Eunice at the store front.

Eunice chanced a look at the witch's reflection. She was pointing at her. No, that was ridiculous. She was pointing at the shop.

"*Merci beaucoup*, Madame Laveau." The petitioner pressed a coin purse into Marie's hand and kissed those fingers. "I can't lose him. He's my life."

Eunice was aghast. *My word, that woman is giving up a week's worth of crawfish. That grasping witch. No wonder she held on to her home after her husband disappeared. In what kind of a world are God-fearing women forced to resort to this nonsense, just that they might hold enticement for their husbands? She should be whipped for such chicanery.*

Eunice studied the delicate features framing Marie's patrician nose. Her skin appeared a shade lighter than Eunice's own aging complexion. Laveau might have passed for white to a careless eye. No wonder she bewitched so many.

Southern men, taking up with a colored mistress. It was a shame, producing such a.... And to think, now George Plantis did the same.

What God hath joined together.... Eunice turned to give Marie a piece of her mind, but the glistening in the witch's eyes stopped her.

"Slaughter at midnight, when the hand touches. Be done before the final bell." Marie Laveau flicked her eyes from the old woman to Eunice, then back to the fish on her hook. "Capture all *du sang,* you hear? Every drop of that fresh blood, you put in a bowl under your husband's bed. His *virilité* be returned to him like he young again, and he have appetite for you alone. You be seein' me next week for a balm to ease your pains, eh?" She placed a hand on her hip, thrust it raucously forward.

Flaming red, the old woman brushed past Eunice into the butcher's.

Eunice prayed away the words of that disgusting spell.

Amidst the clamor of the others now striving for Marie's attention, Eunice tried to escape.

The witch stepped into Eunice's path. *"Comment c'est, madame?"*

Eunice shook her head. *The nerve, speaking to me as if we were equals.*

"A woman of your stature, shopping here for *souper*? Maurice have the finest meat in the city, *oui,* but maybe you *cherche* for something else?

Eunice shook her head again and found it hard to breathe as the bodies pressed close around her. "Excuse me."

Marie looked her in the eyes, bold as brass. "No? Maybe you find it without even aware you search for this thing."

The power in those eyes, with their hint of secrets, whispered to Eunice. Her intended rebuke died in her throat. Instead, she sputtered, "I merely lost my way."

"We only lose our way when we don't keep our eyes open, eh?"

Heads nodded. Eunice stiffened under their scrutiny. This woman, fit for no more than cleaning her chamber pot, made a mockery of her.

Eunice straightened her back and opened her mouth. Marie held up her hand as if to catch the words that never came. "*Je m'appelle* Marie Laveau. *Je suis coiffeuse.* I fix your hair if you like. Just ask your jewel how to find me." Marie winked. "She not know much, that one, but she know the way."

"Who? I...." *Was that a reference to Pearl?* Eunice shuddered. Witch indeed. "I will not be needing your services. *Any* of them." Eunice glanced at the *gris-gris* around many of the women's necks.

"We often know not what we need, 'til time tells us so. Storms come on sudden. But if God *souriant* on you, I pray he continue." Marie Laveau dipped in a combination of a curtsy and a bow, her turban bobbing low. "Until we meet again, *madame. Adieu* and God bless."

With that, Marie Laveau sauntered off, skirts swinging. Her flock scurried behind.

Eunice shivered. Pray for her? The audacity.

Eunice stumbled along unfamiliar streets, her fluster impairing her sense of direction. She could not be far from her original route, but she felt in a different city. Just as she located a street sign she recognized, the delicious scent of roasting pecans overtook her. It lured her to a confectioner's shop she had not noticed before. In the window, a handsome display of pralines. Perhaps this was where Harriet had purchased that decadent praline bread pudding with the caramel-pecan sauce. When William had left on his last long trip, that pan had made eating alone bearable.

She composed herself by counting the coins in her reticule. Yes, she could afford the delicacy, and not have to ask William for another allowance. She entered.

The shop was very small. Not cramped per se, but much smaller than Eunice was typically accustomed. She was forced to sidestep awkwardly to allow another customer, colored no less, to exit. But that scent. It drowned her indignation.

"Might you have a full pan of—" Eunice's heart nearly stopped as abruptly as her words.

Harriet stood behind the counter, wearing a tignon, a dusting of flour on her cheek, and a smile that straightened as her eyes found Eunice's.

"How many others do you work for?"

"This shop is mine, Missus." Harriet placed a glass cover over those glorious *petit fours*, the raspberries plump on top, and a trail of vibrant juice running down the side of lemony butter-cream frosting. "For now."

"That cannot be."

"I assure you it is quite legal." Harriet's voice had an edge Eunice had never heard before.

"That's not—" Eunice's hands twisted her reticule. "What I mean to say is, you cannot possibly have time to tend my house, cook, and bake to fill this establishment."

Harriet stood taller. "Lots of things become possible when you have no choice. When I lost my Isaac to the saffron scourge, I begged the *loa* to carry me to him, but they refused. This shop was our *rêve*—our dream. I could not lose it as well. I do what I must." With the hem of her apron, Harriet wiped a stray drizzle of raspberry from her otherwise pristine counter. "That's how I came to work for you, Missus. Marie Laveau, she counseled me. She said, 'Go to that white woman on Royal Street. Clean, bake, worry about sleep in your next life.' Said I should set my pride at my husband's marker, so I can bake for us, for his memory, for me. So I do." Harriet's eyes shimmered, then a single tear cut its way through the flour on her cheek.

"That woman," Eunice's venom for the Voodoo queen spilled from her lips, "digging her fingers into everyone's lives as if she is some great puppeteer. Is no one safe from her absurdity? She is the epitome, *the epitome* of everything wrong with New Orleans."

"Missus, say what you like in your home. But in my shop, I ask you not disrespect Miss Marie so. She brought me to you. It's because of her I still have this shop. You've enjoyed my labors."

"I won't have you talking to me in such a way." Eunice turned on her heel, made sure to slam the door on her way out.

Dust, the stink of fish ripening in the sun, and the day's heat assaulted her. At her back, the memory of pecans, raspberry, and lemons. Could she blame Harriet for being taken in by the witch? If someone like Pearl could.... Well, Harriet hardly stood a chance did she? While balking at Harriet's impertinence, it would hardly be Christian of her to expect Harriet to deny herself that clearly God-given gift of baking. And what a gift it was.

Those delicacies inside begged for Eunice to dip a fingernail into. Rich chocolates, flaky croissant crust, and there, the praline bread pudding, the caramel and pecans swirling together, still steaming.

After a suitable delay, she slipped back into the shop.

Harriet straightened.

Eunice pointed. "When you come this afternoon, I expect that entire pan." She cast the handful of coins on the counter, then scurried back out. God would forgive her this weakness, surely.

***

Eunice stood in the hallway as Pearl rapped at the door. She'd instructed the servants to inform Pearl that she was indisposed. Indefinitely.

"Eunice, you vile creature," Pearl cried. "I admire your ire, but our spat must wait. I simply *must* speak to you!" She knocked again. "You would not like me saying this here, through your door where anyone could hear."

Eunice drew a step closer.

"I lit four candles for you at St. Louis before coming here."

Eunice's hand hovered above the lock as she weighed their friendship. Pearl was a flighty woman. If Eunice didn't guide her, who would? And, candles for her? Why? Eunice drew back the bolt.

Pearl's flamboyant coiffure left little doubt as to the source of her gossip.

"Do not be all day coming in." Eunice stood aside to make room for Pearl's petticoats. She called primly, "Harriet, bring the kettle."

Pearl had not yet sat on the sofa when Eunice rounded on her. "When a woman reaches a certain age, insinuating that she is past her prime is in bad taste. Why, I might've never spoken to you again, had you not seemed so urgent."

"I am sorry I jested." Pearl hurried close to Eunice. "You simply must forgive me when my mouth has its own gumption. I am here now in your time of need. If you can forgive the source of my information."

"That depends."

Pearl crossed the room, studying William's bookcase. She trailed her fingers along the bindings. "I...."

If Pearl hesitated in earnest and not simply to make Eunice suffer, the news must be terrible. "Pearl?" Eunice fought the panic rising in her gullet.

Pearl turned, eyes down as she worried a pattern into the rich Wilton carpet with her toe. "I happened to compliment Marie on her new headdress. When I heard how she'd paid for it...." Pearl's voice smoothed out, taking on a sing-song pitch. Like the Voodoo queen's. *"Rich white man, done fallen in love with a mademoiselle and paid me a pretty penny to make a charm to bring her affection. Love must be earned, I told him."* From facial expressions to tone to the way she set her hand on her hip, Pearl channeled the witch.

Eunice hugged herself, disbelief and incredulity building.

Pearl sauntered. *"He insisted. It's no use, I say, but he keep paying, so I keep praying...for the one he wrongs."*

"Leave off your silly impressions," Eunice barked. "That woman. Praying for people she doesn't have the right to."

Pearl shook her head. "I don't know what came over me. What was I saying?"

"The man, and this negress? Who is it?"

"Maybe it's better I don't say." Pearl quieted as Harriet arrived with the tea. The woman stood silently as she began setting.

Slow as molasses. "I'll set it myself, Harriet,"
Eunice snapped.

Harriet jerked straight up, revealing plated pralines. She
eyed Pearl, then Eunice. "Yes, Missus." Harriet left, but
with no hurry.

Once Harriet left, Eunice closed on Pearl.
"Not William."

Pearl nodded slowly. "Unless another Mr. Billbray lives
on Royal Street?"

Eunice fanned herself. "I'm certain you've misheard."

"No." Pearl draped an arm around her friend. "She sold
me a *gris-gris* that worked, Eunice. My mother and my
husband are finally civil between them. Maybe Madame
Laveau can help you, too?" Lavender, cinnamon, parsley,
and dragonroot, a horrible mixture of scents filled the air
as she revealed two red satchels nestling against her cross.
Pearl lifted one free, teasing it past her audacious curls, and
dropping it near the unfinished tea setting. Eunice shifted
to get distance from the blasphemous bag. The aromas were
harder to escape as its contents spilled over the tabletop.

"Such foolishness, I would never...."

"Every bit of prayer can help, Eunice."

Eunice could not meet Pearl's eyes.

***

Two days later, Eunice paced down St. Anne's Street.
While the area was well-kept, she again seethed with
resentment as free blacks and mulattos strolled by in fine

clothes. The women shaded themselves with fashionable parasols. What did men see in them?

Eunice had gone behind William's back and inquired with his business partners about the two days' travel. They'd admitted that William had no need to travel for business. Then, at her distress, tried to fix their fumble by recalling a discrepancy William chased down.

Betraying him further, she had searched his bureau and found receipts for flowers she never received.

Not my William.

She'd bruised her knees praying at St. Louis, bargaining with God for William's lost devotion. She'd bared her soul under the seal of the confessional, humiliating herself in her fear, her sorrow, at William's obvious betrayal. Pere Antoine had admonished her, claiming that her own flaw, a lack of wifely attentiveness, was to blame.

She had altered her demeanor. Praised him highly, even came to him in his bed—and still he had left early that morning for his trip.

His passion had wandered, it was certain. But *William.* With a negress slave? Or a free woman? A free negress would be worse. No, she'd need to hear it first hand from the source's mouth to believe it. Then she might discover the means to remedy the situation. *You're just grasping!* Eunice teetered on a precipice. Although she'd dismissed Pearl's claims of the strength of this conjury, the bag left behind haunted her steps. She'd let Harriet clean it up. But, perhaps there was some truth in the woman's power? Pearl had sworn on her grandmama's grave, Marie Laveau used pure holy water and prayed to the proper saints while doing her magic. Why else would Pere Antoine have condoned her rituals? And Pearl's father was a pastor after all.

A nameless terror gripped Eunice as she looked up at the residence of Marie Laveau.

"This is how the flock goes astray. Following other lost sheep." Eunice crossed herself, then forced her breathing to slow, keeping her gaze cast downward in an attempt to calm herself.

She wrung her hands, appallingly bare of gloves with the unusual heat that had settled over New Orleans. The air had been still and stale, and yet people tittered about an unseen storm.

Peering around first to make certain no one paid her any mind, she crossed to Laveau's home. The many windows of the quaint little house had their shutters flung wide in the oppressive heat. No hint of wind cooled the homes, yet the still air carried the heavy drum beats, chants, and murmured prayers.

Banda, they're Banda dancing.

The sounds lured Eunice around the corner onto Burgundy Street. The tall rickety fence that surrounded the humble little house hid her. Confident of her privacy, she perched on tiptoe to watch the ceremony unfolding beneath the backyard's magnolia trees.

Three men gyrated past, arms and legs flailing in a mess that defied patterns. Laveau herself vacillated between two drummers. A woman, visibly pregnant, knelt before her, a halo of smoke forming as Marie swirled a large shell above her head. The atrocious stink made Eunice pinch her nose.

"Thank you, *Madame*. Thank you for my *bebe*." Even at this distance, Eunice could see that the woman's face glistened with tears.

Laveau held the shell in one hand, gently cupping the woman's face with the other. She dipped a finger in the ashes. As the drums silenced, she drew a cross on the woman's forehead.

"Your *bebe* is from God, my child. Through me, God watches over you both. Pray with me." She knelt, taking the woman's hand. "Hail Mary, full of Grace, the Lord is with thee. Blessed art thou among women, and blessed is the fruit of thy womb. You want a safe *bebe, oui?* Then do not miss the services, not even when the water's high. You find a church. You pray for *bebe*." Marie handed her a sachet. "Keep this close." Laveau reached into a box at her feet to withdraw a live, writhing snake.

It was a snake that tempted Eve.

A man twirled towards it, bowing his head.

To keep sight of him, Eunice slipped through a shadowed gate. She drew closer as Marie offered the snake purchase around the man's neck. He spun away and the chanting grew louder.

"We offer ourselves in service to God," Marie cried.

To God?

Eunice watched and waited as Marie completed the ceremony. Unconsciously, she began to sway to Marie's beat.

***

Eunice drew her collar tightly around her neck and shivered in spite of the heat as she hurried home, barely noting the early darkening of the sky. She replayed the ceremony in her mind, recalled Laveau's warning as she'd handed the mother-to-be a single white feather in parting.

"The feather is a powerful magic, *ma chérie,* for good and evil. This one has been freely given, blessed by the Virgin for protection over your birthing. Beware the feather if found, for it always bodes evil."

Last night, after Harriet had prepared Eunice's bed for her retirement, Eunice had found a single white feather resting upon the pillow. At the time, Eunice had brushed it aside. Now she wondered how it had worked its way out of the down stuffing in such pristine condition. A sign from God? The same God?

Her home in sight, Eunice could no longer worry away the winds, which pushed her off course as she crossed the street.

Eunice flung open her front door, coming face to face with a wide-eyed Harriet. Harriet, always present, attentive, except today was her one day *not* to be here. The memory of Harriet in her shop, back straight, eyes unwavering, flashed back. What did she think of her Missus? With her improper friends and a good Christian husband buying trinkets and gifts for another. Servants saw all. Harriet must have seen irrefutable proof. Might she also have an opinion on the *gris-gris* left by Pearl?

Why do I care?

A shutter slammed. Eunice shrieked.

Harriet spoke without leave, her words tumbling out in a desperate rush. "Water's wicked, and the winds, too. Captains ran from their ships, not fully secured. My shop's already secured, so I came to help the others, but they have homes to protect, too. Forgive me, I did not stop them. They say it's bad Juju. I can't say they're wrong. I almost left too, then I remembered Mister Billbray was off, leaving you—" Harriet stopped. "I mean to say, there's no job serving if there's no home to serve. It can't be done alone."

"Careful. This is my house, not your shop," said Eunice, but found her ire limp. She thought of William. "Harriet, what do you know of found feathers?"

"A feather, Missus?"

"My pillow last night. I found a single white feather. Did you place it there?"

Harriet crossed herself. "I don't do evil curses, Missus. A found feather is a bad omen. This is worse than I feared."

A gust blew through the still open door, knocking the Meissen vase from its stand. The piece shattered, its golden handle sliding down the entryway.

Both gasped.

"I'll go latch those shutters down." Harriet pushed the door closed. "Unless you were…."

"I'll be in my room." Eunice fumbled for the words she knew should be said. "Thank you." That didn't taste like the soured milk she had expected.

Harriet started to speak, but a terrible banging interrupted from the sitting room, and she hurried off.

Did William, away on his *business,* worry over her now? Alone, for all he knew, against a coming storm? Save for Harriet, what *would* she have done? She'd never had to latch the shutters down, prepare for a storm. William…. Eunice paused before her window. The Spanish moss hanging from the old oaks whipped fit to break.

A particularly strong wind let loose a terrible howl through the upper floors. Eunice wanted to howl back. Instead, she sank into the plush coverlet and covered her ears, but nothing could drown out that anguishing sound.

At a sharp rap on the door, Eunice jolted upright.

She smoothed her hair before answering, "Come in."

"Missus, you haven't shuttered your room yet. It takes more hands. Even God may not save us from this JuJu."

"Good heavens! Enough with this magic hullabaloo." Eunice stood. "What has it to do with God? My friends are becoming heathens in their willingness to play with your demons. Even I was tempted. Watched the witch dance with my own eyes. What good are the promises of demons if God will not save you?"

"Not demons. The *loa* are like your angels. They speak in God's name. I think they speak now. Warning. We need this home secured."

Glass shattered, a branch spearing through it. Shredded leaves, shards of bark, and rain streamed through the breach.

Eunice shrieked.

"Missus, God has left us no time for hysterics. Help me."

Eunice registered her servant's urgency. "Harriet, finish securing the hurricane shutters outside. I'll attempt the indoor ones."

Harriet nodded and ran from the room.

While Eunice strained to reach the upper window, Harriet worked below. She wrangled the heavy black storm shutters with a long pole. With every attempt, the wind swept them out of her grasp. The pole cracked and crashed into the house. Eunice twanged with guilt as wreckage whipped around her servant, hit her, cut her. Harriet struggled on.

The house thrummed. Where the drumbeats of Marie's Banda dancers had soothed, this rhythm paralyzed.

She'd lost William, but she refused to lose her life. She'd put this into God's hands. She knelt. Roaring wind swallowed her prayers as they left her mouth. The wind snapped the window closed with an ear-splitting crack. Eunice called upon God as she fell back. As she lay on the floor she wondered if Harriet's sacred spirits could hear *her.* A cracking bang came from outside. If only William were here, he'd take charge. But Mr. Billbray was not here; Harriet was, had returned of her own free will to help Eunice.

Where was Harriet, now?

Eunice raced downstairs, throwing her shoulder against the front door.

"How can I help?" she shouted over the wind.

"The other pole!"

"Where is it?"

"Shed!"

Eunice hunched forward, fighting through the wind. She wrapped her arms around the pole. The wind ripped it free.

Watching it fly away, Eunice lunged one step at a time back to Harriet, who grappled with her own pole.

"Let me help you." Eunice steadied its base so Harriet could catch the latch to wrangle it shut.

Eunice cried out as the rain pelted down. She fought to breathe. At any moment, a falling branch could kill her.

"Leave off, Harriet. We've done what we can."

Harriet refused. "We have to make it safe, Missus. The bones foretold the water will rise again. Don't you feel the threat? I can smell it."

"We're far enough from the water, aren't we? We'll be safe." The words rang hollow even in her own ears. Dread soured her stomach like over-spiced étouffée. Eunice was not used to such decisions or labors, yet Harriet showed decisiveness that Eunice did not possess.

Yes, William must have chosen to shelter with his mistress, abandoning his weak, useless wife. She drew in a bitter breath as the rain battered them from above. "What do we do now, Harriet?"

"Axe from the shed, Missus," Harriet screamed over the wind. "For if the water rises. Hammer too. Heavy tools. The best knife from the kitchen."

"Why? Shouldn't we be getting food? We can't break the house apart to build a boat, for heaven's sake!" *Or did the woman mean to murder her? Could she blame her?*

"For the roof. If the tides come this far, the roof might save us. We'll chop through."

Eunice crossed herself. "It's already coming."

Water, lapping up the street. And them, the only ones still outside.

Harriet grabbed Eunice by the arm. "Tools first, then inside. It's all we can do." Eunice let Harriet drag her against the wind, back to the shed. A moment to catch her breath, then Eunice pushed back outside with not only the hammer, but a saw as well. Harriet clutched the axe to her chest. They fought their way back to the house, where the front door refused to open. Eunice screamed. She shifted her grip on her two tools, pushed again. The door yielded.

Harriet lit an oil lamp for Eunice before scurrying to the kitchen for the carving knife. With that flame providing a flicker of hope, Eunice climbed to higher ground. Her bedroom. She pressed herself into the brick of the fireplace. After cursing the heat this week, now she yearned for warmth. There was nothing left to do but pray.

The wind screamed in answer. Ashes flew up, choking her. Her lamp snuffed out.

In the dark, she thought of Harriet downstairs, alone. Had losing her husband given her this strength, or had Harriet always been like this? Maybe they all were. Perhaps it was not their difference in countenance, but rather their inner strength, that led men like her husband away? Did men want women who had weathered storms?

She remembered the power in Marie Laveau's eyes. Her confidence. Was that possible, even for her?

She said one Hail Mary in the darkness. Two. After the third, Eunice yelled for Harriet. The wind's banshee requiem drowned out her voice.

Then the wind dropped off. An eerie voice carried to her from the corridor outside her room. Harriet chanted, her voice rising and falling in plaintive tones. *"Bon Dieu, Bon Dieu*, I call your *invisibles.... Mystères, Agwe*, Shell of the Sea, pull back the waters. *Bondye, Agau*, I honor your powerful *loa* with my promise. Protect this house and those who dwell within it."

Eunice took reluctant comfort in the sing-song prayer. It sounded not unlike Marie Laveau's. When Harriet paused, Eunice called to her again, voice quavering.

Stomping feet answered.

"Patience, Missus. I'm coming."

Eunice leaned out the door as Harriet approached. She clasped her hand around Harriet's, and she felt the woman shaking as mightily as she did. She'd been as afraid as Eunice, but she hadn't acted it.

"You're very brave, Harriet." Eunice meant it, meant it beyond how Harriet was handling the storm.

"I'll fetch the tallow and match safe."

Eunice clutched her arm desperately. "Don't leave me, Harriet. Please."

They held fast to one another.

Eunice imagined how many Hail Marys her priest would require when she confessed her broken faith.

Confound it, he's not here. She forced her question out. "Who is *Bon Dieu*?"

"*Bondye* is our good God."

"And *loa*. They're the spirits?"

"The *loa* carry the message. I arranged for your protection. Offering my service. My *gris-gris* might protect me, but I feared it wasn't powerful enough to protect you too, Missus." Harriet lifted a small burgundy bag from between her breasts.

Why would this woman bargain with her god? For *her*? Eunice had treated her so badly in the past, and she'd spoken ill of her breeding.

And still, Harriet had stayed when her William had abandoned her. Despite the fear drumming into her with the winds, a peace settled around her shoulders.

"Perhaps between us," Eunice said, "our Gods will show mercy when we've no men to save us."

Eunice reached into her bodice. Her chain tangled in the cord of the small *gris-gris* she pulled free. She held both—the cross blessed by the priest who shamed her, and the saffron bag from Marie Laveau. Marie had filled it with beans; the leg bone of a purple martin, its song silenced; and herbs chosen especially for her concerns. Lavender, basil, cinnamon, even the tang of the bay leaf. The earthy scents eased her mind more than the priest's words and incense ever had.

She slipped her crucifix gently into Harriet's pocket. "Our Father, who art in Heaven, please protect Harriet."

The winds screamed back to life, more vicious for the moments of silence.

"Do you not feel the waters rising, Missus? It's in my bones."

Eunice hesitated. "Is it?"

"Surge is coming." And with that, Harriet arose. With deliberation, she dragged the tools to the closet. "We need to get higher, now."

Eunice eyed the panel offering access to the attic, the hook to pull the stairs down. She hefted the butcher knife.

"I'd much rather be using this to cut into your bread pudding."

"If we survive this, I could teach you how to make it, if you'd be willing."

"Now, there's no sense tampering with perfection. But I am curious of your secret. Perhaps I could watch."

Hip to hip, she stood with Harriet against the rain attacking them from above, the water rising below, and the winds of change blowing.

Thoughts on "Hail Mary, Hail Marie" from Victoria Kelsey:

The favorite story that we wrote as a team, for me, was "Hail Mary, Hail Marie." The reason I love this story so much is because I feel like we created a character, and that character evolved so much throughout the story. And every one of us contributed to that evolution, taking the character from a rather two-dimensional person to a fully realized character with flaws and depths that even she didn't realize she had. The story certainly didn't start out that way, and neither did Marie! That's kind of a parallel of our team experience as a whole; we started out rough, but by the end we were clearly melding together and creating something pretty okay!

Thoughts from Wayne Hills:

On the selfish side, [my favorite story] didn't make the final cut for the collection. But as for those we are sharing, "Hail Mary, Hail Marie" [is my favorite] because of the same reasons listed by Victoria. That character and universe could be an entire novel in itself.

"The whole experience was like a black hole. It sucks everything into it, including light and hope and dreams. And then it crushes it for eons before eventually evaporating into nothing as the hot death of the universe sets in and all matter dissociates from everything, leaving an eternity of nothingness in its wake. Oh, no, wait, I thought I was describing what an abusive relationship is like. Working with my teammates was the opposite of what I just described."

—S W Fox

Essays

Whether or not you decide to ever try your hand at collaboration, we felt it was important to shine a spotlight on all the solidarity there is in this endeavor. A lot of people shape our writing experience and the final result. They help us when we're stuck, challenge us to do better, lift us up when we are down, push us to the next level, and ultimately, they keep us with pen in hand (or hands on keyboard).

This next section of the book is a tribute to writing groups, be they official or otherwise. To our first readers, betas, editors, workshop partners, and best friends. Not all experiences are gold, or what we initially hoped for, but each adds another chapter to our journey as writers. And none of us would be where we are today without them.

Hackneyed Hammocks

Jack Woolverton

Hammocks are simultaneously God's greatest achievements and Satan's most brilliant perversions. They are also direct parallels to writers and the writing groups which they haunt. Oh, those wondrous parishioners of poets and plagiarists that ply their pithy prose with perfect punctuation. How can we not compare thee to a summer's day, or at least the perilous, swinging embrace of maniacal rope?

I have waded through a virtual morass of writing groups. Some yield writers of utmost pretension and gravitas. Others present factions of giggling erotic romance writers who can be identified through the fact they are still chortling over the word "morass." Most are a motley collection of in-betweens, but all are unique. Writers often feel the need to find a place that best facilitates their scrumptious scribbles. It's a search for figuring out not only which hammock fits *your* butt the best, but also what it's made of, and where's the best shady spot.

For me, college provided the first, angst-ridden webbing of group writing. Many of us pined away at our journals, convinced in some misguided quantum quandary that we were both the best artists ever and also the mangiest curs to e'er birth a sentence. Then our good ole Prof made us share our misery with each other, encouraging "constructive criticism" of the most personal efforts of our lives. Everything followed a curriculum here—a set standard of instructions that was meant to offer encyclopedic expository expression. Aside from the Irony Essay— essentially an academic way to troll intellectuals—this hammock was a mass-produced swing that cost a lot, but failed to provide all the stretch I needed.

Structured classes were one-size-fits-all hammock prototypes, but in my next step I resembled a blind man entering a hammock IKEA. I knew I had talent, but like learning the mystic secrets of unhooking bras, I fumbled around with it. The muse called to me, but you have to understand, I'm an idiot. For years it's been a toggle of impassioned flourishes of aspirational effort and sudden guillotine stops where, as you might infer, I lost my head. I substituted hammocks for Adirondacks—or maybe iron maidens. During these times, a smattering of random writing groups formed the crests of these undulating allegories.

I lost my virginity to the first group. Or, at least, I made significant strides to interact with actual human beings who took writing seriously in a non-academic setting. We met in our small-town bookstore and spoke in hushed tones of the majestic magic inherent in every writer's lifeblood. Craft was investigated, plots holed, and encouragement divvied between bouts of manic inadequacy. I lasted all of three meetings before the commitment to attend sacrificed itself to my lack of discipline. To make up for my utter failure, I decided to join an online writer's group. Or five.

I found some Egyptian-cotton hammocks that gave me both a comfortable sense of belonging and anonymity. Thousands of writers of all skill levels popped on and off at their leisure, and once a year an automated Happy Birthday would flitter through my private messages to make me feel special. Of course, by the time I actually utilized a group, two years had gone by and all I had left was a moldy shrine to some forgotten god of sloth. Even if you get involved with these groups, the physical distance inherent within them allows for easy detachment. That's why many sites have adopted gimmicks:

Critique others, earn points to post your stories for critique, and hey, join our forums for virtual coffee stickers! Or, *We're the only serious writing group on the net. Established in antediluvian 1998, many of our members have gone on to best-seller lists. Only join if you're serious about your writing. Seriously.*

These sites, while motivating, never held up for my personality. Many writers are fragile, delicate sugar-lace just waiting for the right fat guy to take a lick and send them to oblivion. I'm fat, and a guy, and sugar-lace, so I think I'm allowed to say that. Gimmicks work for some people, but after the novelty wears off, the writer is usually left with a monthly subscription fee and a morbid sense of false obligation. I still lurk in a couple of the better communities, but they aren't inspirational for me. The holes in these hammocks are too big, and sometimes they swallow you, and you're never seen again.

In 2016, God, fate, and the addiction of a gambling man made me realize my social status is irrelevant. I love to write, and occasionally I'm damn good at it, according to my mom. I paid a considerable fee to enter a giant competition I felt I had no chance to win, but that offered both peer review and critique from established judges. Given my propensity for great decision-making, I also joined a beta group in that competition. Since then, those people have evolved into the best group of writers I've had the honor to scribe with. Our cartel of calligraphers grows organically, and it offers heartfelt advice, encouragement, and knowledge with a camaraderie that shares both sorrows and triumphs. It harbors a diverse crew of writers who boldly share a variety of refreshing perspectives. Every piece of the hammock is made of the perfect combination of materials, and woven seamlessly into a tapestry of artistry and support. We swing well together.

As a result, am I a successful author that writes every day, past discipline problems vanished? No. This backyard hammock gets dusty, but never forgotten. My writing group keeps me honest, though they never pressure me. Their support holds me aloft, and I know it will never fail. This hammock is alive, breathing, and definitely not deranged. Okay, maybe a little deranged, but in the best possible ways. I still flip over at the worst possible moment, like when the dog left a pile underneath. Even so, I have never felt more that I can be successful, and I owe that to my group.

Now, I greet all new members of our group with a hammock joke. Sometimes obscene, other times innocuous, it's my way to welcome them to our interwoven community of writers tangled up with all our hang-ups and differences in one massive backyard. It's my way to say, welcome home.

Writing in the Wilderness

Nathan James

2014

The instructions seemed simple enough: Write a complete story in exactly 42 words (not including the title) that answers the question, "Is something crawling on me?"

Well, not simple. Telling any kind of story in 42 words is rarely simple, and 17 years had passed since I'd last written fiction, let alone to a prompt, but I had just started a blog that not even my mother was reading. Three months of pitching my writing into the empty chasm of the internet can be less than motivating.

So, I decided to go for it. I made myself a strong cup of coffee, grabbed a notepad and a pencil, and dug my heels in to write an entry for this challenge hosted by an online writing community. Who knew? Maybe I'd find an audience for my blog.

I spent ten hours total on it, fretting over every word, plugging in and yanking out that first comma until I'd erased a hole in the paper. I posted it on my blog. It stayed there for about fifteen minutes before I took it down to revise it. To make sure it was perfect. I revised it three more times. My partner had to talk me down from deleting my blog completely. Here's what I came up with:

Anatomy

Uncrumpling notebook paper, he found his own
face staring back at him: his masseter muscle dissected,
bleeding, needles poking his retinas. A student's drawing
perfectly placed on his chair. He will feel that gaze stalking
his nape as he teaches tomorrow's lesson.

What was I so nervous about? How could something I had loved to do since I was nine years old shatter my self-confidence so completely?

1995

"This is it," Professor Friedman said as he pointed to a book the size of a loaf of bread, "...your community, your lifeline, your paycheck."

He grunted when he lifted it and flashed the cover at us. The neon-blue words *1996 WRITERS MARKET* hung above an orange clip-art typewriter. Some of my classmates only gave the book a been-there-done-that glance from their desks. Others of us were curious. We stood and gathered at the front of the classroom. A woman flipped it open and read an open call for parenting articles. Then she read listings for sci-fi novels, nature poetry, and one call for a short story with an aardvark theme.

"You and every other writer in this country will battle it out on the pages of this book." The professor smirked in a way that only a war-torn veteran of the process can. He handed the book to a classmate, who checked listings in favorite genres.

"You will need to be meticulous—every participle held firmly in place, every modifier clear as a bell rung on a winter's morning—because when an army is this large, only the flawless will stand out to agents," my professor added kindling to the fire. "This is what it is like to leave the nest of college and live on your own in the wilderness."

He probably didn't sound as much like a Broadway actor as I make him sound, but that's very much how I remember that day. I also remember leaving the classroom sweaty. It was the last semester of my junior year.

2014

I checked my blog non-stop on the day that everyone read the contest entries. That's how the contest worked. Bloggers would write and post a response to the challenge by a certain deadline. After the deadline, everyone would read all of the entries and vote for their three favorites. Many of them left comments and encouragement on the entries.

A few comments trickled in early—at least I'd found people to fill the seats finally—and they were saying positive things. A wave of instant gratification struck me

that I'd never associated with writing before. It's sad, really.
The years of college writing workshops had trained me
to wait for readers' responses before deeming my writing
worthy. And there's an inherent problem in that because
writers are competitive. Not all, of course, but many of
my classmates had been vultures, gliding into the room
on the wind of their own egos, flapping until the next poor
sap offered them a manuscript to tear apart with beaks
or talons. Maybe I just went to a college with a lot of
@GuyInYourMFAs, a Twitter account mocking pretentious
English majors. Or maybe I had been a @GuyInYourMFA.

I read the other contest entries with my pretension
sensors turned all the way up. I left comments and
subscribed to some of the blogs of writers whose styles
I dug. When I returned to my own post, there were 21
messages. Twenty-one people had stopped by my site and
took in my thoughts. I had missed that feeling of being
read. I had missed using my voice.

1997

I won second place. It was just a poetry competition in
a local newspaper, but there were cash prizes and the town
had three colleges in it, so it was something. They asked me
and the other two winners to read my work in front of an
audience. When I arrived at the venue, a theater, it turned
out I knew the winner. He was a friend of a friend. The
only time the three of us had hung out together he'd said
something incredibly pompous. We were playing Scrabble,
and I pointed out the dictionary in case anyone challenged a
word. He scoffed and said, "We won't need that; I'm in the

Honor's College." The Honors College was our university's program for fast-tracking the straight-A high school students. Hackles up, I turned to him. "All that means, Justin, is that you're good at bullshitting."

That had been the year before.

Back in the theater, Justin laughed when he saw me. "Aren't you a writing major?" he asked.

"Yeah."

"Huh. I just wrote this in between biology classes. It's crazy that a biology major won a poetry contest over a poetry major."

I know it sounds like I'm turning him into every villain in a John Hughes movie ever, but I swear he was this annoying.

A half hour later, after actively avoiding any further interaction with Justin, I stood at the podium reading my *award-winning* poem and all I could think about was what Justin said.

Maybe this wasn't my gig. If I couldn't compete with him, how was I going to get work published up against other capital-W Writers? Does the audience know that a science guy beat out the poet for the grand prize?

The room spun. My pulse quickened. I searched the audience for vultures, thought I'd spotted a few. I sputtered out my poem—something about raisins and the blue patterns of china plates—the audience politely clapped when I finished. The third prize winner began to read.

It would be another seventeen years before I would let someone read anything of mine.

2014 – 2016

I won second place. It was just an online writing competition but it was something. The commenters were so enthusiastic about my entry. The editors of the online community quickly encouraged me to write for their other contests: personal essays and short stories. I began writing in genres I'd never considered before. Science fiction, memoir, sonnets, all the time gaining confidence, rediscovering my talents, finding out how age and experience had shaped my writing abilities.

Members of the community mentioned links to online magazines and print journals that only published a genre of writing I'd never heard of before: flash fiction.

They celebrated when one of their stories or poems were published and told me if they could do it I could do it. I made excuses; I thought they were just being polite.

They suggested self-publishing. Write a collection of flash fiction stories or poems and make a chapbook. Writers did it all the time, they said. In their Facebook group, they linked to calls for submissions of every size and shape. It was like that gigantic book Professor Friedman had displayed, only offered piecemeal. I learned what it felt like to be in a "room" of writers who weren't in direct competition with each other. We helped each other with whatever our goals were. Even the writers who were submitting to the same contests had no problem giving considerate feedback to improve the other's work.

I marveled at them. My college experience really had been toxic. And then I grew sad because I realized that I could have had this all along.

Over the next year, I submitted to a few small publishers. They rejected me. My writing community picked me up, dusted me off, encouraged me to submit other work. In between rejections, I got published online, posts on my blog were recognized by WordPress, and the writing community invited me to be one of their editors. Someone submitted one of my posts to a contest. The contest picked my post to be read at their conference in LA.

Standing at another podium, I read my words to a room of over 2,000 people. Justin wasn't there; my hands did not shake. I read my essay confident that I had written something true and worthwhile. I imagined all of the people who had helped me over the past two years to get me here standing behind me. I was nervous, but by expanding my view, the wilderness had become manageable. I looked into the audience as I read and I did not see a single vulture.

The Girl at the Bottom of the Stairs

Colette Bennett

There was a time when watching other writers succeed brought only bitterness to my tongue.

It wasn't that I envied their triumphs—although envy would have been easier to cope with. The darkness that squirmed in my gut was worse, and I longed to spit it out. No matter how I tried to fight it, it summoned me to a staircase within myself that I could not resist descending, no matter how much I dug in my heels. A girl that wore my face waited in the depths, perfectly content to tell me the same thing no matter how many times I visited.

You are not good enough.

The girl lied, but I believed her. She was all I knew how to be. As a teenager, I faithfully scribbled my inner thoughts into journal after journal with deadly purpose, sitting alone on my parents' back porch at two in the morning, cigarette clamped between my lips. Time spent on the page seemed inherently solitary. Writing, I believed, was not for happy people.

I made my way into adulthood, stumbling all the while. I wrote stories but showed them to no one. I scribbled poetry. I peered at the covers of countless books on the shelves of bookstores, wondering how so many people worked up the courage to come to the page not just once, but again and again.

I crept up to the edges of writing groups, first lurking in the background online, then daring to type a few words here and there. In a passing flash of bravery, I joined a local one, only to never show up at meetings.

Part of me wanted to be heard, but terror lay low in my belly. I would have to share my private kingdoms, dare to invite strange faces to explore their hills and valleys. They were the only worlds I was ever happy in, and these intruders could lay siege at any time.

You're not good enough, my doppelganger whispered.

Over the years, another voice pulsed quietly in my chest, so different from that girl who lived deep in my gut. And from that voice, my real stories came, first just in whispers, then spilling through the page and soaking the floorboards.

I had mastered the art of losing myself in other people's stories. But I was afraid to tell my own.

Late last year, a friend mentioned an online writing group and offered to introduce me. For the first time, my fears began to soften. Warm and friendly voices bantered in the comments beneath each post. The members discussed storytelling with objectivity and hope. We shared a common goal: to show our work to the world. At least, I thought I wanted that, too.

Fear is a funny thing. As I watched fellow members post about their successes, a strange terror rose in me. I was closer than ever to writers doing the work to publish, showing up to the page no matter what. And it terrified me.

Her velvet voice rose up in my gut: *Not good enough.*

Despite her entreaties, I couldn't walk away. I watched the group nervously, wanting to participate, wanting to cheer for people's success. Again and again, her voice returned to crush my own.

But I longed to defy her, and that drove me to the doors of the first writing conference I'd ever set foot in. I almost didn't go. If I couldn't tell my writing group about my successes, at least I could say I tried. Maybe, I hoped, I might even hear something that could dislodge this terrible emotion, allow me to write, to stop running away. Maybe that growing pile of stories in my desk drawer could be published, too.

At the conference, I discovered writing journals, talked to authors, and saw for the first time all the tools at my disposal. It was empowering and encouraging. Even so, there were times I felt like an imposter, too. I looked at countless booths dedicated to MFA programs and felt ashamed I didn't have one. I wondered if I could ever be taken seriously by well-educated, literary people.

I also couldn't hear the voice anymore. And in that silence, I made a choice.

I put pen to paper and words tumbled out, a fairy tale about my shame and fear of being what I have known all along I was meant to be. My fear had softened. And I knew for the first time that I belonged there, whether I was writing or not.

Action, it turns out, is a powerful magic I never knew I had.

If I close my eyes, I can still see the girl at the bottom of the stairs, her head heavy with grief. I dare to draw close, and I see the tear-trails of grief on her face. I reach out and embrace her. In my arms she dissolves, leaving nothing more than age-old dust behind.

Scribes United!: Writing Just Might Be an Exact Science

In which the author observes the scientific tendencies of one notable writing group

Abstract: This article explores the remarkable first year of an extraordinary writing group, *Scribes United!,* and how its members and the community they have built work together to form a cohesive and supportive whole, despite being scattered across the globe. A metaphor is explored: specifically, how the group in question compares to a biological organism.

Cayce Osborne, Author and Lead Researcher
Madison, WI

A writing group is an organism. One with many cells. Each unique writer within the organism contributes to the health and success of the whole. Like any such creature, *Scribes United!* embodies the seven essential, complex properties of life:

Organization: Each unique writer feeds the energy of the organism, fueling productivity. The group members exist in their own environs, while supporting one another and striving to make their shared virtual environment pleasant and rewarding. These writers are the basic units of the organism's life.

Homeostasis: Regulation of an organism's internal environment is crucial. *Scribes United!* maintains a positive mood and weathers adversity remarkably. Tactics for achieving this balance include, but are not limited to: pep talks, constructive criticism, sharing resources, selective membership, hilarious gifs, celebrating achievements, pie, cathartic bitch sessions, and general all-around good cheer.

Metabolism: Writing groups, like any other living creature, require energy. The group leaders are particularly talented in this arena, introducing new projects and encouraging conversation when the inevitable lulls occur. All group members are welcome to contribute energy-generating content and have been consistent in sharing new publications, contests, victories, and venues through which the group members might gain exposure for their writing.

Growth: Living entities must grow. Not only do new members enrich a group such as *Scribes United!,* but they also encourage boundary-pushing in existing members, offering new perspectives that engage and energize the rest of the group. This growth is more than merely accumulating matter via increased membership. It is an intellectual growth as well, harder to pin down but much more valuable.

Adaptation: An entity that does not change over time will die. Some of these changes may be brought on by outside factors, others merely byproducts of expanding membership. But this change is fundamental and is one of the things that makes *Scribes United!* unique. As the world of social media changes for the worse—becoming more divisive, more cruel, more partisan—this writing group stands out as a beacon of positivity. If anything, the changes that this author has observed over year one display a marked increase in delightfulness, perhaps even in response to the darkness that seeks to encroach on virtual communities. Such adaptation is to be commended.

Response to stimuli: One can observe this organism's deftness of response each time a new writing contest or prompt is announced. Much like phototropism, the phenomenon by which the leaves of a plant turn toward the sun, these writers will bask in the excitement of a new opportunity. Responses to stimuli are often conveyed through motion; in the case of *Scribes United!*, this is displayed in the speed with which a writer will run toward their laptop when a new prompt is announced, the frenzy with which they will toil as a contest deadline looms, or the cavalcade of support that ensues when one of their ranks is wronged. If only it were possible to bottle such enthusiasm.

Reproduction: The ability of *Scribes United!* to produce new organisms may be the most astonishing property of all. Each completed story by one of its members is a world unto itself, capable of eliciting joy, sorrow, empathy, fright: the full emotional range. These writers send their offspring out into the world fearlessly, hoping for the best yet knowing that should the worst occur, the *Scribes United!* family will be there to help them grieve, help them heal, and ultimately, get them writing again.

In conclusion, the author must applaud *Scribes United!* and all of its members, especially those who can claim the honor of administrator. For surviving their first anniversary in the wilds of the internet not only unscathed, but richer, more dynamic, and more cohesive than when the group began. The term "safe space" is overused and even derided in certain circles. But such spaces are vital, especially for those who toil in solitary; writers being a prime example. These oases are to be protected, and celebrated, and held up as an example to those who seek to tarnish them.

Long live *Scribes United!*

My People

Jennifer Palmer

I have always loved writing—both the action itself and reading the results. However, my search for a place to express this love and cultivate it with others has been a long, sometimes grueling, experience.

My writing escapades became serious when I began to write a novel in high school. Though writing is primarily a solitary activity, a local library hosted a writing group, Hyperbole, geared specifically for teens. I was nervous as all get out the first time I went, but after attending a few times I realized—wait, I got this. I can do it. I don't need a writing group to get these words down on this paper. I don't need to go to the library once a month to sit in a little conference room and talk about writing with other teenagers. I got this. Despite our closeness in age, I knew these weren't my people.

However, Hyperbole is where I first met Carmen. We ended up attending and graduating from the same college, and we both worked at the aforementioned library for a space of time. In fact, she is the Teen Assistant and works with Hyperbole now. So it wasn't a total wash.

Before I move on, a super quick side note—I went through a significant medical experience during the summer of 2013. Due to the aftereffects, I am now eligible for vocational rehabilitation services. I used to go twice a week for occupational therapy, and I got to know the therapists pretty well.

I shared my love of writing with them along with my frustration that I wasn't doing it enough for myself. One of the assistants threw out, "A friend of mine leads this writing group. I can give her your information if you'd like."

Fast forward two weeks, and I am walking up to an independent bookstore one city over. "Joe's Bookstore" the sign reads. I enter and think, *oh snap.*

The bookstore is an old, repurposed house two blocks away from a major performance center in the city. Despite its location, once you cross its threshold it gives off these homey vibes, what with the used books lining the bookshelves on the walls with that old book smell wafting through the air.

I find the writing group upstairs, three women and one man. We introduce ourselves and they share their current projects.

"I'm writing a collection of poems," Vanessa says, "based on flowers and what they mean according to this book I've been reading."

"I write sonnets," the man says, chest hair peeking out of his white, v-neck tee.

My gosh, they're so hipster.

I gave it a try and attended two meetings, but haven't returned since last year. Just not my people. The OT assistant didn't take it personally when I told her though.

Let's back up. When I talked about Hyperbole earlier, that is the teen writing group at the library system's Headquarters branch. Another writer's group meets monthly at the Cyrill-Westside branch, the location closest to my home. I used to attend that one fairly regularly, because another one of my friends from college facilitated it. However, I felt awkward in that group.

I am easily the youngest of this group's participants, though I believe I have the most extensive educational background in writing, having earned a Bachelor of Fine Arts in Creative and Professional Writing. Now, I know that education does not trump factors such as talent, drive, etc., but I believe it does give me an advantage, particularly when it comes to taste. As such, I feel this struggle between asserting myself with my knowledge and respecting my elders, because most of them are at least thirty years older than I. Once again, not quite my people. I'm still on the email list, though.

And then, just when I thought all hope was lost, a light shone through the darkness—*Scribes United!*

In this Facebook group, I've found a miniscule corner of the world where I feel I can be me, me without putting up too much of a facade. I mean, yes, I still tend to present my best side while interacting there (who doesn't?), but I know that if/when I need to, I can reach out for support, get sage advice, or offer encouragement myself. We help each other, whether through sharing information about contests, beta-ing each other's pieces, or giving a "go get 'em, tiger" motivational speech, such as the one I received from Josh F., someone I have referred to as the group dad. Josh doesn't know me outside of Facebook, but he still took the time to cheer me up over Messenger after one particularly bad weekend. And that is merely one example of the caring camaraderie *Scribes United!* provides for its members.

We have cultivated one heck of a community, replete with an anthology, playful competition, and inside jokes (hammocks and pie, anyone?).

I've found it. These are my people; this is my place. Cheers to that.

Essential Friendships

Meagan Noel Hart

At thirteen, I crafted elaborate adventures for my friends. These novellas, hand-scratched into the nonjudgmental paper of school notebooks, involved teenaged versions of my best buds, their hottest crushes (real or fictionalized), and some ridiculous road trip we'd been able to bargain, lie, or luck our way into. What could've been simple preteen lust fulfillment turned quickly into ghost stories, kidnappings, and natural disasters. Sure, we accidentally held hands, but it happened in a darkened gas station, on a lonely desert highway, as a tornado threw sand and our antagonists to the wind. We always solved the mystery, finally got those two crazy kids together, and did it with a sense of humor.

And by we, I really do mean *we*. Sure, I was the only official writer. But, after every "chapter," I'd pin my head to the phone to regale my besties with the tale, getting endorphin highs when they thought I was funny, and taking them seriously when they said, "No, no, no, I wouldn't say that," or "Oh! You should totally make this happen."

Decades later, I realize how important those sessions were. How much they shaped my writing. How much I needed them.

This was my first writer's group.

***

The pressing drama of high school ended these sessions. I still scrawled away in notebooks, but my writing was brief, unfocused, or overly fixated, and I barely remember my pieces from that time.

But the goofy parody songs my friends and I crafted on long bus rides? Things like, "Slow down, you walk too fast, we can't let this wedgie last," sung to the tune of "Feelin' Groovy?" Those I memorized. Our verbal editing sessions, often taking place as we bumped around on brown leather bus seats, the smell of teenage angst clogging the air, are as dear to my heart as my epic preteen fictions.

Is it any wonder that when I entered college-level creative writing that I thrived on critique, reading every chicken-scratch comment or mark? That this is when I started really writing again? Even if I got indignant about the girl who didn't comment on a single line of prose, except to tell me I'd used my quota of ellipses for the rest of my life—workshops were my lifeblood. To keep writing, I pursued an MFA. And I relished every moment of my nerve-wrecking thesis because my classmates were my readers, editors, shoulders to cry on, and promoters.

It shouldn't be surprising that I wrote practically nothing after I graduated.

***

Writers are sold on solitude. That our only real friends are the ones in our head. That it's okay to be the weirdo sulking in the crowd, the eccentric one. To go to extremes to be alone, to isolate ourselves in remote cabins, or expensive New York lofts, and fantasize about the verbs that best capture jumping off a roof. Supposedly, the road to success is to lock ourselves away, shut out the world, and WRITE.

We are sold a myth.

It takes but a short skim of famous authors' front matter, back matter, and interviews to see this. When the "how much," "how often," and "what inspired you?" questions are over, the author usually offers a heartfelt thank you to a friend, editor, or their family. Or a sheepish mention of "my writers group."

Even Stephen King, lauded for his five-hour-a-day writing regime, dedicates a whole section of *On Writing* to the importance of his early readers, and the countless revisions he makes thanks to them.

Writers may be awkward creatures. Sometimes social, sometimes reclusive. Many find it difficult to navigate standard social expectations, no matter how real our characters.

But alone we fail.

***

Eventually, I entered a contest. One that encouraged contestants to share their work and offer each other feedback while waiting on judges' responses. A private forum full of writers, waiting to talk about writing, share their work, read, and comment. Even beta.

"What's a beta?" I once posted.

"They're the second set of eyes. They offer feedback before you submit." A fair, technical answer. What they should've said was, "The most essential gift a writer can receive."

Here, I met other writers who wanted to share, write, be anxious, spit ideas, and laugh together, work together, cry together.

But I only talked to them during that yearly contest.

The only writing I did was for that yearly contest.

Then, a portion of them formed an online group and invited me. The group grew and changed but always, always focused on supporting each other, whether our words hit the page or only our dreams. Whether our stories sat on an editor's desk or private desktops.

***

Compared to famous authors, my writing stats remain small. But I've done more writing my first year with them than in the six that preceded. Submitted more than in the fifteen before. And have published more than ever.

But that's not the best part.

The best part is I feel thirteen again. Rushing to my besties to see if I'm nailing it or failing it, and getting the same earnest honesty in return. These days, the feedback is more sophisticated, but it warms and fuels me just the same. And now, I get to return the favor.

Finding a good writer's group isn't just networking. It isn't reserved for novices and is hardly a thing to be ashamed of. And it isn't easy.

But it *is* necessary.

It is the lifeblood of inspiration and growth.

To succeed, you'll need one. The members may already be in your network. Or you've yet to meet them. They may not even be writers.

But you'll know when you've found your group.

It will feel like giggles in the back of a classroom. A rambunctious sleepover. A tight hug. And like pouring your heart out in a bathroom stall to the only person that just "gets" you.

It will feel like friendship.

It will feel like home.

Thank you…

…for reading *Writing Alone and Other Group Activities.*

We sincerely hope you enjoyed these stories, essays, and quirky authors! If you did, **please consider leaving a review on the site you purchased it from**. Reviews are the lifeblood of authors from small publishers; you might be surprised how much extra attention it garners for our contributors.

Speaking of our contributors, the following section allows them a short space to talk about themselves. Please "like" them on Facebook and follow them on Twitter to see what they are publishing next.

Thanks again!

Scribes Divided

"A single voice crying into the wind is inaudible. When many howl at once, each trying to rise above the others, a cacophony rattles windows but remains unclear. However, when these voices work together, a harmony is formed. A symphony, complex and vibrant, produces a sound richer and far more resonant than any single voice could achieve. Scribes Divided brings together those disparate voices, and through this collective, an unmistakable beauty is revealed.

Scribes Divided is a network of independent authors, linked by the desire to have their unique compositions heard. In an age of mass-media and conglomerate publishing houses, they have chosen a different path. Scribes Divided is owned, edited, supported, and published by its members. No one is left to sing alone."

Writings to Stem Your Existential Dread was the first volume under the Scribes Divided imprint. Twenty-two authors crafted an anthology with fifty-three flash fiction tales, filled with wonder, joy, horror, passions, and magic.

Dread Naught but Time was Scribes Divided's second volume. Using both the theme of time and song-lyric prompts, our authors told twenty-six amazing short stories that will leave you breathless and wanting more!

Anthologies are available at any e-tailer or may be ordered through your favorite brick-and-mortar location. Connect with us on Facebook and Twitter @ScribesDivided.

About the Authors

Serena Armstrong

Serena Armstrong is an insurance broker's assistant from the Southern Highlands region of NSW, Australia. She started reading at an early age and her love of stories and fantasy worlds has only gotten stronger over the years, compelling her to write her first novel. She is in the process of editing *Fledgling Light,* Book One of the Fledgling Trilogy, but participates in short story and flash fiction competitions to hone her skills. You can connect with Serena at www.facebook.com/fledglinglight.

Taree Belardes

Taree Belardes is a dedicated California Girl, recently transplanted to North Carolina where she's reveling in the rain. An energetic healer under the tutelage of a host of Master Teachers, her days are now happily spent as a floral designer.

Taree writes mainly short fiction and was thrilled to be part of the winning team of writers which sparked this publication. Her short story "Thyme Flies" occupies a spot in the anthology, *Dread Naught but Time,* while her diminutive "Reflections" won the recent Fiction in a Nutshell competition with *The Acorn.*

Her poetry has appeared in *The Topanga Messenger*, and she has garnered honorable mentions from NYC Midnight's Short Story Competition, Writer's Weekly, Booklocker, and *The Acorn*'s Tiny Story Contests.

She is currently working on a children's fantasy novel, a political exposé, and a historical novel that chronicles the coming of age in Southern California during the Summer of Love.

She writes mostly at night, illuminated by the moon.

Colette Bennett

Colette Bennett is a journalist with ten years of experience in storytelling and a particular passion for fantastical worlds. Her previous work can be found on CNN, The Daily Dot, Colourlovers, Gamasutra and Engadget. Her fiction and essays appear in *NonBinary Review* and *The Corona Book of Science Fiction*. She is hard at work on her forthcoming YA sci-fi novel, *Chasing the Ema*.

Myna Chang

Myna Chang writes flash and short stories in a variety of genres. Her work has appeared in *Daily Science Fiction*, *Copperfield Review*, *Dead Housekeeping*, and other venues. Read more at mynachang.com.

J.L. Davinroy

J.L. Davinroy spent much of her youth in Cleveland, Ohio lost in books and the stories in her head. As an adult she finally decided to write this stuff down. She works as an accountant and lives with her husband, three children, two dogs and an overgrown garden in a quiet, Illinois suburb of St. Louis. She spends her free time chasing down the perfect nachos on the back of her husband's Harley, picking dog hair off of her clothes, and being habitually late to everything.

Her work has been featured in the flash fiction anthologies *Writings to Stem Your Existential Dread, Dread Naught but Time*, and *72 Hours of Insanity, Vol. 3*. Connect with her at www.facebook.com/jldavinroyauthor, on Twitter @jldavinroy, and her website www.chronichumanity.com.

Allison deHart

Allison deHart is a full time English/Creative Writing teacher and part time musician. She resides in the beautiful mountains of Southern California with her husband (who has authored several books), and her sons. She has her bachelors degree in Creative Writing from Cal State San Bernardino and her Masters in teaching from Chapman University.

Josh Flores

Josh Flores manifested in Chicago with Spanish as his first language, the struggle to learn English well led him to read. He devoured comics and men's adventure novels. Eventually, he exchanged Doc Savage, James Bond, and Sherlock Holmes for authors. He scoured thrift stores and used book stores for Poe, Bloch, Beaumont, Ellison, and Bradbury. Horror wasn't a specific genre but whenever Josh found it, it never failed to draw out raw emotions. Those emotions beckoned Josh to write. At ten years old, he two-finger-pecked short stories on an old electric typewriter. He hasn't stopped writing since. That scares Josh.

S W Fox

S W Fox is a person who lives in holy matrimony
with another person. Fox is a Marine veteran who
knows Chinese, survived cancer, pretends to race
cars, and occasionally launches rockets. But all those
accomplishments are boring and trivial when compared
to being a level 80 Stay at Home Person of two incredible
little people. Also his spouse person is exceedingly patient
and even more exceedingly beautiful. Or something to
that effect.

Meagan Noel Hart

Meagan Noel Hart lives the quintessential author's life,
teacher by day, writer by night. And she loves it. She
can't regret following her passions, after all. Her work
spans many genres, but usually comes tumbling out as
flash fiction or poetry. When she's not chasing words,
Meagan can be found baking cakes, playing video games,
and spending time with her family. She currently lives
in Baltimore, Maryland with her husband, two adorable,
rambunctious sons, and a small herd of pets. Meagan
teaches literature, publishing, and writing at Stevenson
University under her married name. Her work can be found
most recently in *Daily Science Fiction*, *A Twist in Time
Literary Magazine*, and *Dread Naught but Time*. She has
three books of short fiction, including a horror collection
Whispers and Fangs, and her flash story "Quantum Love
Letters" is nominated for the 2019 Pushcart prize. Follow
her at www.facebook.com/MeaganNoelHart.

Shari Heinrich

Shari Heinrich is an award-winning author. She writes young adult fantasy where magic drives her characters. Filled with sass and heart, those teens won't back down when it comes to protecting their friends, their family, or their dreams. She has been published in *Conclave*, and her most recent award is placing 18th of 4,650 participants in the 2019 New York City Midnight Short Story Challenge.

When Shari's not out writing in her backyard, you'll find her tending her vegetable garden, and looking for ways to deter the deer from eating the crops. Maybe she's riding her bike, enjoying the central Ohio countryside. When she sits still, it's to lose herself in a book. Or she's playing "fetch" with her cats after they've skewered her big toe to say it's time to throw the toy across the room. Again.

The photography bug bit her about the same time as the writing bug. She can't resist bringing her camera when she's writing outside. She swears she doesn't use the camera for procrastination when the characters shyly resist telling their stories.

You can follow her writing journey at www.ShariHeinrich.com.

Wayne Hills

Wayne Hills is the alter ego of Miguel A. Rueda. Miguel is one of 10 children including an adopted brother, two step-siblings and one half-sister. His childhood is chock-full of fascinating accounts of sometimes extraordinary stories, which can account for his truly outrageous imagination.

In his spare time, he enjoys: motorcycling, rescuing dogs from high-kill shelters, loving his wife, daughter, two step-sons, four grand-boys, and all things nerdy.

To sum up his outlook on life, "Biker-geek," would be appropriate.

He has published several short stories under both his given and pen-names.

waynehillsauthor.wordpress.com.

www.facebook.com/AuthorWayneHills.

Carrie Houghton

Carrie is a school librarian from suburban Maryland. Her work has been published in the Scribes Divided Anthology *Writings to Stem Your Existential Dread, Fiction War Magazine, Tales from the Cliff,* and *Spectrum.*

Nathan James

Nathan James received his degree in Creative Writing from Western Michigan University. He works as an editor in the educational publishing industry in Chicago. His essays, poetry, and short stories have been featured in numerous media outlets, including WordPress Discover, *Wizards in Space Literary Journal,* and BlogHer's Voices of the Year.

Pamela L. Keil

Pamela's plot has many twists that include studying biology in the mountains of North America, and then moving to the spectacular flat earth of Australia. In that setting, she interacts with characters that include native marsupials, birds, insects, and seven-year olds. Her story includes scenes of birdwatching, experimenting with native foods, telling stories about Australian animals, and helping young people resolve conflicts in daily subplots. She loves the many national parks in her world, but would prefer fewer seasonal climaxes caused by drought and fire, and is worried about a sad ending to the story arc of climate change.

Victoria Kelsey

Victoria Kelsey is a resident of the world, having moved around enough to enjoy residency in more states and countries than she ever thought possible. Her poetry has been published in the Open Mouse, United Amateur Press, and the *Deseret News*. This anthology exhibits her first published short fiction.

Erin Nickels

Erin A. Nickels is a lifelong native of Long Island, New York. She has three children with her high school sweetheart, and appreciates their unconditional love and the support they've provided in her writing career. Erin is an award-winning author, journalist, columnist, and pop culture analyst. Her publication list will grow to include her first novel in 2020. Erin was recently appointed as an Ambassador for the Kindleigh organization, and spends her time spreading joy and good will through random acts of kindness. She lives by the mantra ingrained in her by the late Donald Hiller, her father, who taught her to "Be good, be careful, but most importantly…be cool."

Cayce Osborne

Cayce Osborne is a writer and graphic designer from Madison, WI. She currently works in science communication and public engagement at the University of Wisconsin-Madison. Her fiction has been published in *Exposition Review* and the *Dread Naught but Time* short story anthology from Scribes Divided Publishing. She also collects her work on her website at cayceosborne.com.

Jennifer Palmer

Jennifer Palmer would say that she's a library assistant by day, writer by night, but she's working the closing shift these days....

Palmer's shorter work has been published in *Balloons Literary Journal, borrowed solace, Tales from the Cliff, Writings to Stem Your Existential Dread*, and *Dread Naught but Time*. She has published a YA fantasy novel, *Burst*, under the pen name H. C. Daria, so you should definitely check it out. /wink wink/

When she's not derping on the computer, Palmer enjoys reading, dragging herself to the gym, and indulging in puns. More of her work can be found at hcdaria.blogspot.com.

MM Schreier

MM Schreier is a classically trained vocalist who took up writing as therapy for a mid-life crisis. Whether contemporary or speculative fiction, favorite stories are rich in sensory details and weird twists. A firm believer that people are not always exclusively right- or left-brained, in addition to creative pursuits Schreier manages a robotics company and tutors maths and science to at-risk youth. Selected work and publication listing can be found at: mmschreier.com

Jessica Wilcox

Jessica Wilcox (formerly Gilmartin) hails from the suburbs of Buffalo, NY with her (new) husband and three children. When she's not writing, she is teaching immigrants and refugees in the city, reading, practicing Tae Kwon Do, and dreaming of moving back overseas. Her story "Surviving" was a runner up in the 2016 Fall Writing Contest through The Write Practice and can be found on the Short Fiction Break website. Her stories can also be found in *Writings to Stem Your Existential Dread* and *72 Hours of Insanity Vol. 3.*

Jack Woolverton

Jack Woolverton is a 2007 graduate of Mount Vernon Nazarene University with degrees in English and History. Life has often twisted in macabre, profane ways for his family, but what's a writer without trauma? His wife wishes he'd write more happy stories. His kids aren't allowed to read his stories. And, he has a cockatiel named Basil, who is bent on world domination.

Made in the USA
Columbia, SC
01 November 2020